W9-AMX-374

Also available from
Diana Palmer

Magnolia

Renegade

Lone Star Winter

Dangerous

Desperado

Heartless

Fearless

Her Kind of Hero

Nora

Big Sky Winter

Man of the Hour

Trilby

Lawman

Hard to Handle

Heart of Winter

Outsider

Night Fever

Before Sunrise

Noelle

Lawless

Diamond Spur

The Texas Ranger

Lord of the Desert

The Cowboy and the Lady

Most Wanted

Fit for a King

Paper Rose

Rage of Passion

Once in Paris

After the Music

Roomful of Roses

Champagne Girl

Passion Flower

Diamond Girl

Friends and Lovers

Cattleman's Choice

Lady Love

The Rawhide Man

Wyoming Tough

Coming soon

Midnight Rider

DIANA PALMER

WYOMING FIERCE

HARLEQUIN®

entertain, enrich, inspire™

ISBN-13: 978-1-62090-599-9

WYOMING FIERCE

Copyright © 2012 by Diana Palmer

Excerpt from MIDNIGHT RIDER
Copyright © 1998 by Susan Kyle

This edition published by arrangement with Harlequin Books S.A.

® and TM are trademarks of Harlequin Enterprises Limited or its corporate affiliates. Trademarks indicated with ® are registered in the United States Patent and Trademark Office, the Canadian Trade Marks Office and in other countries.

Printed in U.S.A.

Dear Reader,

I wanted to do Cane Kirk's story from the minute I found him lurking in my brain. He was a man with serious issues. But then, a man without a single flaw would be boring.

The story developed on the computer screen in front of my eyes. I had a basic plot, but the characters themselves wrote this book. I have to admit that the part about the rooster isn't exactly made up. I had one of those problem roosters myself not too long ago.

One day I looked out my front door and saw a red rooster and two white hens grazing on my lawn. I live in town, so this was rather a surprise. I thought they'd go home and that would be the end of it. The next day they were back. I tried putting them out the gate and closing it. They just came back in the minute I opened it. So the hens moved out back and laid me two nice eggs every day, and the rooster went back to wherever he came from. Except that he started reappearing atop my seven-foot-tall solid wood fence every morning at daylight like clockwork.

I chased him out of the yard daily. But he started to fight back. He had spurs and he could fly. I got spurred twice before I figured out how to protect myself. I learned to carry a garbage can lid out with me to keep him at bay. So I was running him all over the yard (I can't exactly run—I was sort of hobbling him all over the yard), and it was upper eighties in temperature. We hobbled, then we wobbled, then he was walking and panting and I was walking and panting, but I couldn't get closer than seven feet away from him. I never could outhobble or outwalk him. But there are sites on the web that can teach you the way of the rooster and how to catch one. No, it's not what you think. I like chicken soup, but I'm not eating such a valiant feathered opponent. He retired with his laurels to a more suitable location.

Anyway, I feel for poor Cort Brannt at the end of this book. When you get to it, you'll know why.

As always, thank you so much for your kindness and your loyalty over the long years.

Your biggest fan,

Diana Palmer

To Cinzia (no ice cream trucks!) and Vonda and Cath,
and all my DP Girls!

CHAPTER ONE

BOLINDA MAYS WAS HAVING a hard time concentrating on her biology textbook. She hadn't slept well, worrying about her grandfather. He was only in his early sixties, but he was disabled and having difficulties paying his utility bills.

She'd come home for the weekend from her college in Montana. The trip was expensive, considering the gas it took to get her back and forth in her beat-up but serviceable old truck. Thank God she had a part-time job working for a convenience store while college was in session, or she'd never have even been able to afford to come home and see about her grandfather.

It was early December. Not too long before Christmas, and she was having final exams the next week. Really cold weather would come soon. But Bolinda's stepfather was making threats again, about turning her grandfather out of the house that had once been Bolinda's mother's. Her death had left the old man at the mercy of that fortune-hunting fool who had his fingers in every evil pie in Catelow, Wyoming. Bolinda shivered, thinking how impossible it was going to be for her, trying to pay off her used textbooks that she'd charged on her credit card. Now she was going to have to try to pay for her grandfather's utility bill, as well. Gas was so expensive, she thought miserably. The poor old man already had to choose between groceries and blood pressure meds. She'd thought about asking her neighbors, the Kirks, for help. But the only one of them she knew well was Cane, and he resented her. A lot. It would be dicey asking him for money. If she even dared.

Not that he didn't owe her something for all the times she'd saved people from him in the little town of Catelow, Wyoming, not too far from Jackson Hole. Cane had lost an arm overseas in the Middle East, after the last big conflict but while he was still in the service. He'd come home embittered and icy cold, hating everyone. He'd started drinking, refused physical therapy, refused counseling and then gone hog wild.

Every couple of weeks, he treed the local bar. The other Kirk brothers, Mallory and Dalton, always paid the bills and they knew the owner of the tavern, who was kind enough not to have Cane arrested. But the only person who could do anything with Cane was Bolinda, or Bodie as her friends called her. Even Morie, Mallory Kirk's new wife, couldn't deal with a drunken Cane. He was intimidating.

Not so much to Bolinda. She understood him, as few other people did. Amazing, considering that she was only twenty-two and he was thirty-four. That was one big age difference. It never seemed to matter. Cane talked to her as if she were his age, often about things that she had no business knowing. He seemed to consider her one of the guys.

She didn't look like a guy. She wasn't largely endowed in the bra department, of course. Her breasts were small and pert, but nothing like the women in those guy magazines. She knew that, because Cane had dated a centerfold model once and told Bodie all about her. Another embarrassing conversation when he was drunk that he probably didn't even remember.

She shook her head and tried again to concentrate on her biology textbook. She sighed, running a hand through her short, wavy black hair. Her odd, pale brown eyes were riveted to the drawings of internal human anatomy, but she just couldn't seem to make her brain work. There was going to be a final next week, along with an oral lab, and she didn't want to be the student trying to hide under the table when the professor started asking questions.

She shifted on the carpeted floor, on her stomach, and tried again to concentrate. Music started playing. Strange. That sounded like the musical ring of her cell phone, the theme from the *Star Trek* movie…

"Hey, Bodie, it's for you!" her grandfather called from the next room, where she'd left her cell phone in her coat pocket.

She muttered something and got to her feet. "Who is it, Granddaddy?"

"I don't know, sugar." He handed Bodie's cell phone to her.

"Thanks," she whispered. "Hello?" she said into the phone.

"Uh, Miss Mays?" came a hesitant voice over the line.

She recognized who was calling immediately. She ground her teeth together. "I won't come!" she said. "I'm studying for a biology test. I've got a lab, to boot…!"

"Aw, please?" the voice came again. "They're threatening to call the police. I think they'll do it this time. The newspapers would have a field day…"

There was a pregnant pause. Her lips made a thin line. "Oh, damn!" she muttered.

"Darby says he'll come get you. In fact," the

cowboy added hopefully, "he's sitting right out-side your house right now."

Bodie stomped to the window and looked out the blinds. There was a big black Kirk ranch truck parked in the driveway, with the lights on and the engine running.

"Please?" the cowboy asked again.

"All right." She hung up in the middle of his "Thank you!"

She grabbed her jacket and her purse and slipped into her boots. "I have to go out for an hour. I won't be too long," she told her grandfather.

Rafe Mays, used to the drill, pursed his lips. "You should get combat pay," he pointed out.

Bodie rolled her eyes and walked out the door. "I hope I won't be long," she said before she pulled it shut.

SHE GOT INTO THE TRUCK. Darby Hanes, the Kirks' longtime foreman, gave her a wistful smile.

"I know. I'm sorry. But you're the only person who can do anything with him. He's tearing up the bar. They're getting tired of the weekly routine." He pulled out into the road, after making sure she had her seat belt on. "He had a date last night up in Jackson Hole. Ended badly, I'm guessing, from all the cussing he did when he got home."

She didn't reply. She hated knowing about Cane

Kirk's girlfriends. He seemed to have a lot of them, even with his disability. Not that it made any difference to her. Cane would still be Cane no matter what. She loved him. She'd loved him since she graduated from high school, when he presented her with a bouquet of pink roses, her favorite, and a bottle of very expensive floral perfume. He'd even kissed her. On the cheek, of course, like a treasured child more than like an adult. Her grandfather had worked for the Rancho Real until his health failed and he had to quit. That had been while Cane was still in the military, after the second Gulf War, before the terrible roadside bomb had robbed him of most of his left arm, and almost of his life.

She supposed Cane was fond of her. It wasn't until last year that everyone had discovered her almost magical ability to calm him when he went on drinking sprees. Since then, when he went on benders, Bodie was recruited to fetch him home. There had been a brief period of time when he'd gone to therapy, been measured for a prosthesis and seemed to be adjusting nicely to his new life.

And then it had all gone south, for reasons nobody knew. His bar crawls had become legendary. The expense was terrible, because his brothers, Mallory and Dalton, had to pick up the expense. Cane got a monthly check from the army, but nobody could entice him to apply for disability. He went to show cattle, with a cowboy who handled the big bulls for him, and he was the idea man for the Kirk ranch. He was good at PR, worked to liaison with the national cattlemen's lobby, kept up with current legislation that affected the cattle industry and generally was the spokesman for the Kirk ranch.

When he was sober.

Lately he wasn't. Not a lot.

"Any idea what happened?" Bodie asked curiously, because Darby would know. He knew everything that went on around the Rancho Real, or "royal ranch" in Spanish, named by the original owner, a titled gentleman from Valladolid, northwest of Madrid, Spain, who started it way back in the late 1800s.

Darby glanced at her and grimaced. It was dark and very cold, even with the heater running and the old but serviceable coat Bodie was wearing.

"I have an idea," he confessed. "But if Cane ever found out I told you, I'd be standing in the unemployment line."

She sighed and fiddled with the fanny pack she wore in lieu of carrying around a cumbersome purse. "She must have said something about his arm."

He nodded faintly. "That would be my guess.

He's really sensitive about it. Funny," he added solemnly, "I thought he was getting better."

"If he'd get back in therapy, mental and physical, he'd improve," she replied.

"Sure, but he won't even talk about it. He's sinking into himself," he added quietly.

"There goes that theoretical physics mind working overtime again," she teased, because most people didn't know about Darby's degree in that field.

He shrugged. "Hey, I just manage cattle."

"I'll bet you sit around in your room at night imagining the route to a new and powerful unified field theory." She chuckled.

"Only on Thursdays," he said, laughing out loud. "At least my chosen field of study doesn't leave me covered in mud and using shovels and trowels in holes around the country."

"Don't knock anthropology," she said firmly. "We'll find the missing link one day, and you can say you knew me before I was famous, like that guy in Egypt who's always in documentaries about pharaohs' tombs." She lifted her rounded chin. "Nothing wrong with honest work."

He made a face. "Digging up bones."

"Bones can tell you a lot," she replied.

"So they say. Here it is," he added, nodding toward the little out-of-the-way bar that Cane frequented. Out front was a stop sign that local drunks often used for target practice when they went driving around in four-wheel-drive vehicles late at night. Now it said "S….p." The two middle letters were no longer recognizable.

"They need to replace that," she pointed out.

"What for? Everybody knows it means stop," he said. "Why waste good metal and paint? They'd just shoot it up again. Not much in the way of entertainment this far out in the country."

"Got a point, I guess." She sighed.

He parked in front of the bar. There were only two vehicles out there. Probably those of employees. Everybody with any sense would have left when Cane started cursing and throwing things. At least, that was the pattern.

"I'll keep the engine running. In case somebody called the sheriff this time," he mused.

"Cane and the sheriff are best friends," she reminded him.

"That won't stop Cody Banks from locking him up if someone files a complaint for assault and battery," he stated. "The law is the law, friendship notwithstanding."

"I guess. Maybe it would knock some sense into him."

He shook his head. "That's been tried. Mallory even let him stew in a cell for two days. Finally bailed him out, and he went back and did it again that same weekend. Our black sheep there is out of control."

"I'll see what I can do to rein him in," she promised.

She got out of the truck, ran a hand through her short black hair and grimaced. Her brown eyes were somber as she hesitated on the porch for just a minute, and then, finally, opened the door.

The mess was bad. Tables knocked over. Chairs everywhere. One was upside down behind the bar in a pile of glass, and the place smelled like whiskey. This was going to be an expensive mess, too.

"Cane?" she called.

A thin man in a Hawaiian shirt peered over the bar. "Bodie? Thank God!"

"Where is he?" she asked.

He pointed to the bathroom.

She went toward it. She was almost there when it slammed open and Cane walked out. His long-sleeved beige Western shirt with the fancy embroidery was stained with blood. Probably his own, she thought, noting the caked blood around his nose, which was bruised, and his square jaw. His sensual mouth had a cut just at the corner, where blood was also visible. His thick, short, slightly wavy black hair was mussed. His black eyes were bloodshot. Even in that condition, he was so attractive that he made her heart pound. He was tall and broad-shouldered, with long powerful legs encased in tight jeans; his big feet in boots that still had the mirror polish on them despite his exploits. He was thirty-four to her twenty-two, but right now, he seemed much younger.

He glared at her. "Why do they always bring you?" he demanded.

She shrugged. "My unusual ability to subdue charging tigers?" she suggested.

He blinked. Then he chuckled.

She went forward and took one of his big hands in hers. The knuckles were bruised and swollen and smeared with blood. She couldn't tell if it was his or somebody else's. "Mallory's going to be mad."

"Mallory isn't home," he said in a loud whisper. He even grinned. "He and Morie went to Louisiana to see a bull. They won't be back until tomorrow."

"Tank won't be happy, either," she added, using the nickname that family used for Dalton, the youngest brother.

He shrugged. "Tank will be knee-deep in those old Tom Mix silent cowboy movies he likes. It's Saturday night. He makes popcorn, takes the phone off the hook, locks himself in and saturates himself with black-and-white cinema."

"That's what you should be doing, instead of wrecking bars!" she muttered.

He sighed. "A man's got to have some recreation, kid," he said defensively.

"Not this sort," she said firmly. "Come on. Poor Sid will have to clean up this mess."

Sid came around the bar. He was huge, and dangerous-looking, but he kept a few steps away from Cane. "Why can't you do this at home, Cane?" he groaned, looking around.

"Because we've got delicate *objets d'art* in glass cabinets," Cane replied reasonably. "Mallory would kill me."

Sid glared at him. "When Mr. Holsten sees the bill for replacing all this—" he waved his hand "—you may be getting a visit..."

Cane pulled out his wallet and pressed a wad of hundreds into the bartender's hand. "If that's not enough, you let me know."

Sid grimaced. "It will be enough, but it's the principle of the thing! Why can't you go up to Jackson Hole and wreck bars?"

Cane blinked. "It would take too long to get Bodie up there. I'd be arrested."

"You should be!"

Cane's black eyes narrowed and he took a step forward.

Sid backed up.

"Oh, come on," Bodie grumbled. She tugged on

Cane's hand. "I'm going to fail biology because of you. I was studying for exams!"

"Biology? You're majoring in anthropology," he argued.

"Yes, but I still have to pass the minimum required courses of study, and that's one of them! I couldn't put it off any longer so I had to take it this semester!"

"Oh."

"See you, Sid. Hope not soon," she added with a laugh.

He managed a smile. "Thanks, Bodie. Especially for..." He gestured toward Cane. "You know."

"Oh, yes, I do know." She nodded.

She pulled Cane out the door and onto the porch. "Where's your coat?" she asked.

He blinked as the cold air hit him. "In the truck, I think. I don't need it. 'S'not cold," he said, his voice beginning to slur.

"It's below freezing out here!"

He gave her a woozy look and grinned. "I'm hot-blooded."

She averted her eyes. "Come on. Darby's waiting. I'll drive your truck out to the ranch. Where's the key?"

"Right front pocket."

She glared at him. "Going to get it for me?"

"No."

Her bow lips made a thin line. "Cane!"

"Go fish," he teased.

She glanced around him at Darby.

"No," he said, putting his hand over his pocket. "Not giving it to him."

"Cane!"

"Not!" he repeated.

"Oh, all right!"

She pushed his hand aside and dug into his pocket for the keys, hating the deep, sensual sound that came out of his throat as her fingers closed around them. She was flushing and hoped he couldn't see. The contact was almost intimate, especially when he suddenly stepped closer so that her small, pert breasts flattened against his broad chest.

"Nice," he whispered, his lips brushing the thick waves of her short hair. "Smells pretty. Feels good, too," he added, his one good hand pushing her chest against his so that he could feel the sudden hardening of her nipples.

She gasped.

"Yes, you like that, don't you?" he whispered. "I wish my shirt was off, and I could feel your bare breasts against my chest...."

She grasped the keys and jerked away from

him, her face blazing. "You shut up!" she said under her breath.

He made a face. "'How dare you!'" he mimicked in a high-pitched tone. "How Victorian you sound." He laughed shortly. "I know all about you college girls. You all sleep around and you want taxpayers to make sure you get birth control so you can do it."

She didn't reply. Lots of people thought the same thing. She wasn't getting into another fight with him, which was what he wanted. He was goading her. Odd, he'd never done it in such a sensual way before. It was affecting her, and she didn't like it.

"Go on, get in," she muttered, almost forcing him into the truck beside Darby.

"And fasten your seat belt!" she added.

He gave her another woozy smile. "No. You do it."

She let out a cuss word and then flushed and apologized.

"No need to say sorry for that," Darby muttered, glaring at Cane. "I feel the same way."

Cane glared at him. "Not riding with you!"

He got out of the truck in spite of Bodie's protests, and when Darby got out to try to force him in, he raised a fist and got into a fighting stance.

It reminded both of them that he had a black belt in an Asian martial art discipline.

"Oh, all right, you can ride in your own truck and I'll drive!" Bodie raged.

He grinned, having gotten his way. He went like a lamb to his own truck, waited for Bodie to flick the remote and let him in. He even fastened his seat belt.

She started the truck, waving Darby to go ahead.

"You're more trouble than cattle!" she told Cane.

He smiled at her. "You think so? Why don't you slide over here next to me?" he added with a raised eyebrow. "We can discuss cattle."

"I'm driving."

"Oh." He blinked. "Okay, I'll slide over next to you…" He started to unfasten his seat belt.

"You do that and I'm calling Cody Banks!" she told him, digging out her prepaid cell phone and showing it to him. "You wear a seat belt when the truck is in motion. It's the law!"

"The law." He scoffed.

"Yes, well, you unfasten that belt and I'm calling him, just the same."

He made a face but he stopped fiddling with the belt. He stared at her, his face hard, his black eyes snapping. Actually she only had about five minutes of phone time left on the device, and she didn't want to waste it calling the sheriff when she might need it for emergencies. Cane could afford a high-tech cell phone and a plan to go with it. Bodie was lucky to have even a cheap one.

"What happened this time?" she asked, not sure she really wanted an answer. But at least it would keep him talking.

His jaw tautened.

"Come on," she coaxed. "You can tell me. You know I won't repeat it."

"Most of what I tell you, you wouldn't dare repeat," he muttered, averting his eyes.

"Yes."

She waited, not pushing, not prodding, not even coaxing.

He seemed to sober a little. "I had on the damned prosthesis. Looks real, right? At least, until you get close up." He looked out the window at the passing dark silhouettes of bare trees and pasture. "I took her up to my room. It's been a long time. I was hungry." Fortunately for Bodie, he couldn't see the brief anguish that skirted across her face. "I started to take off my shirt and when she saw the straps that held the prosthesis in place, she stopped me dead. She said it was nothing personal, she just couldn't do it with a man who was crippled like that. She had to have a whole man."

"Oh, Cane," she said softly. "I'm sorry."

"Sorry. Yes. She was sorry, too. I took off the damned prosthesis and threw it at the wall. Then I flew home." He laid his head back against the headrest. "I couldn't think about anything else. The look on her face, when she saw that thing… haunted me all day. By sundown, I couldn't stand it anymore. I had to get that memory out of my mind. Had to!"

She bit her lower lip. What could she say? Of all the things to happen. She hated knowing that he had women. That wasn't even her business. But for a woman to treat him that way, after all he'd been through, as if he was less than a man because he lost part of his arm fighting in a conflict sanctioned by his country. It was unthinkable.

"I can't live like this!" he burst out. "I can't go through the rest of my life being half a man, being pitied…!"

She stopped the truck. "You stop that!" she said harshly. "You're not half a man! You're a hero! You ran right over the damned IED, knowing it would blow up, to save the medics in the jeep behind you! You knew your vehicle had better armor, you knew the bomb would explode when the column went past. You made a sacrifice, saved God knows how many lives by saving those medics. And some stupid woman makes a remark out of ignorance, and you throw away that heroism, that act of gutsy courage, like a used tissue. Well, I won't let you do it! I won't!"

He gaped at her through a drunken haze. He shook his head.

She started the truck going forward again. Her face felt hot.

"How do you know that, about me?"

"Tank told me," she said gently. "The last time I had to go get you from a bar. He said it was tragic, not only what happened to you, but that you wanted to forget something that won you a silver star."

"Oh."

She drew in a long breath. "Why do you date women like that in the first place?"

"Most of the women around here are married or ugly."

She glared at him. "Thanks, from the ugly brigade, I mean."

"I didn't mean you," he said easily. He pursed his lips and studied her. "You're not ugly, but your breasts are too small."

The truck almost ran off the road. "Cane!" she exclaimed.

"Don't worry about it, a lot of men like small breasts. I just like nice big ones. And a soft, sweet belly to sink against when I get inside all that delicate, wet…"

"Cane!" she exclaimed again, flushing.

"Oh, come on, you know about that," he said, leaning his head back. "Nothing so cushy as a woman lifting to you on cool sheets, feeling you thrust into her, swelling and swelling until you burst and she cries out with the pleasure."

"I get sex education in school!"

"Well, you get the basics, but they don't tell you how good it feels, do they? Or that men come in different sizes and shapes. I'm well-endowed my-self. Not too big, but I can…"

"Will you please stop?" she raged.

He glanced at her. "Getting aroused, are we?" He chuckled in a deep, soft, sensual tone. "You're not really my type, kid, and you're too young, but I could make you get off like a machine gun firing."

She swallowed, stepping on the gas.

"But I don't think your grandfather would ever forgive me. That's probably why you go to college out of state, so he won't know what you're up to. How many lovers have you had?"

"Can't we talk about the weather?" she asked, trying not to sound desperate. She was aroused, unbelievably aroused. He wouldn't know it, but she was still a virgin. Despite that, the imagery was giving her real problems.

He stretched and grimaced. "Sure. It's cold."

"Thank you."

"Do you like the man to get on top, or do you like to get on top? I can go deeper that way," he said as easily as if he was discussing the weather.

She groaned.

"Real deep, in fact," he murmured, getting drowsy. "I remember this one woman, she was small and I was afraid I'd hurt her. But she got on top and pumped me like a shotgun, screaming the whole time. We went all night long." He grinned. "She liked to try new positions. So one time…"

"I don't want to hear about your sexual acrobatics, Cane!" Her voice was high-pitched and desperate.

He rolled his head against the headrest so that he could see her face. "Jealous?"

"I am not jealous!"

He smiled. But the smile faded. "You'd have to get on top," he said coldly. "I don't have two arms to prop on anymore. I don't even know if I could do it now. I wanted to find out. I wanted to see if I could still be a man…."

"Cane, there are men all over the world who have lost arms and legs and who can still have sex," she pointed out, trying to restrain her embarrassment. "People find a way!"

He drew in a long breath. "I won't have the nerve to try again," he said in a haunted tone. "She said I was a cripple." His eyes closed. "A cripple. She wanted a whole man...."

She pulled up at the front of the house and blew the horn. She almost jumped out when Tank came onto the front porch.

CHAPTER TWO

"DAMN IT, CANE," TANK, aka Dalton, muttered under his breath as he helped Bodie get his brother out of the truck and up onto the porch. "Why do you do this to yourself?"

"He does share," Bodie replied. "He did it to the bar also."

Dalton groaned.

"I paid the bar tab, and extra." Cane sighed. He pulled away from his brother. "I want her to take me upstairs." He pointed to Bodie.

"No way. I have to go home. I'm studying for biology finals."

"Won't go if you don't go with me," Cane said obstinately.

Dalton grimaced. He looked at Bodie, pleadingly.

"Oh, all right. But then I have to go home, and somebody will have to drive me."

"I'll take you home," Dalton promised. He smiled. "Thanks."

She shrugged. "You're welcome."

She got under Cane's good arm, shimmering all over at the feel of that powerful body so close to hers, and guided him up the steps.

"You owe me, pal," she muttered.

His hand slid over her arm, his fingers accidentally brushing the rounded underside of her breast in the process, and dragging a helpless shock of pleasure that echoed from her throat.

"Mmm-hmm," he murmured.

She got him into his room. He pushed the door closed behind them and let her guide him to the bed, but when he went down, he pulled her with him.

"Now," he breathed, his hand under her back. "I want to find out something...."

She opened her mouth to ask what and his was suddenly teasing around it, nibbling at her upper lip, teasing the underside with his tongue. The mastery of the caress left her helpless. She just lay there, shocked, tempted...tingling all over with new sensations.

He unsnapped the bra and, leaning on the stump of his left arm, proceeded to unbutton his shirt while his lips were playing with hers. Seconds later, he'd pushed up her shirt and bra and his bare, hair-matted, muscular chest was pressing down against skin that had never been touched.

"Small," he groaned, "but firm and soft and sweet."

His thumb and forefinger were teasing the nipple, making it hard. She shivered.

"Yes." He bent his head and his mouth suddenly opened, hot and moist, right on top of the nipple. He pulled at it tenderly, rasped it against his tongue and finally took all of her into his mouth and suckled her.

She came up off the bed shuddering, trying to contain the hoarse, pulsing cry of pleasure that accompanied the action.

His lean hand was behind her, pushing into her jeans as he shifted, so that he could bring her hips into intimate contact with him. She felt him swell, felt the size and power of him, in a contact she'd never shared with a man in her whole life. Repressed, raised religiously by a grandfather whose morals were still Victorian, she'd kept herself chaste. Now this man, this playboy, was trying to use her like one of his women, make her into his toy, to salve the ego that another woman had hurt.

She was trying to remember all that while one long leg curled around her and his mouth grew more insistent. She was so engrossed in new sensations that she barely heard the knock on the door until it was repeated, loudly.

"Cane! Bodie needs to go home!"

Bodie sat bolt upright, gaping down at Cane, whose expression was a cross between shock and shame.

"On my way!" she called, hoping her voice didn't sound as unsettled as she felt. She fumbled her bra back in place, pulled her shirt down and stared at Cane in shock.

His mouth was swollen from its long contact with her body. His breathing was fast. But the alcohol suddenly seemed to catch up with him. He stared at her, blinked, started to speak and fell back onto the bed, snoring.

She got up and opened the door.

Tank looked in past her and sighed. "Thank God," he mused. "I was afraid he might try to get out of hand." He looked her over, and apparently didn't see anything to concern him. She was mussed, but that could have come from manhandling Cane into bed. Or so she guessed.

"He's a handful all right. I thought I'd never get him into the bed. He's heavy!" she muttered, trying to bluff.

"Yes, he is." He shook his head. "I wish he'd stop picking up women in bars," he added coldly. "At his age, he should be thinking about a family."

"Some men never settle down," she replied, going ahead of him downstairs. "He seems to be one of those."

"You never know. We're in your debt, again," he emphasized, and smiled gently. "Isn't there something we can do for you?"

She smiled and nodded. "Yes. Drive me home, please. I still have to study."

"Come on. Yes, I remember finals. No fun."

"Yes, but I only have one more semester to go. If I pass everything, I get my degree."

"Then what?"

"Then, on to my master's." She sighed. "With digs in between and a nice full-time job this next summer to help pay for it all."

"We could…"

She held up a hand. "You've done so much for Granddaddy. You don't need to do anything for me. I'm happy to help out, any way I can. You're a nice family."

He smiled. "Thanks. Your granddad was one of the best wranglers we ever had. Shame he had to go and get old," he added gently.

"I feel the same way!"

HE DROVE HER HOME. She went inside, just in time to catch her grandfather in a conversation on the telephone.

"But where would I go, Will?" he was asking heavily. "This was my daughter's place…yes, I know you own it. But I can't pay that much in rent!

My little monthly check from the Kirks helps, but I'm still trying to get on disability...yes, I know. I know. All right, I'll try to come up with it. You wouldn't really...? Hello?"

She walked into the dining room. He was standing by the telephone table that had belonged to her great-grandmother, with the freedom phone held in his hand, frozen.

"Granddaddy? What is it?"

He glanced at her, started to speak, thought better of it and just hung up the phone. "Aw, nothing. Nothing at all. You go back and work on that biology. I'm going to read a book. See you in the morning." He even managed a smile.

"You sleep well," she said.

He hesitated. "Oh, did you get Cane home okay?"

She nodded. "Tank drove me back. Cane passed out."

He sighed. "Cane's a good boy. Tragic, what happened to him." He shook his head. "Just tragic." He went into his room and closed the door.

Bodie went into her own room and sank down on the side of her bed, speechless from what had happened in Cane's bedroom. He'd never once touched her. He'd told her things, shocking things, like the intimate details of his dates. But this was different. This was the first time he'd treated her as an adult woman.

She didn't know whether to be outraged, angry or flattered. He was much older than she was. He was rich and handsome. He had a disability that made him forget how dishy he really was to women. But she couldn't forget the look on his face just before he sank back into the pillows unconscious. That had been shame. Real shame.

She sighed. Her whole life had changed in the course of one night. She'd had her mind on education, on getting degrees, getting a job in her field, making some worthy and famous discovery that would set the world of anthropology on its ear. Now, all she could think about was the feel of Cane's mouth on her body.

She couldn't afford to let those thoughts continue. She was poor. Her grandfather was even poorer, and it sounded as if her stepfather had been making threats to him about raising the rent. She grimaced. Will Jones was horrible. He kept all sorts of explicit magazines around the house, and her mother had been furious at the cable and satellite bills because he watched pornography almost around the clock. She'd kept a close eye on Bodie, made sure that she was never alone with the man. Bodie had wondered about that, but never really questioned it, until her mother's death.

The day after the funeral, which her stepfather had actually attended, dry-eyed, he made an intimate remark to her about her body. He said he knew about college girls and he had a new way to make money, now that her mother wasn't around to disapprove. If she'd cooperate, he'd share the proceeds with her. He was starting an internet business. He could make her a star. All she had to do was pose for a few photographs....

Shocked and still grieving for her mother, she'd left his house immediately and gone to her grandfather's rented home with only a small suitcase containing her greatest little treasures and a few clothes. Her grandfather, grim-faced, had never asked why she'd moved in with him. But from then on, they were a team. Her stepfather had tried to coax her back, but she'd refused and hung up on him. He had a friend who liked her. The friend, Larry, wanted to go out with her. She didn't like the look of him, or the way he spent time with her stepfather. She imagined that he had the same taste in reading matter and film viewing as the older man. It gave her the creeps. She opened her biology textbook and sprawled on the bed. She wasn't going to think of these things right now. She'd face them when she had to. At the moment her priority was passing biology, a subject she loved but was never really good at. She recalled her first biology exam. She could understand the material; her professor was an excellent teacher. But she ground her teeth together during the oral biology lab. Her professor, a kind but terrifying man in a white lab coat during orals, had grinned when she rattled off the information about circulation through the lymphatic system. It had been harrowing. But that was only a test. She was certain that the final would be much worse.

She sighed, closing her eyes and smiling. Her physical anthropology class was her favorite. She was actually looking forward to that final. Her roommate, Beth Gaines, a nice girl with whom she lived in a small apartment off campus, was in the same anthropology class. They'd spent days before Bodie came home for the weekend, grilling each other on the material.

"Bones, bones, bones," Beth groaned as she went over the dentition yet another time. "These teeth were in this primate, these teeth were in a more refined primate, this was in homo sapiens... aaaahhhhhh!" she screamed, pulling at her red hair. "I'll never remember all this!" She glared at Bodie, who was grinning. "And I'll never forgive you for talking me into taking this class with you! I'm a history major! Why do I need a minor in anthropology?"

"Because when I become famous and get a job

at some super university as a professor, you can come and teach there with me." She wiggled her eyebrows. "I'll have connections! Wait and see!"

Beth sighed. Her expression was doubtful.

"Only a few more years to go," Bodie teased.

Beth's green eyes narrowed. "I'm not taking any more anthropology classes, period."

Bodie had only grinned, as well. Her best friend was like herself, out of step with the world, old-fashioned and deeply religious. It was hard to be that way on a modern college campus without getting hassled by more progressive students. But Beth and Bodie stuck together and coped.

Bodie opened her eyes. She was never going to get this biology committed to memory by thinking about other things.

She frowned as music started playing. She got up to answer her cell phone, which was playing one of the *Star Trek* themes.

Bodie opened it. "Hello?"

There was a pause. "Bodie?"

Her heart skipped. "Yes."

She moved to the door and pushed it shut, so she wouldn't disturb her grandfather.

"About earlier tonight," Cane began slowly.

"Yes?" She was beginning to sound like a broken record.

He cleared his throat. "If I said anything out of the way, I'm sorry."

She hesitated. "You don't remember?" she asked.

He laughed softly. "I was pretty much drunk out of my mind," he said with a long sigh. "Honest to God, I remember getting into the truck with you. The next thing I remember is waking up with a pounding headache and so sick that I had to run to the bathroom." He hesitated again, while Bodie's heart fell like lead. All that, and he didn't remember anything?

"You should stop treeing bars," she said quietly.

"If I'm going to have memory loss like this, yes, I guess you're right."

"And more specifically, you should stop trying to pick up women in bars," she said with a bite in her soft voice.

He sighed. "Right again."

"You need to get back into therapy. Both kinds."

There was a long hesitation.

"You're not doing yourself or your brothers any favors by behaving like that, Cane," she told him. "One day, paying off the damage won't be enough and you'll have a police record. Think how that would look in the newspaper."

There was a sound, like a man sitting down in a leather chair. The sound leather made was no stranger to Bodie, who'd wished all her young life for a chair so fancy for her grandfather. His easy chair was cloth, faded and with torn spots that Bodie kept sewing up.

"You're not the only person who came home from the military with problems of one sort or another," she continued, but in a less hostile tone. "People cope. They have to."

"I'm not coping…very well," he confessed.

"You have to have a psychologist that you like and trust," she said, recalling her friend Beth's entry into therapy over a childhood incident. "I don't think you liked your last one at all."

"I didn't," he said curtly. "Smart guy, never had a pain or injury in his life, said you just had to pull yourself together like a man and face the fact that you're crippled…."

"Oh, for heaven's sake!" she exclaimed. "You should have walked right out the door!"

"I did," he muttered. "Then everybody said I wasn't trying because I quit therapy."

"You should have told why you quit, and nobody would have said anything," she shot back.

He sighed. "Yes. I guess I should have."

"Aren't you supposed to be on the road in the morning with Big Red for that cattle show?" she asked suddenly, naming their prize bull who was on the show circuit. He'd won all sorts of awards.

Cane took one of the ranch cowboys along with him on the road, to help manage the big bull who was, however, gentle as a lamb on the lead. Having another man who could help if Big Red got out of hand was a smart precaution.

"I'm headed out later, in fact. I just wanted to make sure I hadn't abused your trust," he added gently. "Not good policy, to alienate your only caretaker."

"Tank or Mallory could save bars from you if they had to," she pointed out.

"Well, yes, but not without some broken teeth. You can do it with fewer bruises."

"Nice to know I'm useful," she replied with a smile in her voice.

There was another pause. He didn't like talking on the telephone. He did it reluctantly at best. "You dating anybody from that college you go to?" he asked suddenly.

Her heart jumped. "Why?"

"Just curious."

"I'm too busy studying to run around with men," she muttered. "I wasn't blessed with the size brain all you Kirk boys have. I have to dig for my grades."

"We all have degrees," he admitted. "But we had to dig for ours, too. Well, maybe not Mallory. He's just smart."

"He is."

"When do you go back to school?"

"Tomorrow morning before daylight," she said heavily. "My first final is after lunch tomorrow. It's finals all week."

There was another pause. "You coming back home after you finish those?"

"Yes. I'll be here until the first of the year, through the holidays. Granddaddy would be all alone without me. We only have each other."

"And your stepfather," he said, but without any warmth in his tone.

"Will Jones is not part of my family," she bit off. "Not at all."

"Can't say I blame you for not claiming him," he admitted. "None of us ever understood what your mother saw in him."

Not for worlds would Bodie admit what her mother had said, that she knew she was dying and it was worth putting up with her new husband's quirks because he was well-to-do and was willing to pay her medical bills and take care of Bodie. It had been a little more complicated than that. Bodie had spent the past two years getting undressed in bathrooms and locking her door at night to prevent any unwanted attention from her mother's husband. Then when her mother died, everything had come to a head just after the funeral and she'd gone to Granddaddy's home for good.

"There's no accounting for taste," Cane said.

"Truly."

"It was money, wasn't it?" he asked suddenly. "She was sick for a long time and couldn't work."

Bodie's heart skipped. Her bow lips made a thin line. "Something like that."

"She was proud," he said unexpectedly. "Not the sort of person to ever ask for help."

She didn't reply.

"All right, I won't pry," he said after the silence. "So, I guess I'll see you when you come home."

"Yes," she said, hesitant.

"If I said or did anything to upset you, I'm sorry," he added. "I wish I could remember, but the whole night's a blur. Tank said you looked a little ruffled when he drove you home."

"I should have looked ruffled!" she replied with spirit. "Trying to wrestle a huge, heavy man onto a bed when he's deadweight would cause most people to look ruffled! And then you passed out…"

"Oh." He laughed, softly, deeply. "Okay. That's really what I wanted to know."

She was blushing. Thank goodness he couldn't see. "So, you don't owe me any apologies," she said.

"I guess not. I had this really crazy dream to-

night…but it was just a dream, I guess, after all."
He laughed, while Bodie bit her tongue. "Damned
woman hurt my feelings so bad," he said in a heavy
tone. "I take things hard."

"Women come in all shapes and sizes and dis-
positions," she pointed out. "I don't think women
who hang out in bars looking for men are particu-
larly sensitive. Just my two cents."

"You want to know what they're looking for,
I'll tell you…"

"Don't!"

"It's money," he said flatly. "It was a five-star
hotel, and a lot of rich men have a nightcap. She
was waiting for a patsy to show up, and I walked
in. If she'd seen an empty sleeve, she probably
never would have come near me, with her hang-ups
about disability," he said curtly. "I guess I should
toss that damned prosthesis in the trash can. I
would, except I could buy a car with what it cost."

"They're working on prosthetics that can be di-
rectly connected to nerve endings, so they work
like real hands," she told him. "The whole field
of prosthetics is very exciting, with all the advances…."

"And why would you be reading up on that?"
he asked suddenly.

She hesitated. "Because I have this idiot friend
who thinks he's disabled," she fired right back.

He burst out laughing. "Are we friends?"

"If we weren't, why would I be rescuing you from bars and certain arrest?" she wondered out loud.

He sighed. "Yeah," he replied. "I guess we are friends." He paused. "You're barely twenty-two, Bodie," he said gently. "I'm thirty-four. It's an odd friendship. And just so you know, I'm not in the market for a child bride."

"You think I'd want to marry you?" she exclaimed.

There was a hesitation. She could almost feel the outrage. He'd be thinking immediately she didn't want to marry him because of his arm.

"Just because you know a tibia from a fibula when you dig it up, right?" she continued quickly in a sardonic tone. "And because you know how to pronounce Australopithecus and you know what a foramen magnum is!" she said, referring to the large hole at the base of the skull.

He seemed taken aback. "Well, I do know what it is."

"You wait," she said. "When I finish my master's work and get into the PhD program in anthropology, I'll give you a run for your money."

"That's a long course of study."

"I know. Years and years. But I don't have any plans to marry, either," she added, "and certainly not to a man just because he can tell an atlas from a sacrum. So there."

He laughed softly. "I used to love to dig."

"You can get people to dig for you, and still do it," she suggested. "In fact, when you're doing the delicate work, it doesn't really require two hands. Just a toothbrush and a trowel and no aversion to dust and mud."

"I suppose."

"You shouldn't give up something you love."

"Bones and mud."

"Yes." She laughed. "Bones and mud."

"Well, I'll think about it."

"Think about the therapist, too, would you?" she asked. "I've already lined up a summer job at a dig in Colorado next year after graduation. I'll be away for several weeks. Nobody to rescue you from bar brawls," she added pointedly. "And depending on which specialization I choose, I might go overseas for PhD work, do classical archaeology in the Middle East...."

"No!" he said flatly. "Don't even think about it. I'll talk to your grandfather if you even consider it."

She was surprised and flattered by the protest. She knew he was remembering what had happened to him in Iraq, with the roadside bomb. "Cane, I wouldn't be working in a combat zone," she said softly. "It would be at a dig site, with security people."

"I've seen the quality of some of their security people," he came back. "Rent-a-Merc," he said sarcastically. "Not even real military—independent contractors who work for the highest bidder. And I wouldn't trust them to guard one of our culls!" he said, alluding to the non-producing cows who were sold at auction each breeding season.

"Selling off poor cows because they can't have babies," she muttered. "Barbarian!"

He laughed roundly. "Listen, ranches run on offspring. No cow kids, no ranch, get it?"

"I get it. But it's still cow insensitivity. Imagine if you couldn't have kids and somebody threw you off the ranch!"

"I imagine they'd have a pretty hard time harnessing me," he admitted. "Besides, that's not something I'll ever have to worry about, I'm sure." He hesitated. "You want kids?"

"Of course, someday," she qualified, "when I'm through school and have my doctorate and have some success in my profession, so that I can afford them."

"I think it might be a problem if you wait until you're moving around with a walker," he said.

"It won't take that long!"

"Generally speaking, if you wait to have kids

until you can afford them, you'll never have any."
There was a pause. "I hope you don't plan to do
what a lot of career women do—have a child from
a donor you don't even know."

She made a huffing sound. "If I have kids, I
plan to have them in the normal way, and with
a husband, however unpopular that idea may be
these days!"

He laughed. "Statistically, married people still
have the edge in childbearing."

"Civilization falls on issues of religion and mo-
rality," she stated. "First go the arts, then go the
morals, then go the laws and out goes the civilization. Egypt under the pharaohs, Rome..."

"I have to leave pretty soon."

"I was just getting up to speed!" she protested.
"Where's my soapbox...?"

"Another time. I studied western civ, too, you
know."

"Yes. Sorry."

He hesitated. "You're sure that nothing...
happened?" he asked again.

"Cane, you were too drunk for anything to happen," she replied. "Why are you so concerned?"

"Men get dangerous when they drink, honey,"
he said, and her heart jumped and skipped in a
flurry of delight, because he'd never used pet
names. "I wouldn't want to do anything out-of-

the-way. Maybe it's a bad idea to let my brothers keep calling you when I go on a bender. One day, I might do something unspeakable and we'd both have to live with it."

"The answer to that is that you stop getting drunk in bars," she said in a droll tone.

"Spoilsport."

"You can drink at home, can't you?"

"It's the ambiance of bars. I don't have that at the ranch. Besides, Mavie would throw me out the back door and pepper me with potato peelings if I even tried it."

"Your housekeeper has good sense."

"Good something. At least she can cook.

"Well, I guess I'll let you go," he said after a minute.

"You be careful on the road," she said softly, in a tone far more intimate than she meant it to be.

"You be careful, too," he added. His own tone was oddly tender. "Wear a coat when you go out. Temperature's dropping."

"I noticed."

Soft breathing came over the connection. "I guess I should go."

"You said that," she replied, and her own tone was as reluctant as his.

He laughed softly. "I guess I did. Well…good night."

"Good night, Cane."

"I like the way you say my name," he said suddenly. "Bye."

He hung up abruptly, as if he regretted what he'd just let slip. Her heart was pounding like mad when she put up the phone and opened her bedroom door. She felt as if her feet weren't even touching the floor.

All the same, she did manage to get the material memorized for her biology final. She got up very early the next morning to drive back to school in her battered old vehicle.

She kissed her granddaddy goodbye.

"Good luck on those finals," he told her as he hugged her.

She grinned. "Thanks. I'll need it. I'll see you next weekend."

He managed a smile. "Miss you when you're not here, girl."

She was touched. "I miss you, too. I won't be away that long, and then we'll have the Christmas holidays together. I'll make cakes and pies…"

"Stop! I'm starving already," he teased.

She grinned again and kissed him again. "See? Something to look forward to."

FINALS WERE EVERY BIT AS grueling as she'd imagined. Her first was biology. A lab rat was laid out on a dissecting board with pins stuck in various portions of its anatomy, designating which parts were to be labeled and discussed on the exam.

She felt that she'd sweated blood on the written portion, however, especially trying to recall the methodology of the Punnett Square, used to predict heritability of genetic traits. That was one part of the textbook section that she had problems with. But she hoped she remembered enough of the material to slide by.

The next exam was physical anthropology. That one didn't worry her. She loved the subject so much that she was in her element when she studied it. She breezed through the test. Only two to go at that point, English and sociology.

FINALLY THE EXAMS WERE finished, the teacher evaluation forms at the end of each class were filled out and turned in and she was packing to go home.

"You should stay here tonight...come out with us to celebrate," Beth told her with a grin. "Ted's got this friend Harvey. He's really nice, you'd like him. You never date," she accused.

Bodie just shook her head as she went back to her packing. She wasn't going to tell her friend anything about Cane, for fear of being teased. It was too early in her changed attitude toward him for that. "I have a career in mind. No time for romantic activities."

"There's the holidays, we could go out then," Beth persisted.

Bodie shook her head again. "I'm going home for the holidays and it's just too far to drive back with gas prices what they are. I'm really sorry," she said when her friend looked disappointed.

"Well, I'm going home, too, to Maine," she agreed. "But after the first of the year, when the new semester starts, you really should meet Harvey. He's just so cute!"

"Poor Ted!"

"No! I mean, he's cute. My Ted is gorgeous," she added, wiggling her eyebrows. "He wants to marry me."

"Really?"

"Really." She sighed. "I don't know what to do. I really want to go on to do my master's work in history, but Ted wants to get married now."

"You should do what you want to," Bodie advised.

"Marrying Ted is what I really want to do. Ted and several babies and a nice house with a fence," she said dreamily.

"Babies." Bodie laughed. "I want one, too, but not for years yet. I'm going to be successful first."

Beth gave her a look that she didn't see; her nose was in her suitcase.

"That's why you won't date," Beth guessed. "If you fall in love, that career's going on hold for a while."

"Mind reader," Bodie said. "Now go dress for your date and let me finish packing."

"Ted wants to go dancing. I love to dance!"

"I didn't notice," Bodie said dryly, because it was a familiar theme.

"Okay. Well, you drive safely. I'll see you in January. I hope you have a great Christmas and New Year."

"Thanks. I hope you do, too. And that Ted buys you a nice big diamond," Bodie teased.

"On his salary? Fat chance. But the ring doesn't matter." She sighed. "All I want is Ted."

Bodie just smiled.

CHAPTER THREE

BODIE'S HOMECOMING WAS met with a sense of urgent misery by her grandfather's sudden bout of indigestion. He took a dose of baking soda, an old-time recipe he'd learned from his grandmother, but it didn't seem to be working.

Bodie was worried enough to get him to their family doctor, who diagnosed something that stood her hair on end.

"I think it's his heart," Dr. Banes said gently. "His blood pressure is abnormally high and he has a murmur. I'm having my nurse do an electrocardiogram. I need to send him to a specialist. We have a good one up in Billings, Montana, and he can do an echo, a sound picture, of your grandfather's heart to see if there are clogged arteries."

Bodie's expression was eloquent. "He gets a pension from the ranch he used to work for," she said, remembering the Kirk brothers' kindness in that act. "He's just now eligible for social security, but it won't start until January. He's trying to get disability, too, but it's a long process. We just don't have any money, and there's no insurance."

He patted her on the arm. "We can make arrangements about that," he assured her. "I know you're getting through school on scholarships and grants and student loans," he said. "And you work at a part-time job near the college to pay for your expenses. I admire your work ethic."

"I learned it from Granddaddy." She sighed. "He was always a stickler for earning things instead of being given them."

"He's a fine man. We'll do what we can for him. I promise."

She smiled. "Thanks."

"You can come in with him when we get the results of the trace we're doing. Won't be long."

"Thanks."

ABOUT AN HOUR LATER, she went into the doctor's office with her grandfather. The doctor was very somber.

"I've had my receptionist make you an appointment with a heart specialist in Billings," he told the old man. "Now, don't start fretting," he warned. "We can do a lot of things to help a failing heart. You'll have options and you'll be able to decide…"

"What did you find?" the old man asked shortly. "And don't soft-soap me."

The doctor grimaced. He leaned back in his chair. "I think it's heart failure."

"Oh, no," Bodie ground out.

"I figured there was something pretty bad wrong," the old man agreed, looking no more upset than he'd been all along. "I've had some pain in my chest and left arm, and a lot of breathlessness. That sort of thing. Will I die right away?"

"No one can tell you that. I can tell you that it's actually a fairly common condition at your age, and not necessarily a death sentence. There are medical options. Drugs. Surgical intervention if it will help."

"No surgery," the old man said doggedly. "Nobody's cutting on me."

"Granddaddy," Bodie began.

"Won't change my mind," Rafe Mays told her flatly. "I've had a long life, a good life. No sense trying to prop up a body that won't work right anymore."

"You'll have great-grandchildren one day," Bodie said firmly. "I want them to know you!"

He looked at her. "Great-grandkids?"

"Yes!" she said. She glared at him. "So you'll do what the doctors say, or else."

The old man chuckled. "Just like your grandmother," he said. "My wife was like that. Ordered me around, told me what to do. I've missed that," he added.

"I'll order you around more," Bodie promised. "You have to try. Please. For me."

He grimaced. "Okay. But I'm not getting cut on. Period."

Bodie looked at the doctor with an anguished expression.

"We can do a lot with drugs," he replied. "Wait and get the results of the tests. Then we can all sit down and make decisions. Don't anticipate tomorrow. Okay? I mean both of you."

They both nodded.

"Go home and get some rest," the doctor said, standing up. "You know, most bad news is acceptable when the newness of it wears off. It takes a day or two, but what seems unbearable at first will be easier to manage once you have time to get used to the idea. I can't get that to come out the way I want it to," he said irritably.

"I understand, anyway," Bodie assured him. "Thanks."

"Thanks a lot," the older man said, and shook hands with the doctor. "I appreciate you giving it to me straight. That's why I come to you," he added, and chuckled. "Can't abide being lied to and treated like a three-year-old."

"I understand," the doctor agreed.

Bodie followed her grandfather out the door. She felt the weight of the world on her shoulders.

It was much worse when they got home. Her stepfather was in the living room, waiting for them. It was unsettling to notice that he'd used a key to get in. It was her mother's property. The man had no right to come barging in without an invitation, even if he did own the place!

Bodie said so, at once.

Will Jones just stared at them with a haughty expression. The way he looked at Bodie, in her well-fitting but faded jeans and sweatshirt, was chilling. She glared at him.

"Got no right to barge into my home!" the old man snapped.

Jones shifted his position, in Granddaddy's chair, and didn't speak.

"Why are you here?" Bodie asked.

"The rent," her stepfather said. "I've just raised it by two hundred. I can't manage on that pitiful little life insurance policy your mother took out. I wouldn't even have had that, if I hadn't been insistent before she got the cancer," he said curtly.

"There's a really easy answer," Bodie shot back. "Get a job."

"I work," the man replied, and with an odd smile. "I get paid, too. But I need more."

More to buy his porno, he meant, because Bodie's mother had remarked how expensive it was, considering the amount he bought. It turned Bodie's stomach. She wanted to order him out of the house, remind him that it had been in her family for three generations, like the land. But she was unsure of her ground. Her grandfather couldn't be upset, not now, when he was facing the ordeal of his life. She bit her tongue, trying not to snap.

"I'll take care of it," she told her stepfather. "But the bank's closed by now. It will have to wait until tomorrow."

"Oh, you can write me a check," he said.

She drew in a long breath. "I don't have enough in my checking account. I'll have to draw it out of my savings account. I don't even write checks. I use a debit card for groceries and gas." Her old truck needed tires, but they'd have to wait. She couldn't afford to let Granddaddy lose his home. Not now, of all times.

She would have told her stepfather what his health was like, but she knew it wouldn't do any good. Will Jones had been watching old movies on television at home when her mother died, with Bodie at her bedside, in the hospital. Bodie and her grandfather had made all the arrangements. Her stepfather said he couldn't be bothered with that, although he was quick to call the insurance company and empty her mother's savings account. He'd also been quick to produce a will with her mother's signature, leaving everything her mother had to him. That had been strange, because Bodie's mother had promised everything to her. Perhaps she'd had a change of heart on her deathbed. People did. Bodie hadn't felt bitter at her for making her husband the beneficiary of her property; after all, he'd paid her medical bills.

"I'll come by in the morning, first thing," her stepfather said irritably. "You'd better have the money."

"Bank doesn't open until nine o'clock," she pointed out with cold eyes. "If you come before then, you can wait."

He stood up and moved toward her, his dark eyes flashing angrily. He was overweight, unkempt, with brown hair that looked as if he never cleaned it. She moved back a step. His scent was offensive.

"Don't like me, huh?" he muttered. "Some fine lady you are, right? Well, pride can be cured. You wait and see. I got a real good cure for that."

He glanced at the old man, who looked flushed and unhealthy. "I never should have let you stay here. I could get twice the rent from someone better off."

"Sure you could," Bodie drawled coldly. "I just

know there are a dozen rich people who couldn't wait to move into a house with a tin roof that leaks and a porch you can fall right through!"

He raised his hand. She raised her jaw, daring him.

"Bodie!" her grandfather called shortly. "Don't."

She was trembling with anger. She wanted him to hit her. "Do it," she dared, hissing the words through her teeth. "I'll have the sheriff at your place five minutes later with an arrest warrant!"

He put his hand down and looked suddenly afraid. He knew she'd do it. He knew it would be the end of his life if she did.

He lifted his face. "No," he said insolently. "Hell, no. I'm not giving you a chance to make me look bad in my town. Besides, I wouldn't soil my hand."

"Good thing," she returned icily, "because I'd hurt you. I'd hurt you bad."

"We'll see about that, one day," he told her. He looked around the room. "Maybe you'd better start looking for another place to live. Government housing, maybe, if you can find something cheap enough!"

Bodie's small hands were clenched at her sides. Now he was trying to make her hit him. It was a good strategy: turn her own threats back on her. But she was too savvy for that. She even smiled, to let him know that she'd seen through his provocation.

He glared at her. "I can throw you out any time I like."

"You can," Bodie agreed, "when you can prove non-payment of rent. I'll require a receipt when I give you the money. And if you want to throw us out for any other reason, you'd better have due cause and a warrant. And the sheriff," she added with a cool smile, "because he'll be required."

He let out a furious curse, turned and slammed out of the house.

Granddaddy was looking very pale. Bodie ran to him and eased him down into his chair. "Easy, now, I'm sorry, I shouldn't have said anything…!"

She stopped, because he was laughing. "Damn, girl, if you aren't just like my mother used to be," he said. "When I was a boy, she took a length of rope to a man who tried to take one of our cows, said it had strayed onto his land and it belonged to him. She laid into him with it and beat him to his knees, and then invited him into her house to use the phone so he could call the law and have her arrested." His eyes twinkled. "His pride was busted so bad that he never came back onto the place. Wasn't going to admit to anyone that a woman beat him up."

"My goodness!"

"You're named for her. She was called Emily Bolinda, and her nickname was Bodie, too."

"I'd forgotten that," she confessed, smiling. "You okay?"

He nodded. "Just a bit breathless. Listen, he's going to get us out of here one way or another. You know that. It isn't the money. It's revenge. He hates me. I tried my best to keep her from marrying him. I told her we'd find a way to get enough to support you and her, but she wouldn't listen. She wanted things for you. She knew there was no money for cancer treatments, and no insurance, and she did what she thought was best for both of us." He shook his head. "It was wrong thinking. We'd have managed somehow."

She sat down opposite him. "It's not right, that people can't get treatment because they're poor. Not right, when some people have ten houses and twenty cars and ride around in chauffeured limousines and others are living in cardboard boxes. Taxes should be fair," she muttered.

"Not arguing with that," he assured her. He sighed. "Well, when do we have to go see that specialist?"

"I'm just going to call the doctor's receptionist and find out," she promised, and got up and went to the phone.

She was very worried. Not only about her

grandfather but about the threats her stepfather had made. He was going to bleed them dry. If he couldn't find a way to do it with the rent, he'd find another way to humiliate Bodie. He'd always hated her, because she saw through his act to the filthy man underneath. He'd had plans for her mother's possessions, especially two pieces of jewelry that had been in the family for four generations and were worth a good bit of money. One, a ring, had emeralds and diamonds; there was a matching necklace. Bodie had them locked away. She'd never have sold them, not for worlds. They were her legacy. Her mother had given them to her months before her death. But her stepfather knew about them and wanted them. He was furious that he couldn't find a legal way to obtain them. He'd tried to argue with the lawyer that all her property belonged to him, as her husband, but the lawyer pointed him to a handwritten note, witnesses, that her mother had given Bodie—probably anticipating that Will might try to reclaim them. The note entitled Bodie to the jewelry. No way around that, the lawyer assured Will. No legal way.

So it was war. Not only did he want the jewelry, but his younger male friend wanted Bodie. She'd laughed when he'd asked her out on a date. She knew what he was like because her mother had told her. He liked to date prostitutes and film them.

She'd said that Will Jones had actually mentioned that it would be fun to film him with Bodie, and her mother had had a screaming, furious argument with him over the comment. Over her dead body, she'd raged, and for once, Jones had backed down. But it had chilled Bodie to the bone, knowing that he'd even thought up such a sleazy intention.

She hated the man with a passion. Once, she'd thought of going to the Kirk brothers and asking for help. But they were just starting to get out of the hole. She'd heard that they'd come into a windfall from the sale of several of their prize purebred bulls and that their business was growing by leaps and bounds. That had increased when Mallory had married one of the heirs to the enormous Brannt fortune. Morie Brannt was the daughter of King Brannt, who was one of the richest ranchers in Texas. He'd provided Mallory with two seed bulls rumored to be worth millions. In fact, they were kept under lock and key with a twenty-four-hour guard around them. No way was Mallory risking his prize bulls.

THE APPOINTMENT WITH the specialist had been set up for the following Monday. It was quick work, the receptionist said, because the specialist was usually booked months in advance. But Rafe

Mays's heart problem was so worrying to the doctor that the specialist had promised to work him in.

Meanwhile, she went to the bank and drew out the rent money. Her small savings were wrecked in the process. She'd have to try to get a part-time job here until school started again. Then there would be more medicines to buy, groceries....

She felt like crying, but she couldn't let her grandfather see how despondent she was. There was no money. They lived from check to check, with no luxuries, not even a hot dog and fries on occasion from a fast-food joint. Bodie cooked plain fare, the cheapest food she could prepare, and planned one dish to last at least two days.

It was a frugal, painful existence. She frequently felt guilty at going to college at all. But when she graduated, she could at least get a job that paid a professional wage, so the sacrifices now would be worth it. Master's work might have to wait a bit, though. In June, after graduation, if she got her bachelor's degree in anthropology, she was going to get a full-time job and see if she could catch up the bills a bit before she went back to school. She might have to do the work/study thing, and work one year and study the next. Plenty of people did that. She could do it, too, if it meant leaving Granddaddy better off and less worried. She knew that their financial situation was as frightening to him as it was to her.

He'd suggested asking the Kirks, but reluctantly. She didn't mention that Tank had offered to help and she'd turned him down. She couldn't even ask Tank right now; he was on an extended trip to Europe on ranch business. Mallory and Morie had gone somewhere out of the country, as well.

"You're friends with Cane, sort of," he reminded her. "Wouldn't hurt to just ask him."

She shifted uncomfortably. "He's really sensitive about people asking him for money, especially lately." She didn't add that Cane had almost been a victim of a woman who wanted it, when she'd tried to pick him up in the bar.

"I guess he is. With his disability, likely he thinks that's all women see in him now," he conceded.

Not for worlds would Bodie have mentioned that no woman in her right mind would turn down a man that attractive, disability or not. Cane was so sexy that memories of their brief encounter still left her tossing and turning at night. Her whole body glowed when she thought of him touching her.

She cleared her throat. No reason to go down that road, especially when Cane didn't even remember what had happened. That was a mercy, for a lot of reasons.

"We'll get by," Bodie promised her grandfather.

His eyes narrowed. "Don't you even think of giving up college," he instructed firmly. "Worked too hard, too long, to have one person in my family with a degree. I didn't even finish high school. Had to go to work when my mother got sick. It's a trap. You think you can go back and finish your schooling, but once you make money, all sorts of things come up that needs it," he added solemnly. "You leave now, you won't go back. And that would be a pity, Bodie. A real pity."

She smiled, went and hugged him tight. "Okay."

He chuckled and hugged her back.

"You and me against the world," she said when she drew away, her pale brown eyes were smiling as well as her lips.

"That's how it goes, I reckon." He sighed. "Don't want to go see any specialist," he said heavily. "I don't like people I don't know. Suppose he wants to throw me in a hospital and cut on me?"

"We won't let him," she lied.

He seemed to calm down then, as if he thought she could see the future.

"One day at a time, Granddaddy," she said gently. "Step by step."

He hesitated. Then he nodded.

THE SPECIALIST WAS A MAN only a few years younger than Bodie's grandfather. To the old man's surprise, he was led into an examination room where he was hooked up to some sort of machine that looked right at his heart through his chest. They called it an echocardiogram, a sonogram of the heart.

"Damndest thing I ever saw," he told Bodie while they waited for the cardiologist to read the results. "They let me look at the screen. I could see inside my body!"

"New technology really is amazing," she agreed. She was sitting nervously on the edge of her chair. She'd had a long talk with the receptionist while her grandfather was having his test, about monthly payments. The bill was going to be staggering. It was a testament to Bodie's salesmanship that the payment plan had been agreed on. There was no question of further education after this next semester. Then, too, she had to make sure that her grades held up, so that she'd pass all her subjects and be able to graduate. So many worries. She wondered how in the world she was going to manage any of it.

"Don't chew on them nails like that," her grandfather instructed. "You'll have them gnawed off into the quick."

"Oh." She drew her finger out of her mouth. "Sorry. I'm just nervous a bit."

"Yeah. Me, too."

She got up and found a magazine to read, something about hunting and fishing that she then passed to the old man, who seemed to find it much more interesting than she had.

While they waited, she looked around the waiting room at other people. Some of them had the same worried, drawn expressions that she and her grandfather were wearing. It gave her a sort of comfort, to know that they weren't the only people here with anxieties.

Time dragged on. She stopped watching the clock. There were so many people in the waiting room. Then, suddenly, time sped up and people started going back into the examination rooms. And finally, the nurse called her grandfather's name.

Bodie went with him, prepared to fight her way in if she had to. But the nurse only smiled and put them both in the doctor's office, in front of his desk and padded chair.

Dr. McGillicuddy came in, preoccupied, reading a tablet PC on the way. He glanced at the two worried people facing him.

"We're not going to recommend operating on you," he told the old man at once, and this message was received with great sighs of relief and tears from Bodie.

"Not that it isn't a fairly bad situation," he said as he sat down and put the tablet aside. He clasped his fingers in front of him. "It is heart failure," he said.

"Oh, no!" Bodie burst out, horrified.

He held up a hand. "Not what you're thinking. Not at all. It can be treated with medication and lifestyle changes. It doesn't mean he's a candidate for a funeral home."

Bodie shivered. She'd been so afraid!

Her grandfather smiled at her. "She's my right arm," he told the doctor. "Orders me around, takes care of me. Feeds me good, too."

"No fried foods," the doctor said. "Everything low fat. Go easy on beef and fatty meats, especially salty meats with preservatives. Lots of vegetables and fish."

The old man made a face. "I hate fish."

"You can learn to like it. I did," the specialist said, glowering. "Anyway, my nurse will get the relevant information from you on the way out. You'll have three heart medicines to take. I want you back here in two months, sooner if you have any unusual symptoms. We'll see how the drugs work, first. If they arrest the progress of the disease, we'll be in good shape. If they don't, we can make decisions then about how to proceed."

That sounded ominous, but Bodie didn't react. She just smiled. "Sounds good."

"Yes, it does," her grandfather said heavily. "I hate the thought of hospitals and being cut on. I'm not much keener on some of those tests my regular doctor mentioned."

"I know, I spoke to him earlier," the other man replied quietly. "He said you'd fight tooth and nail to prevent me doing a heart catheterization."

"No, I wouldn't fight, I'd just go home and take the phone off the hook." The older man chuckled.

"So I heard. You know, it's the best way to find out exactly what's going on. If you have clogged arteries or any other problems..."

"Your technician said my arteries looked fine on that thingabob machine," he returned.

"They do," the specialist conceded. "I won't insist on a catheterization right now. But we did a baseline measurement of your heart in an X-ray and we'll take others as we go along, to compare. If your blood pressure shoots up unexpectedly, if your heart enlarges, that will mean the road ahead is dangerous and we have to take precautions."

The old man shifted. "Flying horse."

The specialist blinked. "Sir?"

"Old story I heard," he said. "The king was

going to execute this guy, and he said wait, if you let me live for another year, I'll teach your horse to fly. The king was dubious, but he said, well, okay, what have I got to lose? Guy walks out, and his friend says, are you crazy, you can't teach a horse to fly! The condemned man laughed. He said, in a year, the horse could die, I could die, the king could die...or I might actually teach the horse to fly. Moral of story, time can bring hope."

"I'll remember that," the specialist said with a smile. "Nice story."

"It was in a series I watched on television, about that King Henry VIII of England, a long time ago. Never forgot it."

"I can see why." The specialist stood up and extended his hand. "You go home and take your medicine and call me if you have any problems. Better yet, call my nurses," he said with a chuckle. "They know more than I do!"

Bodie and her grandfather laughed.

"WELL, THAT WAS A RELIEF," he told Bodie on the way home. "I was scared stiff he was going to want to operate on me."

"Me, too," Bodie confessed. "It's such a relief!"

AND IT WAS, UNTIL they got to the drugstore and presented the prescriptions. She asked her grandfather to go and get a can of peaches to take home for supper. While he was diverted, she asked the clerk how much the medicine would be.

She almost passed out at the figure. "You have got to be kidding," she exclaimed in a horrified tone.

"Sorry, not," the young man replied sympathetically. "Look," he said softly, "we can fill the generic version of all three of them. It will still be a lot, but not quite as much."

He gave her a new figure that was the whole rent amount for the next month. She felt sick all over.

The clerk winced. "It's hard, I know," he said. "I have an elderly mother who has a bad heart. We have to buy her medicine. If it wasn't for my job, and my wife's, she'd have to go without. Her social security won't pay for more than a fraction of them, even though she gets them filled at a discount pharmacy and for a small amount of money."

"People shouldn't have to choose between heat and food and medicine and gas," Bodie said in a haunted tone.

"Tell me about it," the clerk agreed wholeheartedly.

She drew in a breath. She was thinking about those two expensive pieces of jewelry at home and how far the money for them would go toward paying the rent and medicine bills. She couldn't let her grandfather die for lack of money. She wouldn't.

She lifted her chin. "Go ahead and fill them," she said quietly. "I have some heirloom jewelry I can sell. It will more than pay for them."

"I hate that for you," he said. "I had to sell my grandmother's engagement ring to pay for a car repair." His eyes were sad. "It would have gone to my daughter one day."

"In the end, they're just things, though." She glanced at her grandfather down the aisle and smiled gently. "People are much more important."

"I can't argue with that. We'll have them for you in about a half hour, if that's okay."

"That will be fine," she assured him.

SHE DROVE HER GRANDFATHER home. Then she dug the necklace and ring out from under her bed, where they'd lived in a photograph box since she moved in. She looked at them lovingly, touched them, then closed the box. Sentiment was far too expensive at the moment. She'd rather have her grandfather than pretty things from a different day and age, even if it was going to wrench her heart to sell them. Her mother had loved them, shown them to her from her childhood…explained the legends that surrounded them. Bodie had grown up loving them, as well, as a connection to a long-ago place somewhere in Spain.

But it was unlikely that she'd have children. She didn't really want to get married, not for years, and she wasn't sure about having a child even then. Or so she told herself. It made it easier to take the box into town, to a pawn shop, and talk to the clerk.

"MISS, ARE YOU SURE you want to do this?" he asked. "These are heirlooms…"

"I have to," she said gently. "My grandfather is very ill. We can't afford his medicine."

The man grimaced. "Damned shame," he said.

Bodie stared at the jewels, vaguely aware of someone coming into the store behind her. "Yes," she said. "I know." She was fighting tears.

"Well, I promise you I won't sell them to any-body," he told her. "I'll lock them up tight until you can afford to get them back. How about that?"

"You would…do that?" she asked, surprised. "But it might be months…"

"So I'll wait months." He smiled.

She had to fight to speak, past the lump in her throat. It was so kind! "Thank you," she managed to say.

"You're welcome. Hold on to that," he added, sliding a ticket across to her. "You'll need it."

She smiled. "Thank you very much."

He counted out a number of bills, more than she'd expected to get for the jewelry. "You be careful with that," he added.

She stuffed it into her pocketbook. "I will."

"See you in a few months," he said, and smiled again.

"Okay. That's a deal."

She turned, almost colliding with a cowboy. She didn't look up to see who it was. Plenty of ranches in the area. She didn't know who worked for most of them.

The cowboy watched her go out of the shop and frowned. "Wasn't that Bodie?" he asked the clerk, who was his brother-in-law.

"Sure was. Her granddad's in bad shape. She couldn't afford his medicine so she pawned her family treasures." He showed them to the other man. "Hell of a shame."

"Yes. It is."

The cowboy opened his cell phone and made a call.

CHAPTER FOUR

BODIE BOUGHT HER grandfather's medicine with part of the money she'd gotten from the jewelry. The rest she hid under her bed for an emergency. She would have to find a part-time job while she was out of school, anything to help bring in a few more dollars.

But she scoured the want ads and couldn't find anybody who was hiring, even temporarily, for the holidays. She could get a job up at Jackson Hole, maybe, in one of the shops, but the sudden snows had closed everything down and at least one road into the area had been shut down. So driving up there even to apply was out of the question now. Not that her junky old pickup truck would even make it that far, she mused darkly, or that she could afford the gas to go back and forth.

She checked at the two local restaurants and the fast-food joints to see if they needed anyone, even to wash dishes, but nobody was hiring.

She went back home dejected, having wasted

twelve dollars worth of gas that she could ill afford just to look for work. She did put in applications in a couple of places, but the managers weren't encouraging.

In desperation she looked for ranch work. Not on the Kirk place, that would be too humiliating even to ask, but on two other area ranches. One rancher did have work, driving heavy machinery. But Bodie had no training and it wasn't a skill she was eager to learn. So she went back home in defeat.

Her grandfather seemed to react well to the medicine after the first few days. He perked up and had more energy, and he was less breathless. Bodie smiled and pretended that everything was all right, but she was very worried. She worked part-time at a convenience store in Billings near the college she attended, but that was a long commute. She couldn't even afford the gas. She didn't know how they were going to afford the medicine next month, or pay the increased rent that Will Jones was demanding, or even have enough for Christmas presents. She went into her room, closed the door and cried. She'd never felt so despondent, and she didn't dare let her grandfather see how worried she really was. It was like the end of the world.

But she dried her eyes and went into the kitchen

to cook, resolved that God was in control of everything, anyway, and would provide somehow. It was faith that kept her going through the worst of times. Often, it seemed that faith was all she had to hold on to.

She went out into the backyard and cut down a small spruce tree, found an antiquated old tree stand and put the tree in it. They had decorations that her mother had stored, some of which were three generations old. Decorating the tree cheered her up and the tree made the living room look alive with color.

At least, it cheered her up until Will Jones came to the door and demanded money for cutting down one of his trees.

"Your trees?" Bodie exclaimed. "My mother planted those trees before she got sick…!"

"It's my house, my land and my trees, and you owe me fifty dollars for that tree," Will Jones said haughtily. "That's what they charge in those tree lots."

Bodie felt the blood drain out of her face. She hadn't even thought about cutting the tree. They'd done it for years. In fact, her mother had planted them for just this purpose.

"You can add it in with the rent," the man said coldly, and he smiled. "How are you managing, anyway? You don't have a job. I guess all that education makes you too good to get a real job, don't it?"

"I've applied for jobs all over town," Bodie said in a quiet tone.

"I guess all the boss jobs are taken, huh?" he taunted.

"You'll get your money," Bodie said coldly.

Jones looked around the room, trying to find something to complain about. "Needs dusting," he muttered when he drew a finger across the dining room table.

"I haven't cleaned house today. I was looking for work," she reminded him.

"Not many jobs going, I guess. I got one." He gave her a leering stare. "You get desperate, you just come see me."

She could guess what sort of job it was. "I can manage."

"My friend Larry really likes you," he said. "A lot. He'd like to spend some time with you, at my place. You'd be chaperoned, if that's what worries you." He laughed as he said it, and Bodie felt sick to her stomach. She could imagine what he was talking about. He'd mentioned in the past how he'd love to film her with his friend Larry.

"You can pick a woman up on a street corner for that sort of work," Bodie said coldly.

He gave her a hard look. "You're so lily-white,

aren't you?" he scoffed. "Upstanding young woman, never put a foot wrong, won't play around with any men. You gay?" he asked.

"No," she said. "But I wouldn't be ashamed to admit it, if I was."

He made a sound in his throat. "Everybody knows about you college girls," he said sarcastically. "You're like them—you just don't want anybody around here to know it."

"I'm not like that," she said. "I'm a person of faith."

"St. Bolinda," he muttered. "Well, you might get a shock one day. It wouldn't hurt you to learn a little humility. Looking down on other people, making out like you're so much better than they are, with your sterling morals. You need taking down a peg."

"And you're just the guy to do it, right?" she asked with a bite in her voice.

"Maybe I am," he shot back. "You're only allowed to stay here if you pay rent and do what I say." He looked around the house. "Maybe the house needs fixing and you and your old family member will have to leave while it gets done. Maybe it will take a year or so to do it, too." He was thinking aloud. He smiled with contempt. "Nobody would say you'd been evicted if I did that, and you wouldn't have a legal leg to stand on."

"Anybody could see that the house isn't in that bad a shape!" she shot back angrily.

"Middle of the night, something could happen to the roof," he said, pursing his lips thoughtfully. "Couldn't prove a thing, either."

She felt her blood run cold. She couldn't afford the rent here, how would she afford it someplace else? The cost of moving alone was out of her reach right now. She had just a few dollars, barely enough for groceries and gas. She felt the terror all the way to the pit of her stomach.

And he knew it. He smiled even more widely. "Scares you, don't it?" he mused. "Good. You think about that. You don't keep me happy, why you could have to move tomorrow. It could be an emergency."

"I'd tell," she said.

"Tell what?"

"What you just said to me," she retorted.

"Yeah? Prove it." And he laughed.

She just stood there, horrified.

"Yep. Maybe you'll need those repairs real soon. And I want to be paid for that tree by, let's say, the weekend." His face went hard. "Otherwise, you'll come over to my house on Saturday and spend a little time with Larry. Not a big thing to ask, is it? Just spend a few hours with my friend and me."

"I'll die first," she said huskily.

His eyebrows arched. "Yeah? Can't afford your grandfather's medicine now, how will you afford it next month? How about the rent next month?" He pursed his lips again. The way he looked at her chilled her blood. "I could make all those problems go away. Even put your grandfather's medicine on my credit card. You'd be grateful for that, now, wouldn't you?"

She couldn't even speak she was so angry.

"You just think about it," he added with a short laugh. "You'll come around to my way of thinking."

She'd starve first, she'd die first, she was still thinking of things she'd do first when he left. Her grandfather, out watering his roses, hadn't heard a word of it. He came back in a minute later, frowning.

"Was that Will?" he asked angrily. "What did he want? We paid his rent."

"I cut down a tree."

"Oh, my God, he's not going to charge us for the tree my own daughter planted on her own land?"

She forced a smile. "Of course not. Everything's fine. How about a piece of cake and some decaffeinated coffee?" she asked innocently.

She debated going to the Kirks. Anything, even humbling her pride, was better than her stepfather's solution. She'd pawned her mother's jewelry.

There wasn't anything else of value that she could even pawn. No job, no money, no hope and Granddaddy with a condition that could kill him quickly.

In the middle of her despondency, her old truck developed a noise that sounded very much like the brakes would need relining. She had no money for repairs. If only she had some real skill, some way of making extra cash! But digging up old things wasn't really going to help at the moment.

She sighed and rubbed the rock in her pocket. It was something her late mother had given her. Her grandmother, who had a rock collection that was sizable, had picked it up near the place she lived as a girl. The rock had been in the family for three generations now. Bodie called it a "worry stone," because she used it to soothe herself when she was upset. She loved its smooth contours. It was heavy for its size. She wondered why it was so heavy. Maybe it had some sort of ore mixed in with it. She didn't study geology. She wished she had. Many of her grandmother's rocks were perched on windowsills inside the house. Bodie didn't even know what sort of rocks they were. She didn't care. They were treasures to her.

"You're brooding again, girl," her grandfather observed when she joined him in the living room, her hand busy in her jeans pocket. "Got that rock going." He chuckled. "Your grandmother used to carry it around in her own pocket and rub it when she had something on her mind. Guess it runs in the family."

"I guess so." Bodie laughed. She pulled it out and turned it over. The rock was oddly heavy, shaped sort of like a wedge. It had a dark gray color and it was shiny on the outside. Inside, where a piece was broken off, she glimpsed a different composition. "I wonder what sort of rock it is."

"It's just a rock, sugar," he said, sighing. "Your grandmother liked unusual looking ones, but none of them had diamonds inside. Pity."

She laughed and repocketed the stone. "Yes. It really is."

He shoved his hands into the pockets of his faded and stained blue jeans. His hair was white. He was tall and thin, and he looked pale.

"You okay?" she asked, worried.

He shrugged. "Just a little indigestion. Must be that Mexican stuff we had last night." He rubbed his stomach. "I love it, but those spices are pretty hot."

She grimaced. "Sorry. I didn't realize I'd put so much chili powder in it."

"Not your fault. You like things hot. I used to, but my old taste buds don't work so good anymore."

She smiled. "Just the same, I'll tone it down a notch next time."

He grinned. "Thanks."

She picked up her coat. "I'm going out for a bit."

"That truck squeals like a pig," he commented. "The brakes may be going. You be careful. Need to have those brakes relined, anyway."

Not for worlds would she have told him that she didn't have the price of a full tank of gas, much less anything for repairs. His retirement check that the Kirks provided wasn't due until after Christmas, and they still had to get through utility bills. Her grandfather's social security wouldn't start until January. That would be too little too late, especially with the truck apparently dying.

She groaned when the brakes squealed at a stop sign, because there was a deputy sheriff in his car behind her. But he didn't stop her. She let out a breath of relief as she drove, cautiously, toward the Kirk ranch. She knew this was going to be a mistake, but she was out of options.

When she pulled up at the front porch, she didn't see any vehicles around. That was an ominous start to what seemed like the worst sort of idea, anyway. She hadn't seen Cane since that night she'd brought him home from the bar, or spoken to him since his unexpected phone call. Actually, she was nervous about seeing him again, and her heart was pounding like mad when she rang the doorbell. She almost wished nobody was home.

But that was cowardice. She had to find some way to solve her financial problems before she was forced to do what Will wanted. Robbing a bank would be easier for her, but she couldn't manage a solution that would spare her pride in any way at all. Just asking Cane Kirk for a loan was going to be traumatic enough. She had no collateral, so going to a bank was useless. She had to consider her grandfather. He was the most important thing in her whole world. She'd do anything to keep him safe; even, as a last resort, going out with her stepfather's friend. Even then, she promised herself, if anything off-color was even mentioned, she'd leave and find some other way to pay for her grandfather's meds if she had to beg a job digging ditches.

She waited, breath hushed, but no sound came from inside the house. She started to push the doorbell again, grimaced as she thought how painful it would be to even ask Cane for help, and turned on her heel. She might as well go home and find a pretty dress and get ready to go on a date with Larry. She made an awful face. The man was horrible. Just horrible. No sane woman...

"Hi, there."

She jumped at the sound of Cane's deep voice behind her.

She turned around, flushed. "Oh. Hi. You startled me." She put a hand to her chest, flushed and laughed nervously. "I thought nobody was home."

"I was out back looking at Darby's new whittling knife. His sister sent it. An early Christmas present, he said." He cocked his head and studied her. "You need something?"

Was it that obvious, she wondered silently. She bit her lip. "I was just wondering…"

"Hey, there," Darby interrupted, coming up on the porch from behind Cane. "I heard that god-awful racket your truck was making. Your brakes are going, girl. Need to get that seen about before you have a wreck."

"Chance would be a fine thing," she said heavily. "I just paid for Granddaddy's new heart pills. Not much left over for brakes, I'm afraid."

"Pull it into the shed and have Billy reline those brakes, will you?" Cane told Darby at once. "Check the rest of it while you're at it."

"Sure thing," Darby said, holding his hand out for the keys.

"Oh, no, really…!" she tried to argue.

"Give him the keys," Cane directed. He raised his eyebrows and grinned. "Unless you want me to fish them out."

She scrambled them out of her pocket and dashed them into Darby's hand. Both men chuckled.

"I seem to recall making you go fish for my keys, the last time you came here," Cane remarked.

"At least you're staying out of bars, lately, I gather?" she shot back, her pale brown eyes twinkling.

He chuckled again. "Somewhat. I've got to ride fence. You can come with me. It'll pass the time while they get your truck squared away." He gave it a contemptuous look. "Paint's the only thing holding the doors on," he said scathingly.

"It's a very nice truck," she argued. "It just has some little flaws."

"Yeah, like an engine that only hits on two cylinders and a carburetor that backfires every time you start it."

"The radio works fine!" she retorted after a minute, having searched hard for one virtue she could ascribe to her ride.

He laughed. "Okay. Point to you."

They walked into the barn. "Hey, Roy, saddle Pirate for her, will you?" he asked.

"Sure thing, boss."

The mare that Cane usually rode was already saddled and hitched to a stall nearby. Pirate was an older horse, neutered and quiet.

"You still don't think I can ride," she muttered.

"Hell, you can ride Buzzsaw if you like," he

stated mildly. "I just don't want to have to pay the hospital bills when he throws you into a tree."

She made a thin line with her lips. "I could ride him if I wanted to."

"Right."

"Some people aren't good on horses."

"Like you, college kid," he joked.

"I know how to date projectile points," she murmured.

"Me, too. We can have a competition one day."

She sighed. It was a pointless argument, and she didn't want him to get out of the good mood he was in. She hated having to ask for help. But he could see the shape her truck was in. He'd probably guess she was in over her head with her grandfather. He might even offer help and save her pride. She hoped he would.

BUT HE DIDN'T MENTION money. They rode lazily across the fields, where a light coat of snow had fallen that morning. It was going to be gone by afternoon, because the temperature was already above freezing. It just looked pretty, against the leafless trees and the dull beige of stubble where wheat had grown earlier in the year.

"Maybe it will snow for Christmas this year," she said.

"Not likely," he replied.

"It could happen."

He shrugged. "I suppose."

She fingered the reins, feeling the rocking chair movement of the horse. He was old, but he was gentle and trustworthy. She was never going to be a good rider. She hadn't the correct seat, for one thing, and for another, she was mostly afraid of horses. She wasn't going to admit that to a cattleman, however.

"Why is your grandfather taking heart pills?" he asked out of the blue.

"He has heart failure, the doctor says," she replied heavily. "I've been worried sick. They've got him on three or four medicines to keep it under control, and they say it's not going to be fatal. Scared us both to death. He thought it was just indigestion. So did I."

He reined in his mount and stared at her curiously. "Isn't he old enough for social security?"

She sighed. "It starts in January. At least that will help."

"Insurance?"

She shifted restlessly. This was getting personal, and it was hurting her pride to talk about it, more than she'd thought it would. "Yes, he does have that," she lied. "And it helps pay for his medicine, too. So does that check you guys send him every month for retirement. You don't know how grateful he is for that."

His dark eyes narrowed on her face. He didn't say anything. He moved the horse forward again.

They spotted a fence post that had been knocked half down by a fallen tree. Cane dismounted, lifted the small tree off with his one good arm and tossed it aside. He righted the fence post, glaring at the way it sat.

"Damn. I need a shovel and somebody to hold the wire while I nail it back." He glanced at her.

"I don't carry a shovel in my pocket. Sorry." She twisted her lips and her eyes twinkled. It made her feel proud that he didn't seem disturbed by not being able to do the job alone. His disability seemed to affect him less when he was with her.

He made a face at her. He pulled out his cell phone, called Darby and told him the location of the post that needed resetting.

"Better get to it this afternoon or tomorrow," Cane said over the phone. "Just in case any nervous cattle decide to run this way. Highway's pretty close by."

He listened, chuckled. "Right. See you." He closed the phone and repocketed it. "He said it would be bad luck if a convertible drove by and a cow decided to hitch a ride."

She laughed. "There was this story on the news,

about a cow that got loose from a slaughterhouse and was spared. The guy who wrote the story called it a cow. It was a steer." She shook her head. "People who don't live on the land just don't know the difference."

"As I recall, I had to educate you on the subject. You thought a yearling heifer was a cow. They're not cows until they're two years old and they've been bred."

She gave him a speaking look.

"We're not all born knowing ranch vernacular, I guess."

"Really!"

"Let's ride down this way. We've had a lot of trees go down this fall. Weather's gone crazy, it seems."

"Yes, I noticed."

"I've got to get Darby to find us a nice tree to cut down for Christmas, to decorate." He glanced at her. "You've got yours up already, I imagine."

She laughed. Her mania for the yearly Christmas tree was well-known locally. "Yes, I do." She didn't add that she'd had to pay her stepfather for cutting it down. "I love Christmas. It's my favorite holiday."

He got back into the saddle, laboriously. She pretended not to notice, to save his pride. It was really hard for a cowboy to be missing part of an arm. Even with the prosthesis, mounting wouldn't have been much easier. It didn't have the ability to lift.

"I was thinking," she began, trying to find a way to approach the subject.

"Don't do too much of that," he advised dryly. "It can be deadly."

He sounded grim. She reined in the old horse and stared at him. "What makes you say that?"

He rode over to a small stream that ran through the property, dismounted and let the horse drink, still holding gingerly to the reins. She did likewise.

"You've lived with that problem for some time now," she pointed out, indicating his arm. "You're coping very well, it seems to me, except for an occasional bout of alcohol."

"Looks are deceiving." He sighed, looking out over the barren landscape. "That's how I feel inside," he commented, indicating the bare look of the pasture. "Dead. Useless."

"If you lose your brain, that's how you'd feel, sure," she said, moving to face him. He was so much taller that her head was barely up to his shoulder. "But you're still able to do a lot of stuff. You can show cattle, you can market them, you can talk to potential buyers, all those things. That's a real skill." She moved uncomfortably. "I'm not good with people. I'm shy and it's really hard for me to talk to people I don't know."

"You talk to me."

"Sure. I know you. Well, as much as you can know a person you see from a distance," she qualified. "You don't make me feel awkward."

"I don't?" He moved a step closer, so that she could feel the heat and power of his body. Her breath caught, and he laughed softly, deeply. "Are you sure about that, Bodie?"

He smelled of spice. She loved the cologne he used. He was always immaculately clean, even his fingernails. As he moved closer, both her small hands pushed into the soft fabric of his shirt and she felt thick hair and muscle underneath.

His good hand speared into her short, thick black hair and tilted her face up, so that he could see those pale brown eyes at point-blank range. He wasn't smiling now.

"You have eyes like a wolf I saw once, up close," he said quietly. "Ran into him way back in the forest when I was hunting deer one fall. Damndest thing, he came almost right up to me, stared at me for a minute, and turned and trotted away. Big fella, too, gray and powerful. I never saw an animal like him."

"Don't Native Americans say that they have

totem animals?" she asked. "Maybe a wolf is yours."

His hand became caressing in her hair. "I only have a drop of Native blood. Lakota, they say. I've never been sure." He smiled tenderly. "Maybe we should have somebody do a family history, for when the kids come along. I love kids."

"Me, too," she managed to say.

His dark gaze fell to her mouth. "You're so young, Bodie," he murmured huskily. "Probably too young for what I'm about to do."

"What are you…about to do?" she whispered brokenly, hanging at his lips.

"This…"

He bent and drew his lips gently across her mouth, teasing it to open, just a little. Then his mouth came down on it, hard, twisting, demanding. She gasped into his lips, shocked at the pleasure that shot through her as she tasted him.

"Why does this feel so familiar?" he whispered. But he didn't answer his own question. His hand slid down to her back and forced her body into the hardening contours of his own. "Oh, what the hell, I'm starving…!"

His mouth crushed down over hers and he pulled her against him. Her hands worked feverishly at buttons until she got them against his skin, spearing into the thick hair that covered his chest.

She opened her mouth, inciting him, inviting him, to come inside it. And he did. His tongue thrust into the dark softness, and she cried out and shivered.

"Yes, you like that, don't you?" he asked against her lips.

He backed her into a tree and his hips crushed down against hers, letting her feel the sudden swelling of his body. "You know what that is, too, don't you?" he ground out against her open mouth.

She shivered as he moved against her. His mouth was hungry, hot and hard, forcing her lips apart, moving insistently between them. His hand went to the front of her jeans and started to move the zipper down.

She wanted to resist. She really did, but her body was on fire. She'd dreamed of having him do this again, she'd burned from the memory of the last time, the time he didn't even remember.

"Cane," she moaned, and arched her back helplessly as her mouth answered the demand of his.

And then, suddenly, he went still against her. Some deep buried instinct made him stop and pull back. He was flushed and breathless, and his eyes were blazing as he looked down at her.

The accusation in his eyes made her uneasy. "You started it," she accused shakily as he moved quickly away.

"You invited it," he shot back, furious that he'd given way to temptation.

She shivered, cold now that she didn't have the heat of him against her body. She watched him absently do the shirt buttons back up again. His face was like stone. He was coldly furious, and it showed.

"Why did you come here?" he asked suddenly.

She flushed. "I… Well, I…"

"You didn't just show up at my door," he continued with visible suspicion. "You came here looking for something. What do you want, Bodie? Spit it out," he said icily, when she hesitated.

She swallowed. "I was wondering if you could loan me some money."

The expression on his face was so distasteful and contemptuous that she knew she'd damned herself in his eyes forever. She'd reduced herself to the level of that woman in the bar who wanted him for what he had, and dismissed him because he was disabled.

He smiled. It was the most chilling smile she'd ever seen on his lips.

"And what would you be willing to do for it?" he asked with contempt. "More of what we just did? Would you go to bed with me for money? Earn it on your back?" he demanded heatedly.

She moved back a step. "I'm sorry," she choked

out—humiliated by his tone, by the way he was looking at her. She went as red as a beet. "I'm sorry! I'll manage. It was a stupid thing to do. I'll leave the horse at the barn. And thanks for what you asked Darby do for the truck, but I'll just manage, really!"

"Manage. On brakes that don't work?" he gritted.

She swung into the saddle, clumsily because she was so embarrassed. "I'm sorry," she said, fighting tears. Her whole life was going down in flames because she'd been stupid. "I'm so sorry! I should never have asked you that!"

"Why not? The only thing women ever want from me is money, isn't it? Because that's the only thing that would make a woman even consider sleeping with a cripple!" He was furious, absolutely furious. "I thought you were different, you little tease." He spat the words. "You're no better than a call girl, Bodie. A common prostitute, willing to do anything for money!"

She swallowed, hard, sick at heart and cold inside. Tears stung her eyes. "I'm sorry," she managed.

She turned the horse, clumsily, and rode off quickly before she said or did anything even more stupid.

CANE STOOD AND WATCHED her, confused and unsettled by what had happened between them, because it seemed so familiar, as if it wasn't the first time he'd touched her, kissed her like that. He kept going back to that night he was drunk. He couldn't remember what he'd done, but he had a feeling that he'd done something and that it had encouraged Bodie to ask him for a loan.

For money! She was just like every other damned woman, out for what she could get. He was furious, not only that he'd been suckered into kissing her that way, but because she'd put him in a position where he felt guilty that he'd sent her away upset.

He pulled out his phone, called Darby, spoke to him quickly. He hung up, mounted his horse and rode slowly back toward the barn. He didn't want to get there before Darby left with Bodie. Right now he didn't care if he never saw her again.

CHAPTER FIVE

BODIE WAS CRYING LONG before she got back to the barn. But she wiped her eyes on the tail of her ratty old gray hoodie and tried to smile when she encountered Darby.

"Just leave him right there, we'll deal with unsaddling him," the older man said with some concern. "Come on. I'll drive you home. We'll have your truck back there first thing in the morning. Got a few more little things to do to it," he said with a kindly smile.

"No, it's okay, I'll just take it home now," she protested.

"Bodie, we've got the tires off," he said with a gentle smile. "You can't drive it yet."

"Oh."

"Come on." He led her to one of the ranch pickups and helped her into the passenger seat. He drove off. Just as they left the yard, she saw Cane coming toward the barn slowly. It was obvious that he didn't want to have to say anything else to her.

She bit her lip so hard that it drew blood.

"Cane has moods," Darby said gently. "You know that. He's as likely to bite your head off as to smile at you some days. It isn't personal. He gets to thinking about the military and what happened to him, and he just doesn't deal with it well."

"He needs to get back into therapy."

"He did. Lasted a week. Then he got into an argument with the psychologist and wouldn't go back." He glanced at her and winced. "You have to not take things so hard, Bodie. Look, once you hit thirty-five you won't give a damn anymore," he added with a chuckle. "You won't get so upset over things that happen and you won't let the world bother you as much. Trust me."

She sighed. "I wish I was thirty-five now, then," she said heavily. She grimaced. "I asked him for a loan. Gosh, of all the stupid things to do!"

"A loan?"

She had to tell somebody. It was killing her! "Grandaddy's got heart failure, Darby. He has to take these expensive pills and now my stepfather's raised the rent. He even charged me fifty dollars for a tree I cut down that Mama planted, to decorate for Christmas. He says he's going to do something drastic to the house so he can say it needs repairs and throw us out." She fought tears. "Dear God, I've tried every way I know to get a job, but nobody's hiring except Jake Hall, and he needs a heavy equipment driver. I just can't learn that sort of work. I'd do dishes, scrub floors...I can't get anything. We're out of money and the only way I can get any is to do what...what my stepfather wants."

"Which is?" he asked coldly. "Tell me, Bodie."

"He wants me to spend some time with his friend Larry this Saturday," she said heavily, "and take pictures of us. Nothing really bad, just some posed ones..." She hurried over that part of it. "He says if I'll just do that he'll make it right about the rent and help pay for Granddaddy's medicine. I can work near my college in January, I've got a job there set up for when the semester starts, but until then, I can't do a thing." She slumped. "The rent will come due before then. I've pawned my grandmother's jewels, I've sold everything I can sell to get money, but not enough to settle the rent with Will." She tasted blood on her tongue from her lip. She could still taste Cane there, too, and it was unsettling to remember the pleasure he'd given her, even if he felt contempt for her afterward.

"Damn!" Darby bit off. "Listen, kid, I have a little money saved..."

"No." She glared at him. "Absolutely not. I'd have asked Tank if he was home, and he wouldn't have made me feel like a prostitute for doing it.

He even offered, before. He knew I was having a hard time with Granddaddy." Her face went hard. "I'll never forget how Cane looked at me, what he said to me. I'll never forgive him!"

"It was too soon after that women tossed him over for being disabled, I guess," Darby said, seething inside at his boss's actions.

"At least you guys will get my truck in good enough shape that I can drive it," she said. "Thanks for doing that."

"We do what we can to help out," Darby said. "I could call Dalton…"

"No." She drew in a long breath and smiled at him as he pulled up at her porch. "Granddaddy doesn't know what's going on. He thinks we're square with Will on everything, that we have no financial problems. I don't want to tell him. He's in really bad shape, even with the medicine." She shrugged. "I don't even know how long I'll get to have him around. He gets breathless, his heart beat's funny, he's pale and sick to his stomach a lot." She winced. "I need to take him back to the doctor, but they want to be paid up-front these days. I told Cane we had insurance. We don't have a thing. I've got the heart specialist's bill to see to monthly now, as well as our local doctor…" She looked at him with pure desperation. "How are people supposed to live in an economy like this? Why doesn't the government do something?"

"I guess they're afraid they won't get reelected if they do anything wrong, so they just don't do anything. It's all about going back into office, not about helping people." He shook his head. "We should only elect poor people to public office, you know," he said philosophically. "They'd know what it was like to live from paycheck to paycheck, and they'd do things to help the working people and the disabled."

"Chance would be a fine thing." She opened the door. "Thanks for listening, Darby. You won't say anything to Cane?"

"Not if you tell me not to," he replied after a pause.

"I'm telling you. I don't want pity. I'll do what I have to do, so that Granddaddy doesn't have to live in a shelter or on the street." Her face set in hard lines. "I hope Will gets his just deserts one day."

"People do get back what they hand out, even if it takes years," Darby said quietly. "But don't you do anything desperate, you hear me? Give me a day or two to see what I can figure out. Okay?"

She smiled. "Okay," she lied. "Thanks, Darby. Thanks a lot."

"My pleasure. I wish I could do more."

She watched him drive away. Tomorrow was

Saturday. She had one nice dress. She could stomach a little discomfort for money, if it would keep her grandfather alive. She could never let him know. It would kill him. But she was strong. She could do what she had to do, up to a point. She wasn't taking the dress off, not even if Will did evict them....

DARBY WENT BACK AND helped his men fix up the truck for Bodie, but it was in really bad shape, and the work took until late Saturday afternoon.

Darby had worried about what to do, because he was sure Bodie would go over to Will's house and do anything he asked, within reason, if it would save her grandfather a roof over his head. He wasn't about to approach Cane. The other man was surly and distant and snapped if anyone spoke to him.

But Dalton came home, thank God, just as Darby finished working on the truck. He went immediately to see the youngest of the Kirk brothers.

"I need to talk to you," he told Tank.

"Sure. What's up? Cane drinking again?" he asked worriedly.

"It's not Cane, it's Bodie," he said quietly, and then he told him what had happened the day before, and what Will wanted Bodie to do. "She's likely heading over there pretty soon," he concluded. "She'll do whatever she has to, in order to keep a roof over Rafe Mays's head."

"Damn! And Cane let her walk into that?" Tank exploded.

"He doesn't know. She made me promise not to tell him anything after he was so mean to her," Darby replied. "But I didn't promise not to tell you," he added.

Tank laid a big hand on Darby's shoulder. "Thanks, pal. I owe you one. I'd better get over to Will Jones's place before he does something to her that all the psychologists on earth can't fix."

"I owe you one for that. I'm fond of her."

He smiled. "Me, too."

He went into the house, picked up the phone and called Rafe Mays. "Hi, Rafe. It's Tank. Is Bodie there?"

"No," the old man replied, sounding odd. "I think she went to Will's house. Worries me something fierce, I know what that snake's capable of. Tank, she won't tell me what's going on, but I overheard her telling Will he'd better keep his promise not to throw us out of this house. He's making threats, and she's just an innocent, you know. Damn!" He coughed. "Got indigestion so bad I can't hardly talk. I'm going to take a dose of baking soda and see if it won't get easy. Tank, can you go over there and make sure Will's not doing anything to my girl?" he asked weakly. "I hate to ask, but I'm too sick to do it myself. Got no way to go, either, her truck's gone."

"It's over here," Darby said. "We're fixing it for her."

"That Larry came to get her," he added coldly. "She was all dressed up, white in the face. She said she really wanted to talk to Larry and her stepfather, that she was having dinner with them. It's more than that. She looked scared to death...!"

"I'm on my way. You just sit tight, and don't worry, okay?"

The old man sighed. "That little girl is my whole life, Tank," he said heavily. "Don't let them hurt her."

"You know I won't. Take it easy. I'll see you soon."

"You tell her...I love her."

"I'll do that, too."

He hung up. Odd, the way Rafe sounded. It was disturbing. But at the moment, Bodie was the more urgent problem.

"You home?" Cane asked as he came into the room. He blinked. Tank was livid. "What's going on?"

"Bodie's selling herself to Will Jones for the rent payment," he said bluntly. "I hear she asked you for a loan and you sent her packing, so she's doing what she has to do to keep Will from throwing her grandfather out on the street."

"Good God Almighty!" Cane exploded. "She never said anything about that!"

Tank glared at him. "Maybe she figured you were smart enough to know that she wouldn't ask anyone for money if she wasn't desperate."

"She has a job near her college…"

"It's part-time and she doesn't work there except during school. She tried to get a job around here, even cleaning out barns, and there was nothing available. Will's threatened to do something to the house so he can evict them. They'd have to live on the street, and her grandfather's in bad shape. He has heart failure and all sorts of medicine that she can't afford, either. Will even charged her for a tree she cut down on her mother's place for Christmas!"

Cane felt two inches high. He'd never get over this if she was assaulted by Will and his stupid friend, trying to get enough money to stay afloat. Why hadn't he asked her what she needed the money for? Probably, he thought, because he'd felt so guilty at making advances to her. She was very young. But that was no excuse to treat her the way he'd treated her.

"Where are you going?" Cane asked as Tank started out of the house.

"To save Bodie."

"I'm going with you," Cane said, and followed him out.

WHEN THEY GOT TO Will Jones's house, all the lights were on inside. Tank pounded on the front door.

"Just a minute!" Will raged.

Tank pounded again.

Will came to the door, flushed and disconcerted. "Mr. Kirk?" he faltered.

"Invite us in. That way you won't have so many fractures to explain," Cane said, edging in front of his brother.

"But, uh, it's not convenient…"

Cane shouldered in past him. On the sofa, a young man with his shirt unbuttoned was getting up. Bodie was sitting there, white-faced and disheveled, with her dress pulled off one shoulder and her hair ruffled. She was crying.

"Dear God," Cane whispered. He went to her and started to pull her up. She winced and jerked away from his hand, shivering. Cane froze, sick to his stomach. "Tank!"

Dalton went around him, picked Bodie up in his arms and carried her to the door. He stopped, staring coldly at Will. "There may be charges pending. If I were you, I'd get a good lawyer."

Cane followed close behind him. As they started

out the door, he glanced at the side table. There was a laptop computer with a camera hooked up to it. On the screen was Bodie, being kissed by Larry, with her shoulder exposed. He almost exploded with anger. Without even thinking, he brushed against the table with his hip and accidentally, on purpose, pushed it onto the floor. It landed with a crash.

"You broke my computer! I'll sue you!" Will raged as he picked it up.

"Accident. So sorry, but I'll gladly replace it," Cane told him icily. "I'll have my attorney contact you. And the sheriff."

"Wait!" Will was flustered, almost shaking. "Wait, we can work this out! She came here voluntarily, you just ask her!"

"What about her rent?" Cane asked coldly.

"What rent?" Will said unsteadily. "I mean, it's paid up for two months. She don't owe me anything. Not anything. Not nothing. I'll swear to it!"

"You'll need to," Cane told him. He turned, his black eyes on Bodie's averted face. "Let's go."

He held the door open for Tank. Bodie was sobbing. Cane had never felt so low in his whole life.

Tank put her beside him, with Cane on the other side, and he drove her back to her grandfather's house. But trouble was waiting.

When he got out to open the door and try to explain things to Rafe, he found the old man lying on the floor in the living room. He was icy cold.

Tank came back out, hesitating as he opened the door. "No, don't get out, Bodie," he said gently. "Oh, God, there's no nice way to say this. Your grandfather's…gone. He's gone, baby. I'm so sorry!"

"Gone? You mean he went out…?" She was so shocked that words weren't making sense. "You mean, my granddaddy…is dead, Tank?" she whispered. "He's dead?"

Tank nodded. "I'll call the EMTs and the sheriff and stay here with him until they get here. You go home with Cane. You can stay with us until… we get things sorted out."

"He's dead. He's dead." She was white. She started shaking. Her whole life had fallen apart in the past few minutes. She felt empty and numb inside.

"I'll take you home," Cane said gently. He would have comforted her, but she slid away from him as he got behind the wheel and started the truck. She acted as if she couldn't bear to even look at him. He didn't blame her. Her life had been shattered.

CANE TOOK BODIE HOME TO the ranch, opened the door and hated having only one arm because he couldn't just pick her up and carry her inside and hold her.

She got out of the truck, her head bowed and looking so defeated that it made him sick. He wanted to go back and beat the ever loving hell out of Will Jones and his friend.

Mavie came out onto the porch and hugged Bodie close, rocking her as she cried. "What happened?" she asked Cane.

"Her grandfather's dead," he said, leaving out the rest for now.

"Oh, you poor baby. Come on. Let's get you inside and upstairs to bed. I'll loan you some nightclothes, okay?"

"Thanks, Mavie," Bodie choked out. "It's just, it was so sudden! He said he had indigestion, that it was just a stomachache. I'd never have left him…!"

"It wouldn't have made any difference, Bolinda," Cane said gently. "It was probably instantaneous. My grandfather died like that. He just fell down. It was over in seconds. I was standing right beside him and I couldn't do a thing."

She didn't look at him. "Thanks," she said weakly. "That helps, a little."

"I'm sorry." He bit off the words. "Really sorry."

She knew he meant more than sorry for her grandfather dying, but she didn't say anything. She just nodded.

Mavie helped her up to bed. Bodie was crying so hard that she could barely see where she was going. Behind her, down the stairs, she heard Cane cursing.

CANE WAS SICK AT HEART. He'd treated Bodie like a prostitute negotiating a night in a motel, and there was nothing, nothing, he could do to fix the heartache he'd created for her. She'd gone to her stepfather's house and done things she'd never forget in an attempt to save her grandfather's home. Now her grandfather was dead, and Bodie had to live with herself. It wasn't going to be easy, not for a woman who had been totally innocent and a person of faith.

All that could have been avoided if Cane hadn't been such a pain in the neck. He'd been smarting, still, from the rejection of that woman in the bar who'd only wanted his money. But damn it, he knew Bodie wasn't like that! He knew she wasn't the sort of woman to ask for money on a whim, or for something frivolous. He even knew her grandfather had heart trouble. It hadn't occurred to him how bad her financial situation really was until now, when it was too late to do her any good.

He sat down heavily on the sofa. He was remembering that photograph on Will Jones's computer, and the sight of Bodie's tragic white face, numb with tears. His eyes closed on a shudder. He hoped that computer's hard drive wasn't recoverable, after he'd crashed it onto the floor. At least Bodie would be saved whatever notoriety Will had planned. There was gossip that he had some covert porn website that he produced images for. Obviously he'd planned to use Bodie and his friend to provide him with more content. God only knew what he really had in mind. Bodie was so innocent that she probably didn't realize just how far the man might have gone if Cane and Tank hadn't shown up at his door.

He leaned back against the sofa with a sigh. It was a horrendous mess. Bodie was all alone now, without her grandfather, probably without even a place to live if Will had his way. He had legal title to the property. No doubt he'd toss everything Bodie owned that was still there....

He jerked out his cell phone and called his brother.

"Get a mover, quick," he told Tank solemnly. "Will is bound to throw out Bodie's few things if he gets the chance."

"I'll make sure he doesn't get the chance," Tank said coldly. "We'll move the furniture out of the guest bedroom and put it in storage. We can put Bodie's things there. I'll make sure it's all safely transported. The sheriff's on his way. Cody Banks is a good friend of mine," he added with a cold laugh. "I'll tell him what Will's been doing. I'm sure there's some statute that will cover it, even if Bodie's not underage."

"Have him check out Will's ISP," he advised. "And see if he has a social networking page that feeds into his covert website."

"I can do that, too. If he's got even one photograph of an underage female on it, he'll be arrested."

"I wish we could make sure of that," Cane said heavily. "It's all my fault. All my fault. If I'd just thought before I spoke…"

"Hindsight is a wonderful thing," Tank agreed.

"We'll have to help her with the funeral arrangements," he added. "She won't have a clue. He was a veteran, so there will probably be a little money from the military to help, but I'm fairly certain that she won't have a burial policy."

"Actually she will," Tank reminded him. "We bought a policy for Rafe when he worked for us, and I've kept it on automatic payments ever since."

"Thank God."

"Yes, because regardless of what you think of her, Bodie will turn her nose up at any offer of charity," his brother said quietly. "She's proud."

"Rub it in." Cane grimaced.

"I should," Tank replied. "You're my brother

and I love you, but Bodie will have to live with what she did forever. We did get there in time to save her from anything really traumatic, but what happened is bad enough in itself. She'll consider that what she did was sell herself for money, even if it was for a noble purpose. It won't be easy for her to live that down. Especially," he added angrily, "if Will starts any rumors to the effect that he has special photos of Bodie in a compromising position."

"We could sue him."

"What for, exactly?" Tank asked reasonably. "He can say that Bodie went over there and posed for pictures of her own free will and that she's of age. And with reservations, that's exactly what happened. She won't lie, even to protect her own honor."

"Damn."

"Let me talk to the sheriff," Tank replied. "No way is Jones getting away with this."

"Rafe was worried sick about why she went over there," Cane said. "I imagine she'll think she helped him have that fatal heart attack, as well." He sighed. "I wish Morie was home," he added heavily. "Bodie needs her more than ever right now."

"I'll call Mal," Tank said, alluding to their elder

brother. "When he knows what's happened, he'll come home."

"Good idea."

"Meanwhile, I'll handle this if you'll call the funeral home and get the process started. We can take Bodie over there in the morning to go over the arrangements."

"Rafe had a lot of friends," Cane recalled. "It will be a full house for the services."

"I agree."

"Thanks," Cane said after a minute. "For what you did."

"Thank Darby," Tank replied. "Bodie told him everything and made him swear he wouldn't tell you. But he didn't promise not to tell me."

"She didn't want me to know?" Cane faltered.

"Apparently she thought you hated her."

"Dear God." He swore softly.

"She's naive, in the nicest sort of way," Tank said. "She doesn't even date anyone. She's had no experience of men at all. That will make what happened harder for her."

Cane didn't dare mention what had happened between himself and Bodie, but he thanked God now that it had. At least she hadn't been totally innocent of men when that slimy toad put his hands on her. She would remember how tender Cane had been with her, even if he'd been a total fool later on. He'd loved kissing her. He'd loved it so much that he'd been scared to death of where it might lead. He'd been hurt too many times, and he was overly sensitive about saddling a woman with his disability.

His own insecurities had helped land Bodie in this mess, as much as his unreasonable behavior. He wanted to make it up to her. He just didn't know where to start.

BODIE CRIED HERSELF TO sleep. Mavie sat with her for a little while, before she had to go downstairs and make supper for the brothers.

Cane walked into her room, leaving the door open. He sat down in a chair beside the huge queen-size bed and just stared at her, wincing at the ravaged little face in its frame of thick, wavy black hair. He reached out with his one good hand and tenderly smoothed a loosened strand back into place behind her ear. She looked so very vulnerable.

He recalled a night when he'd been vulnerable, and drunk. She'd brought him up here and helped him down onto the bed. Things were a bit hazy after that, but the sight of her in bed was bringing memories back into focus with startling clarity.

He'd kissed her that night. He'd kissed her with furious, feverish passion and pulled her down against his body, in his own bed. He'd stripped her shirt away and held her bare breasts against his chest, felt her shiver and heard her moan with pleasure....

How could he have ever forgotten such an experience? His dark eyebrows dipped together above the high bridge of his nose as he watched her sleep and remembered the forbidden pleasure they'd shared.

She'd never mentioned it. He'd even phoned her to make sure nothing terrible had happened, because he couldn't remember. She'd lied and said he was too drunk to do anything, but he hadn't been. He'd made love to her. He'd almost gone too far. How could he have forgotten something so shattering?

Bodie in his arms, loving him, holding him, wanting him. Bodie, who was innocent, experiencing passion for the first time with a man too drunk to appreciate her vulnerabilities, treating her as an experienced woman, showing her things that should have come much later in their turbulent relationship.

It was too late to go back and do it over. But, in a way, it was a blessing. That sickening boy, Larry, had a taste of Bodie, but not the first sweet taste of her innocence. That was owned by Cane, who would treasure it for his whole life.

At least she would have something of him to remember that, perhaps, wasn't as distasteful as he
thought it was. He did remember that she hadn't
fought him, not even at first. She'd melted into
him as if she'd only just discovered pleasure. He
could remember even now the taste of her mouth,
the softness of her skin under his hands, the feel
of her sweet young body twisting under his as she
tried to get even closer to him.

The only thing that had saved her was that he'd
been drinking. If he'd been sober, he might not
have been able to stop.

Now that he had the memory, now that he knew
how intimate they'd been, he was surprised that
he hadn't been able to recover that night sooner.
But perhaps he'd been hiding from her, protecting
himself from the possibility of yet another heartache. Bodie was young and impressionable, and
there had been a time when she found him very
attractive.

Not that she would ever again, he thought with
something like desperation. She'd hate him forever
for what he'd done by refusing her shy request for
help. She'd be thinking that she'd never have had
to go to her stepfather in the first place, or lose her
grandfather who was worried sick about her. She'd
be thinking that Cane had failed her. As he'd failed
himself, so many times since his injury.

He took a long look at what he was doing to himself and the people around him, and he didn't like it. He'd been so focused on his own needs and feelings and inadequacies that he'd totally ignored those of his family, and Bodie.

It was time to start looking outward, to stop feeling sorry for himself and put his life back together. The first step in that process was to stop going on benders and get himself back on track. He owed that to Bodie. And to himself.

He got up from the chair, bent and brushed his mouth tenderly over Bodie's dark hair, so lightly that she wouldn't feel it. "I'm sorry, honey," he whispered huskily as he stared at her sleeping face. "So sorry. I swear to God, I'll make it all up to you, somehow."

He went out of the room and closed the door.

Downstairs again, he opened his cell phone and got the telephone number for the local funeral home. There was only one in town. At least he could do this much for Bodie. He could take some of the burden away.

CHAPTER SIX

RAFE MAYS HAD LIVED in Catelow his whole life. Locally he was quite well-known. So the funeral home was full from the time the wake was announced in the newspaper and on the local radio station.

Bolinda, in a black dress that Morie had insisted on buying for her, received visitors in the carpeted room in the funeral home. From time to time, she glanced at the closed coffin where her grandfather rested. He had wanted it that way. "No folks filing past gawking at me, if you please," he'd been fond of saying.

People were kind. Some shared stories from the old man's past, when he was young and handsome and had the pick of the local single women. He'd pursued Bodie's grandmother with flowers and chocolates and even a nice palomino horse before he finally won her. Bodie knew that story by heart, but it was oddly comforting to hear it told. It was as if her grandfather lived on in the memories of people who had cared for him.

"It's time, you know," Cane said from beside her. He was wearing a dark suit with the prosthesis he'd sworn he'd never put on again. With his black hair and snapping black eyes in that smooth olive complexion, he was the handsomest man Bodie had ever known. He could have made a fortune in modeling, but she'd never have told him that. He liked his rugged image.

"Time for what?" she faltered, having been distracted by his amazing good looks.

"Time," he repeated. "I didn't do theoretical physics in college, like our brainy friend over there—" he indicated the ranch foreman, Darby Hanes "—but I do know a little about the concepts involved. All the people we've loved and lost are still alive, you know—they're just separated from us by time."

She stared at him, trying to understand what he was saying.

"Listen," he said, "when you plot a position, you need latitude and longitude. That gives you a fix on the target. But in the broader sense of things, you also need a time. For example, if you went to Laredo, Texas, today, and looked for a particular address, you'd find it. But if you went to the same location, if you could go back in time two hundred years, chances are good that you wouldn't find it back then. You see what I mean?"

She was grasping it. "If I could go back in time a month, my grandfather is still alive, there, in the past."

He smiled tenderly. "Yes. Time separates us from them. Just time."

Incredibly it made her feel better. The comfort was visible in her relaxed posture, the light in her soft brown eyes.

Cane touched her cheek with just his finger-tips, standing close enough that she could feel the heat and strength of his body. "You'll get through this," he said, his voice deep with feeling. "We all have to go through it, losing the older ones in our family. It's never easy. But it's part of the process of life."

She swallowed. "Thanks," she said softly. But she drew back a little, remembering without want-ing to, the things he'd said to her when she'd hesi-tantly asked him for a loan.

He knew that and didn't take offense. He drew in a long breath. "This isn't the time," he said ten-derly. "But I'm sorry. I'm so sorry. I seem to have spent the last couple of months making your life a misery." He frowned. "I don't even know why. You've always been kind to me. I'm not the sort of man who likes hurting women. I never was, even before this happened." He indicated the prosthesis.

She swallowed. "I had to do things…" She stopped and bit her lip.

Cane looked hunted. "Tank's got the sheriff after your sleazy stepfather," he said bluntly. "I hope he finds enough to put him away for life."

"Will's very careful," she said coldly. "There's a girl in town who knows him. She works at the grocery store and she talked to me about him once. She says he checks identification before he films anybody, just to make sure he isn't crossing the line in any way. It would be a crime if he didn't get locked up," she added with more ice in her tones.

"It would be a shame if he didn't," Cane replied. "There are all sorts of ways to trip up people who think they can bend the law."

She gave him a long look. "I'll bet you know most of them," she said with the first hint of humor he'd seen in her in a long time.

He smiled. It made his eyes glow softly with feeling, and he looked at her in a way that he hadn't, before. She couldn't quite decide what it meant, but she was trying to when another friend came up to her to express his condolences. Cane melted back into the crowd.

THAT NIGHT, BODIE SAT ON the edge of her bed, in her pajamas that looked more like a sweat set, and stared into space. She didn't really believe in ghosts, but she was afraid to turn out the light. Her grandfather had loved her; she knew that, as much as she loved him. But there were all these stories people told of things in the dark after a loved one died. She was nervous, and grieving, and upset.

There was a light tap on the door. Cane came in, carrying a cup of hot chocolate. He hadn't been to bed, either. He was still wearing jeans and a soft blue shirt, but in his sock feet instead of boots. His black hair was a little ruffled, as if he'd worried it with his hand.

"I figured you wouldn't be asleep," he said. "Here. It's got marshmallows, too."

She caught her breath. She loved hot chocolate, but especially with the tiny marshmallows in it. "How did you…?"

"Mavie made it." He chuckled. "I just offered transport service."

She managed a smile as she took it from him and sipped it, closing her eyes with delight. "It's wonderful. Thanks. To you both."

He shrugged. "I didn't sleep for two nights after our mother died," he said. "It was a long time ago. We were in our teens. She had cancer."

"So did my mother. It was terrible when I lost her."

He nodded. "Nobody understands, unless they've been through it. It's a long process. Sometimes the treatments work. Sometimes they don't. We always thought our mother just gave up. She was a sad sort of person. She lived for her sons, but she had no real life outside the home. I've often wondered if she had dreams of being something else, maybe an artist, because she loved to draw. She gave up her dreams to raise us."

"She did a wonderful job on the three of you," Bodie said quietly. "Doesn't that have value in our society anymore? Does every woman have to go out and become CEO of some major corporation, or a high military officer, or a politician at the national level? Isn't it acceptable for a woman to just have a family and teach them values and keep them safe and happy through their childhood?"

"I wouldn't know," he said. "I've never had children."

She averted her eyes. "I would like to one day," she said softly. "I want to dig up dinosaurs and make my mark in the world, in a small way," she added with a laugh. "But I want a family, too. No reason I can't do both. Children are portable. One of my friends has parents who are anthropologists. They go all over the world, and the kids go with them. They're mostly home-schooled, but they're way ahead of kids their own level in the educational system." Her eyes were dreamy. "I wouldn't mind that. Carrying my kids to dig sites, I mean, even though I'd be digging up dinosaurs instead of cultural artifacts."

The thought of Bodie with kids, some other man's kids, made him bristle. He glowered at her.

Her eyes widened. "Listen, just because you don't want to get married is no reason to look at me like I'm nuts," she pointed out.

He averted his eyes. "I wasn't."

"Yes, you were."

"Stop that. I'm not arguing with you. Not tonight."

"Ah. You're in truce mode."

He laughed shortly. "Something like that." He studied her pale, drawn face. "I'm sorry it went down like this, that you didn't have time to say a proper goodbye to your grandfather. But remember what Tank told you. Rafe said to tell you he loved you very much. I think he knew what was coming. He wanted to be sure that you knew."

Tears stung her eyes. She bit them back and sipped her hot chocolate. She couldn't taste it very well with the tears clogging her throat. She didn't look up again until she'd finished it, and the tears were only threatening to overflow. She didn't want to show weakness in the face of the enemy. She couldn't forget what Cane had said to her before she went home. Her pride was still lacerated.

He drew a spotless white handkerchief from his pocket and placed it against her eyes, shocking her into looking up. His expression was grim.

"I'm trying to think up ways to make up for what I said...what I did," he faltered. "I'm going to stop drinking, Bodie. I'm going to get back into therapy. Will that help?"

She handed him the cup. "It would be the best thing, for you. Your family loves you. It's not fair to put them through hell because of what happened to you overseas." She searched his black eyes quietly. "I know it's been rough. But you have to try to move on. There's a whole world out there that you're not even seeing. You're hiding, inside yourself."

"Stop that." He averted his face. His eyes were stormy.

"See?" she said.

He turned and glared at her. "Stop reading my mind."

"Sorry. Not intentional." She smoothed back her hair. "I'm afraid to go to sleep, isn't that stupid?"

"Not really. I didn't want to turn out the lights for two days after my mother died. I wasn't really afraid of the dark. I was just...uneasy."

"That's how I feel. My grandfather would never hurt me. I know that." She laughed. "Ancient memories of taboos and spiritualism, perhaps."

He nodded. "Perhaps."

She sighed. "Well, thanks for the hot chocolate. Thank Mavie, too."

He turned down the covers, tugged her arm so that she got under them. "Move over."

She blinked. "What?"

"Move over."

Surprised, she complied. He slid into bed beside her, laid back on a pillow and moved what was left of his other arm so that it was around her head.

"Now go to sleep," he said, and reached to turn out the bedside lamp with his good hand.

She was stiff as a board, and shocked.

"The door's wide-open," he reminded her, nodding toward it. "Even if I had the impulse, I wouldn't act on it when you're grieving and frightened. I may be a rogue, but I hope you think better of me than that."

She relaxed, just a little. "What will your family think, though?" she worried.

"That I'm doing something Quixotic," he murmured, alluding to Don Quixote and his habit of misplaced nobility. "Protecting the vulnerable."

"Am I vulnerable?"

He turned his head on the pillow. His black eyes

pierced hers. "You were the night I got drunk, weren't you, Bodie?" he asked in a deep, husky whisper.

She turned red. "You said you didn't remember," she accused.

"I didn't. Not until the other day." His head rolled back on the pillow so that he could stare up at the ceiling. "Not until it was too late, and I'd said things I can't take back, prompted you into a decision that will scar you for life."

She swallowed. "Oh." She was remembering that night with brutal clarity. He'd been a little rough with her, but so tender and sweet that her mind reeled with pleasure.

"Was it the first time?" he asked tautly.

She hesitated. It wasn't something she wanted to admit, least of all to him.

His head turned on the pillow. In the light from the hall, he could see her face. "Was it, Bodie?"

She bit her lower lip. "Yes. I never... I mean..." she said hesitantly.

Something flashed in his eyes. He turned her face up to his with a tender hand, caressing her cheek as he bent to kiss her eyes shut. "At least," he whispered, "you had something untainted before Will's friend put his filthy hands on you, even if I was drunk at the time."

She started to speak, but his mouth moved

softly onto hers, tasting it with reverence, with aching, breathless tenderness.

"Soft little rosebud," he whispered against her tight lips, "so afraid to open its petals…"

"I am…!"

He chuckled as her indignant reply gave him just the opening he wanted. He pressed her lips back under his, opening them to a kiss that was as reverent as it was masterful. He nibbled at her upper lip, teased the moist underside with his tongue, in a way that made her body go tight in the oddest places.

She gasped.

He drew back, his breath a little unsteady on her mouth. "If you were a few years older, and I was a bigger rake than I already am, I'd get up and lock the door."

She was all at sea. She had no real experience of men, except with him, and she wasn't sure what he was insinuating. "You mean you'd lock me in…?"

His mouth ground down into hers hungrily. "I mean I'd lock myself in here with you and start taking off your clothes!" he bit off.

She gasped under his demanding mouth as he rolled toward her.

His hand was under her shirt, moving up, when footsteps sounded on the staircase. Luckily he wasn't too far gone to hear them.

He moved onto his back, grimacing, and forced himself to breathe normally. "Please try to look like you're asleep so that my brother doesn't throw me out the closest window," he said with a rough attempt at humor.

"I should help him," she managed to reply. But she did close her eyes and try to look innocent.

The footsteps stopped at the open door abruptly. There was a soft explosion of breath, and then a softer chuckle. The footsteps started up again.

Cane let out the breath he'd been holding. He turned his head so that he could see Bodie's shocked eyes, very close to his.

"You wouldn't throw me out a window," he mused, his eyes twinkling. "You'd have nobody to teach you how to kiss."

"Cane!" she muttered angrily.

His thumb moved over her soft mouth. "God, I love kissing you," he whispered. "You're too damned young and I'm out of my mind to even be looking at you. I've hurt you, sent you running, gotten you into one hell of a mess with my temper…"

"You forgot the part where you called me a budding prostitute," she said angrily.

He sighed. "Yeah. I forgot that part."

He looked so guilty that he made her feel guilty for bringing it up. She grimaced. "Sorry. It stings."

"I wanted you."

She blinked. "Excuse me?"

He rolled over, facing her. "I wanted you," he said quietly. "We were alone, I was aching for relief after I kissed you, and frankly, you'd have let me do anything I liked. I would have liked to do a lot." His jaw tautened. "I said things I didn't mean, to make you run. I'm sorry. I should have been honest with you about it. But I can usually only be that honest when I'm drunk." He looked at her chin instead of meeting her eyes. "You're too young, Bodie," he said flatly. "You haven't even lived yet."

"You want me," she repeated it, faintly shocked.

"Yeah."

"You never...said."

He gave her a speaking look. "You couldn't tell by how hard I got when I was kissing you, then?"

She gasped. "Cane Kirk!" she muttered, and hit him.

He grinned. "Want me to demonstrate it again?"

She started to speak when the footsteps sounded in the hall again.

"We're asleep," he reminded her, and turned onto his back, closing his eyes.

The footsteps sounded odd. That was when he realized that there was more than one set of them. He didn't dare look.

There were soft exclamations from at least two people. More subdued chuckling. After a minute, during which Cane hoped they wouldn't look too closely at the people in the big bed, the footsteps moved away again.

When he glanced at Bodie, her eyes were open and she was trying not to laugh.

"What?" he asked.

"Your brothers, Morie and Mavie," she said breathlessly. "You should have seen their faces."

"How…?"

"I was looking past your chest," she said. "They couldn't see me."

He shook his head. "I suppose we do look odd."

She laid her head on his shoulder, against what was left of his arm. "Thank you," she whispered.

"For kissing you?" he teased lightly.

"For being noble," she replied quietly. "For caring that I was in here alone and scared of the dark…and not making fun of me."

He hadn't had a woman in his arms since the accident. He was afraid he wouldn't be able to make love again or that he'd fumble and make a fool of himself with some worldly-wise female who'd laugh at him. But Bodie didn't make him uncomfortable. So he curled his elbow around her, the stump against her waist. She didn't even flinch.

"It doesn't bother you?" he asked tautly.

"Don't be silly." She sighed. "Why should it?"

"There's no hand," he said through his teeth.

"Lots of men have lost arms and legs in the war and during the occupation," she said, her voice sounding a little drowsy now. "Many of them were married. I don't think it would matter to the women they came home to."

He blinked.

She nuzzled closer. "Would it matter to you if I was missing an arm?"

"No." He said it instantly, without thinking.

She smiled.

His chest rose and fell heavily. He was conflicted. Part of him was delighted that Bodie could accept him as a man, as a whole man, and not be disparaging. But another part was uneasy and apprehensive about getting serious with her. She'd just suffered a major loss, compounded by her very unpleasant experience with her stepfather and his friend. She wasn't thinking about it right now, safe in Cane's arms. But it would be in her mind, and when the numbness wore off, that blessed numbness that eased bereaved people through the worst part of the pain and anguish, she would have to deal with it. She might hate Cane for his part in her disgrace. She might blame him for losing her grandfather and forcing her to lower her pride in an attempt to save the roof over their heads.

She might. But right now, she was curled trustingly in his arms, drifting off to sleep. And he was holding her, like precious treasure, drinking in the faint scent of roses that clung to her soft skin.

Tomorrow might bring more heartache, more problems. Tonight he was safe, she was safe, they were together and experiencing a new tenderness in their relationship that felt like a bright new-minted penny on a spring day. He felt reborn, full of hope and subdued passion.

He wasn't going to think about any of it tonight. He was going to savor Bodie in his arms, close against his heart and let tomorrow wait. This might be the only time he'd have Bodie to himself, ever again. He wasn't going to waste a second of the night in worried possibilities. He closed his eyes. He even smiled.

THE NEXT MORNING, when Bodie woke, she was alone. She thought at first that she'd dreamed about Cane holding her while she slept. But then she noticed the empty cup that had held hot chocolate, and saw the dent in her spare pillow where Cane's head had rested. Impulsively, smiling, she buried her face in it. The spicy scent of his cologne still clung to it. She drank it in.

She got out of bed and then she remembered. Today they were burying her grandfather. All the bright happiness was gone, like a light switch being clicked off. She was going to be alone for the rest of her life. The last living member of her family was dead. She had no home left, because Will Jones had possession of her house. All her things, and Granddad's, were here in this room or in the Kirks' storage building.

For some insane reason, she remembered the Christmas tree that she'd cut and paid for, and decorated with such optimism and love. She sat down on the bed and burst into tears.

"Oh, my goodness," Morie said from the door. She went to Bodie and hugged her tight, rocking her as they sat together on the bed. "I thought it would hit you sooner or later," she added gently. "It's all right. Really."

"My Christmas tree," she choked out. "It's such a stupid thing to cry about. It was one Mama planted before she died, so we could have live trees. I cut it down and Will Jones made me pay him for it, because it was on his land…"

"That dog!" Morie muttered.

"It had our old decorations on it. Some of them were my grandmother's. They're all gone…!"

"They are not," Mallory said from the doorway. He walked in, smiling gently at his wife. "Morie remembered the decorations, so we called Tank and had them strip them off the tree. They're in a box, along with all your other odds and ends, in the barn shed. They'll be safe. The building is temperature controlled, so there will be no damage to them."

"Yes, because our prize breeding bulls live there, too," Morie said.

"Oh, that's so kind!" And Bodie burst into tears again.

"We've got you another dress to wear to the funeral," Morie told her gently. "Don't fuss. If our situations were reversed, you'd do it for me in a heartbeat and you know it. Everything's arranged, even the burial plot in the church cemetery where your grandmother, your father and your mother are buried."

"You should see the flowers," Tank said from the doorway. He was wearing a suit and looked very dashing. He had the same dark eyes and hair that his brothers shared. "The church is full already and the florist is stoop-shouldered from carrying them in. You'll have a lot of things to plant."

"Yes, and I hope my college dorm will allow me to dig up the floor for that," Bodie said with faint humor.

"You can plant them here," Morie said gently. "They'll be here whenever you can come home, and your room will be here waiting for you."

She lifted her head and looked at the older woman blankly.

"You're home, now, Bodie," Mallory added, smiling. "We had a family meeting." He shrugged. "So you're now officially part of the family. This is your place in the world, when you're not away at college or on digs."

The tears were drowning her. "I don't know what to say," she choked out. "You guys are so sweet!"

"It was sort of Cane's idea." Tank chuckled.

"He said you couldn't live in a motel." Morie nodded.

"Although we offered to set you up a tent on the road in front of Will Jones's place and have the local newspaper do a write-up on how he stole your mother's land from you," Mallory said with pure venom.

"Which we agreed we weren't going to talk about, yes?" Morie told her husband with wide, speaking dark eyes.

"Sorry," Mallory murmured. "Couldn't resist it."

"Will Jones will get his just deserts one day," Tank promised. "The sheriff has some promising leads on a young lady who is rumored to be underage. If it pans out, Will's going to jail."

"It couldn't possibly happen to a nicer man," Bodie said between sobs.

"We're also having our attorneys look into the legality of your mother's will," Tank told her. "We think there may have been some irregularities, especially since your mother said very specifically that her property was to go to you on her death."

"He had a will," Bodie began.

"Wills can be forged, sweetheart," Morie told her gently.

"It would be nice to have my house back," Bodie said. "But it's just a house, you know. When I finish undergraduate studies, I'll go on to master's and then doctorate schools. I won't be around much." She wiped her eyes on the hem of her shirt. "But thanks for letting me have a space for my stuff." She managed a watery smile. "We all have to have our stuff."

They chuckled.

"He's got more stuff than most people." Morie indicated her husband, giving him an affectionate grin.

"I'm older than most people," Mallory said easily.

"Dear old man," Morie murmured. She got up and kissed her husband's chin. "We should get dressed. We have to leave soon."

"Some of us are already dressed, and look dashing," Tank said, striking a pose.

"Ha!" Cane said from the doorway. "In your dreams. Now, when we speak of dashing men..." He indicated himself, decked out in a navy blue suit with a spotless white shirt and patterned tie.

"Conceit runs in your family, doesn't it?" Morie murmured again.

Cane made a face at her. "Can I help it if I have so much to be conceited about?"

Bodie laughed.

He gave her a teasing smile. "Tell them. I have qualities."

"He does," she had to admit.

"Yes, and it was nice of you to leave the door open," Morie told Cane. "Some of us had suspicions about your motives for sharing Bodie's bed."

"Wicked girl," Cane shot back. "I was the soul of chivalry."

Everybody looked at Bodie for verification of that boast. When she flushed, they all burst into peals of laughter.

"Hence the open door," Cane said with a worldly sigh. He chuckled. "We'd better let her get dressed," he added, more solemnly. "One last hurdle to get through, Bodie."

She nodded.

"You have decisions to make, also," Tank remarked.

"I do?" She thought she'd made them all, about music and the casket and the ministers. She said so.

"No," Tank clarified. "About how you want us to handle it if Will shows up at the funeral home."

"He wouldn't dare," Bodie exclaimed. "He didn't come to the wake!"

"Yes, but he lives in the community and there will be some nasty gossip if he doesn't come to his own father-in-law's funeral. Usually he doesn't care for the opinion of other people. But in this case, he just might."

"I'll have the funeral director ask him to leave," Bodie decided solemnly. "Granddaddy wouldn't like having that man at his funeral. He hated Will."

"A lot of people hate Will," Tank replied. "He's had a hand in every bit of nastiness that ever went down in this community, from what people who grew up here have told us. He's never been arrested, but he's been investigated. They could just never find enough evidence to bring him to trial."

"That can change," Cane said.

"Yes." Tank smiled. "Get moving, Bodie. After the funeral, we'll have a houseful of people coming to help us eat the wagonloads of food our neighbors brought. We live in one hell of a nice place."

Bodie smiled, too. "One of my earliest memo-

ries was of Mama baking cakes and making cas-
seroles for people who had deaths in the family.
The whole church always got together. They had
a list of members they called who provided meals
for the family members."

"That's why we love living here," Mallory replied. "Okay. Everybody out."

"Thanks," Bodie said as they filed out. "Thanks
a lot."

Cane paused at the doorway. "You'd do it for us,
honey." He smiled at her reaction to the endearment, and closed the door.

CHAPTER SEVEN

BODIE CRIED THROUGHOUT the brief ceremony, her eyes on the closed casket, surrounded by what seemed to be mountains of colorful flowers. There were a lot of poinsettias since it was nearly Christmas, red ones and white ones, in profusion. That brought home the realization that she wouldn't be sharing the holidays with her grandfather, and she cried even more. She was suddenly aware of Cane's arm around her, holding her close.

"Hold on," he whispered in her ear. "Almost done."

She nodded.

There was a final prayer and the pianist played "Amazing Grace" as the pallbearers moved the casket through a side room to the waiting hearse.

As Bodie turned with Cane, she saw her stepfather standing across the aisle from them. Her eyes shot fire at him. Cane looked at the man and jerked his head toward the front door with cold meaning.

Will wasn't brave enough to stand up to a

younger man with evident hostility. He shrugged
and moved to the doorway, slowly enough to make
Cane want to go after him.

That unpleasantness dealt with, Bodie followed
the pallbearers with Cane holding tightly to her
hand. He helped her into the limousine and went to
speak quietly to Tank and Mallory. Bodie couldn't
hear what was said, but she was fairly certain it
had something to do with her stepfather.

THERE WAS AS BIG A CROWD at the cemetery as there
had been at the church. Cane held Bodie's hand
possessively, oblivious to the amused attention of
several bystanders, while the final prayers were
said.

A blanket of red, white and blue roses covered
the casket, a present from the Kirks, acknowledg-
ing Rafe Mays's service in Vietnam as a decorated war veteran. The whole area was covered
with sprays and wreaths in beautiful bright colors.
Christmas colors. The sky was dark and forebod-
ing and weather forecasts mentioned the possibility of snow. Bodie wouldn't have minded. She
loved snow, despite the hardships it presented for
ranchers and townsfolk alike.

With the last prayer completed, members of the
community filed by to shake Bodie's hand or hug
her and voice their condolences. It took a long

time, and warmed her heart to have so many people come to pay their respects.

She stood alone at the graveside for a few minutes, saying her own private goodbye to her grandfather.

"I'll miss you all my life," she whispered. "I love you, Granddaddy."

Tears stung her eyes. She wiped them away, took a last look at the casket and turned to leave. It was hard to walk away. It was even harder not to look back.

LATER, AT HOME WITH mountains of food on the dining room table and a buffet line formed because all the cowboys who worked for the ranch also were invited to the feast, Bodie filled a plate with fried chicken and mashed potatoes and peas. She wasn't really hungry, but it would have been an insult not to eat, when people had gone to all this trouble to make dinner for the family. Since everyone knew that Bodie was living at the Kirk ranch—there were no secrets at all in small communities—they deliberately made enough so that the Kirks and the cowboys could eat, as well. It was a kindness that Bodie acknowledged with humility. She hadn't realized just how kind her neighbors really were until now.

"That was quite a turnout," Mallory Kirk said as

they sat around the big dining room table, working their way through desserts that included cakes and pies and puddings. "Your grandfather had more friends than I even realized."

"He was born here," Bodie reminded him, forcing a smile. "His name is on that big veterans' monument downtown."

"We were grateful that he came with the ranch when we bought it," Tank added, sipping black coffee. "He knew everything about the day-to-day operations, and he taught Darby how to organize the work."

"Yes, he did," Darby replied. "He was a good man, Bodie."

She smiled. "Thanks."

"He taught me how to swim when I was a boy," one of the older ranch hands piped in.

"Did he?"

"Yup." His eyes twinkled. "I told him I didn't know how. He picked me up and threw me headfirst into a water hole."

"Good heavens!" Bodie exclaimed. "And you didn't drown?"

"Well, drowning was a good incentive to learn to swim. I started dog-paddling on the spot. Not that Rafe would have stood by while I died," he added. "He said he would have jumped in after me if I'd gotten in trouble. Said that was how his dad taught him to swim." He eyed Bodie and pursed his lips. "Can you swim?"

"Yes!" she said at once.

Everybody laughed.

Later, WHILE MALLORY and Morie watched the news, Bodie sat in the living room with Tank while he tried out a new piece of sheet music he'd bought online.

"I really like that," she said when he finished.

"Me, too," he agreed. He turned on the piano bench. "Any requests?" he inquired with a tender smile.

"Yes," Cane said from the door. "Stop playing."

Tank made a face at him. "You're only jealous because I mastered 'Rach Three' and you never could," he added, referencing a nightmare of a piece composed by Rachmaninoff that very few classically trained pianists could master.

"I could have learned it if I'd wanted to," Cane returned. But he didn't fly up at Tank for the memory of an earlier time when he had two hands and he could play almost as well as Tank. All the Kirks were musical.

"No patience," Tank told Bodie, nodding at his brother. "Mom almost had to tie him to the piano bench to make him listen to the piano teacher."

"I was always more interested in outdoor activities," Cane returned. He sat down on the sofa beside Bodie and crossed his long legs.

"Like shooting other boys with BB guns," Tank pointed out dryly. "Almost landed us in a lawsuit once."

"He shot me first," Cane argued. "He just lied about it. I never lie."

"That's absolutely true." Tank sighed. "I asked him to tell a little white lie, just once, to keep a determined woman from pursuing me. He told her I was home and even brought me the telephone."

"Just helping you out," Cane drawled. "Running away from a problem never solved it."

Bodie and Tank almost bit their tongues through trying not to mention that drinking certainly came under that heading.

Cane glowered at them. "I'm turning over a new leaf," he said defensively. "I set up an appointment with a new therapist and I got Mavie to pour all my aged Scotch whiskey down the drain." He made a face. "She actually laughed while she was doing it."

"That's commitment," Tank had to agree.

Cane looked down at Bodie speculatively. "I'm working on something a little more addictive than alcohol."

"Are you?" Tank pretended innocence. "What?"

Cane's black eyes twinkled. "That would be telling. Weren't you playing?"

Tank turned back to the keyboard. "In fact, I was. The new soundtracks are nice, but you just can't beat Rachmaninoff's 'Second Piano Concerto.'" He began to play it.

Cane looked down into Bodie's eyes for so long that she flushed and averted her face. He chuckled softly under his breath.

THAT NIGHT SHE TOSSED and turned, but she did finally sleep. Her dreams were troubled, though, and she went down to breakfast with dark circles under her eyes.

"Well, you look like death warmed over," Cane remarked as she sat down beside him and reached for the cup of coffee he poured for her.

"Couldn't sleep until about three this morning," she confessed.

"Bad dreams?"

"Fear of bad dreams," she said quietly.

"They'll pass," Mallory said gently. "It only needs time, Bodie."

"I know." She smiled at him. "I'm so grateful to all of you. I wouldn't even have a roof over my head..."

"Nonsense," Tank returned. "Half the town offered you that, at the funeral. A lot of people were fond of Rafe."

"I suppose so." She toyed with her eggs.

"Don't turn your nose up at my rare, carefully nurtured cage-free, home-grown eggs," Mavie said as she slid a platter of crispy bacon and perfectly cooked sausage alongside the platter of home-made biscuits. "I serenade my hens every day to get those eggs."

"Yes, she does, I've seen her standing in the henhouse playing her violin," Cane said, tongue in cheek.

Mavie brandished a serving spoon. "You're in enough trouble without looking for more," she told him.

"What did he do?" Bodie wondered aloud.

"He walked off with a whole platter of cookies I baked for dessert tonight and ate every one," Mavie said indignantly.

"Lies," Cane said, tasting the sausage on his plate. "You made them just for me."

"I did not!"

"You said yourself that I needed feeding up," he pointed out.

"Yes, but not with cookies! You won't even eat a good biscuit."

"I'm allergic to biscuits," he replied.

"Nobody is allergic to biscuits."

"I am. Watch this." He picked up a biscuit and spun it off his plate onto the tablecloth. "See that? I have biscuit apprehension disorder. Very rare. It's even more noticeable if they have butter on."

Mavie burst out laughing. "I give up."

"You might as well," Tank replied. "Nobody wins an argument with him."

"I did, once," Mallory said.

"Well, chemistry isn't my field," Cane drawled.

"It wasn't a chemistry issue," Mallory replied. He finished his coffee. "I was barely in middle school at the time. You said that methane wasn't explosive. Tank lit a match and proved you wrong."

"He damned near blew up the cow who provided him with the raw materials," Cane accused.

"Ah, childhood." Mallory sighed, smiling pleasantly. "They got such a whipping from Dad." He smiled. "Happy memories."

"He put us up to it," Cane said, pointing his fork at Mallory and glowering. "He told Tank to tell me methane wasn't dangerous. He knew I'd argue. I always argued."

"You still do." Tank chuckled.

"Only when I know I'm right."

"Only all the time," Tank mused.

Cane made a face. "Well, anyway, it was an instructive experiment. And it got me out of cleaning the stalls in the barn for quite some time."

"For a whole week," Mallory agreed.

"My grandfather said you guys were experimenting with a way to use methane gas to power the electricity in the barn."

"We are," Mallory replied. "It was an expensive setup, but it's saving us a fortune in power bills. Imagine. Modern technology is impressive."

"Why can't they do that other places?" Bodie wondered.

"Well, there are some places where landfills use it for power," Cane said. "But the setup, as Mallory said, is quite expensive. Only large cities can utilize the concept."

"Wouldn't it be nice if garbage could be used to solve our energy woes?" she wondered aloud.

"Nice, indeed."

"What a subject for breakfast conversation," Morie exclaimed, joining them at the table with an empty cup.

Mallory kissed her tenderly and poured coffee into it for her. "We were discussing energy concepts."

"So I heard." She glanced up. "How are you doing, Bodie?"

Bodie smiled. "A little blue. But I'll mend."

"Of course you will. It just takes time."

Cane pursed his sensual lips. "I have to drive

over to Jackson Hole to talk to a man about a bull. Want to come along?" he asked Bodie.

She was surprised. But it was a pleasant surprise, and it showed. "Well, I...sure."

He chuckled. "We won't be long. I want to look at one of his yearlings. The sire's been written up in major ranching journals. I want to see for myself."

"I like cattle," Bodie said.

"So do we." Mallory chuckled, too.

"We'll go after breakfast," Cane told Bodie.

She smiled and nodded. It would be good to have something to keep her mind off her grandfather. And it was a thrill to have Cane seeking out her company. That in itself was unusual.

CANE DROVE ONE OF THE ranch pickups, his one hand managing the steering wheel effortlessly.

"The rancher's name is Bill Sanders," he told her. "He's a third generation rancher. His father almost lost the ranch to a development corporation a few years ago. They wanted to build a hotel complex on his land. He went to court and fought them for two years. In the end, he won. They went to another part of the state, where people were less resistant to change."

"Jackson Hole is pretty developed, isn't it?" she wondered. "Lots of hotels and stuff."

"Yes. It's commercialized these days. The Teton mountain range is so famous that people come from all over the world just to look at it. Plus, it's unspoiled up here in this part of the state. Fresh air and water are nothing to sneeze at."

"Yes. My grandfather said that I'd live to see people go to war over water. I thought that was funny when I was young. Now, it doesn't seem so far-fetched at all."

He glanced at her, smiling. She looked very pretty in a green turtleneck sweater and jeans. It was warm in the truck, so her old leather jacket was spread over her legs. "You look nice, Bodie. You always do."

She smiled back. "Thanks."

He turned his attention back to the road. "I thought we might have lunch on the way. I know this little place that serves some of the best barbecue in Wyoming."

"I love barbecue," she noted.

"Yes, I know. So do I. The hotter, the better."

"I still have taste buds. They can make it milder, can't they?" she asked.

"As mild as you like, honey," he said, the endearment coming so naturally that he didn't even notice.

Bodie did. Cane didn't use endearments, not to anyone. It was a thrill to hear him use them with her. Perhaps he just felt sorry for her or guilty about his behavior before Rafe Mays died. Whatever the reason, it made her heart lift.

"With French fries," she added.

He grinned. "Can't eat barbecue without fries. They make their own. No frozen ones out of bags."

"Wow."

"And the owner's mother bakes cakes for the restaurant. Some of the best ones I've ever tasted."

"Now you're making me hungry," she pointed out.

He chuckled. "Good. You could use a little meat on those bones."

"I am not thin."

"Yes, you are, a bit. No wonder, considering what you've been through lately." His face hardened. "I wish you'd told me all of it, Bodie. I went off half cocked and said things I'll never forgive myself for. If I'd known how bad things were at your place, I'd never have spoken to you so harshly."

She swallowed. "It was pride," she confessed. "I didn't want to admit that I couldn't take care of my own finances."

"Nobody could function with that sort of tragedy looming." He glanced at her. "One of the cowboys said you even pawned your grandmother's jewelry to pay for Rafe's medicine."

That smarted. She ground her teeth together. "I didn't have a choice," she said after a minute. "Jewelry, even heirlooms, well, are just things. People are more important. Besides, the pawn shop guy promised he wouldn't sell them. I told him I'd be able to redeem them early next year."

He didn't reply. But there was a secret smile on his lips that he didn't let her see.

THE RESTAURANT WAS A truck stop, full of beefy truck drivers. The parking lot was full of semis, lined up like ducks in a row.

"You never said it was a truck stop," Bodie remarked.

He chuckled as he held the door open for her. "Nobody knows where the best food is better than a trucker. Long hauls like they make, you live for good food."

Several men looked up when Bodie walked in with Cane. She felt uncomfortable. She only saw one woman, sitting with a very tall, older man in a back booth.

Cane frowned. Her reaction disturbed him. "Hey, it's okay," he said gently.

She bit her lip. One of the truckers was giving her a look that made her feel undressed. He punched his companion and jerked his head toward

Bodie. The other man looked at her for a long minute and then smiled, and not in a nice way.

Bodie moved a little closer to Cane.

He stopped dead, stared at the trucker and narrowed his eyes. The trucker suddenly noticed his food and stopped looking at Bodie.

"Let's go," Cane said curtly. He caught her hand and led her out of the restaurant. "What the hell was that all about?" he asked curtly. He stopped at the truck and looked down into her eyes. "I've never seen men react that way to you before."

"Me, neither," she said uneasily. "I'm not wearing anything revealing, am I?" she wondered, insecurity in her tone as she studied her own clothing. "Gosh, I felt like I was on offer or something."

He drew in a long breath. He was remembering Will Jones's computer. The man was a techie. He could do anything online. But Tank had seen the image on the computer screen and he said that Will's friend Larry had just been kissing Bodie. That was all. Still, it would have been traumatic for an innocent, who was doing something against her will to try to save her grandfather from being evicted.

"You think I'm cheap, don't you?" Bodie asked in an anguished tone. "That was how those men looked at me, like I was a streetwalker...."

He pulled her into his arms, wrapped her up

tight and rocked her against his powerful body. "I don't know what was going on in there, but no sane man would ever liken you to a scarlet woman," he whispered in her ear. "Least of all, me. I know better than any other man on earth how innocent you are."

Her heart tripped and ran away with her. She felt breathless, excited, as she'd never been in her life.

His hand smoothed her dark, soft hair. "You've had one too many upsets already. We'll find another place to eat. One where families go, not truckers. Okay?"

She managed a smile. "Okay..."

"Hey," a deep voice called to them.

They turned. A tall, burly man with a woman beside him came up to them. Bodie noticed that Cane's posture changed, just slightly, as he moved into a balanced stance. She recalled that he had a belt in martial arts and that Tank said he taught it when he was in the service. Did he perceive a threat?

The other man came up to them and hesitated when he saw Bodie's drawn, pale face. "The owner of this place is a friend of mine. Don't know what caused those two men to make you feel uncomfortable, but the owner tossed them out. You come

back and have a nice meal. Don't let two idiots put
you off some of the best food in Wyoming."

The woman smiled. "I could see how uncomfortable you were," she told Bodie. "My husband
and I do these long hauls together. I drive while
he sleeps and vice versa." She looked up at the
big man lovingly. "We've been married ten years.
Doesn't seem that long."

Her husband chuckled. "Not to me, either, dar-
ling." He looked at Bodie. "Come on back inside.
You can sit with us. If anybody gives you a hard
time, I'll teach them some manners." He turned
his attention to Cane and chuckled again. "Saw
you go into that fighting stance. I wouldn't tackle
you," he added, unaware of Cane's irritation that
another man offered to help Bodie because Cane
was disabled. "You look pretty dangerous."

That was when Cane recalled that he was wearing the prosthesis and the other man didn't realize
he was disabled. He relaxed visibly. "Only when
something threatens my best girl," he said gently,
and smiled down at a visibly flustered Bodie.

"I'm the same way. Come on. This barbecue
isn't something you want to miss!"

He led the way back in with his wife. Cane and
Bodie sat with them, aware of apologetic glances
from the other men present, and ordered plates of
barbecue. By the time they finished, they were

on a first-name basis with their rescuers and even some of the truckers sitting nearby.

"WELL, THAT WAS A surprise," Bodie mused when they were back on the road to Jackson Hole.

"Wasn't it?" He smiled. "People can be nice. I'll be honest, I didn't know what to expect when that human mountain came barreling out toward us. I thought it was going to mean a fight."

"Me, too. But I wasn't afraid. You can handle yourself."

"Yeah. Me and my one arm."

"Stop that," she muttered, glaring at him. "You're missing a hand. That doesn't make you any less a man. When the chips are down, I'd bet on you against anybody else in a fight."

He looked surprised. "You would?"

"Of course."

He shifted a little behind the wheel. His chin lifted. She didn't know it, but he'd felt very defensive when he thought the other man was insinuating that he couldn't protect Bodie. Now, he felt better. She had no doubts about his ability to take care of her. It made him feel two feet taller.

"I'm sorry for what happened to you overseas," she said gently. "I know you don't like to talk about it, but you did a very brave thing. I don't know anyone else who would have been willing to make a sacrifice like that to save lives. Well, maybe your brothers," she amended. "But the point is it's like a firefighter rushing into a building to save a child." She glanced at his hard face and away again. "I think you're the bravest person I've ever met."

He actually flushed. He couldn't even answer her.

"There, I've stuck my toes in my mouth again, haven't I?" she asked aloud, grimacing. "I can't seem to find the right words…!"

"I think you found just the right words." He put on the brakes at a four-way stop and turned to look at her. "I have trouble expressing myself, too. I'm defensive about the way I am. When that trucker said he'd handle it if some other man bothered you, it hurt my pride. I thought he was saying I wasn't man enough to do it." He laughed hollowly. "Then I realized he didn't know I was missing part of my arm. This thing looks pretty real." He nodded toward his left arm, where the prosthesis made it look very normal.

"You take offense sometimes when people aren't trying to hurt you," she said hesitantly.

"Like with that fancy woman in the hotel?" he asked, his face going hard. He looked both ways and put on the gas.

Bodie didn't say anything.

"What?" he prodded.

"I didn't think you were that sort of man," she replied tautly.

"What sort?"

"The kind of man who picked up women," she said quietly. "Okay, so I'm living in the dark ages. I know it goes on. But it seems reckless. You don't know anything about people like that. She might have just wanted money from you, but she might have given you a drug to knock you out, or even had a boyfriend waiting nearby to beat you up and rob you."

"Boy, do you have trust issues," he pointed out.

"I don't pick up men in bars," she retorted.

"Yes, you do." He glanced at her. "You've been picking me up in bars for years."

"You're not listening," she replied, exasperated. "Listen, women who play around with men can have all sorts of diseases, even fatal ones. How would you know? Do you ask for a health certificate before you…" She couldn't even say the words. She turned her attention out the window. "I guess I don't belong in any modern world, anywhere. I think people should get married first."

He cleared his throat. "Well, you have to remember that a lot of people these days don't have those old-fashioned attitudes."

"I noticed."

"And whether you approve or not, people will do what they please."

"I'm not a prude," she said. She moved restlessly. "I just have a more traditional outlook on life."

"Shut down the theaters. Close the bars. Pour out all the alcohol. Live in a house with a picket fence, wear an apron, have a dozen kids."

She flushed. "Don't make fun of me, please."

He chuckled. "It's hard not to, honey. You really are a little dinosaur. Where did you get those strange attitudes from?"

She turned toward him. "From my father, who was a Methodist minister," she said, her eyes frankly hostile, more so when he looked surprised. "He raised me to believe that certain things were wrong even if the whole world said they were right. He lived his faith. He wasn't a hypocrite, mouthing off about values and taking fact-finding trips to Las Vegas."

He frowned. He looked back toward the road. "You never talk about your father."

"Hurts too much," she said heavily. "I was riding with him. There was ice and snow on the roads, and we were going over a mountain pass. The road was closed, but one of his congregation members had just come home from the hospital and was having a crisis of faith. He felt the trip was necessary." She swallowed. The memory was hard. "There was a deer. It was just suddenly there, in the road. I grabbed the wheel…" She bit her lower lip so hard that it bled. "We ran off the road and hit a tree. He died instantly." She closed her eyes. "I killed my father."

CHAPTER EIGHT

AS SOON AS HE COULD, Cane pulled over to the side of the road, into a deserted parking lot, and abruptly pulled Bodie into his arms. He held her, rocked her, kissed her dark hair while she cried.

"You didn't kill him," he said at her ear. "It was an accident."

"I jerked the wheel…!"

"Bodie," he said softly, kissing her eyes free of tears, "if you're a person of faith, then you believe in acts of God, don't you?"

"Well, yes."

"Honey, when your time's up, it's up. Doesn't matter where you are, what you're doing." He smoothed back her dark hair and brushed his mouth over hers. "It was his time. Simple as that. You were an instrument, maybe. That doesn't make you a murderess."

"I loved him so much," she whispered. "Mama did, too. She grieved for so long. She never blamed me. But I always wondered if the cancer didn't come from a broken heart. It's not rational, but it's how I thought. I lost my father, and my mother, and now my grandfather. My whole family, Cane."

"Not all of it. You still have us."

She smiled wetly. "Thanks."

He pulled out a handkerchief and handed it to her. "Wipe your eyes. People will think I made you cry."

She made a face. "You do. All the time."

He glowered at her. "Only when I don't know what I'm doing."

She drew in a calming breath.

"And I'm sorry. Really sorry."

She managed a smile for him. "Me, too."

He tilted her face up and searched her eyes for so long that she went beet-red in her cheeks.

"I like making you nervous," he said in a deep, slow voice.

"Not nice."

"I'm never nice," he pointed out. His gaze fell to her soft, sensitive mouth. "Not ever…" Even as he spoke his head bent, and his mouth crushed down hard over hers. "You still taste of barbecue sauce," he whispered.

"I…do?"

He chuckled softly. "That wasn't a complaint." He sat up and looked in the rearview mirror. "We'd better get back on the road."

"Martians are tracking us?" she wondered with a grin.

"I don't think deputy sheriffs are Martians," he said, as he pulled back onto the highway. "But I don't want to find out, either."

"Good idea," she replied.

He grinned at her. "All the same, if his patrol car starts to levitate, I'm going to break many speed limits getting us out of here!"

THEY WENT BY THE RANCH and looked at the rancher's yearling bulls. Cane was impressed. He made arrangements to have two of them trucked back to the ranch, and he held Bodie's hand the whole time he was talking. Once in a while, he looked down at her with such tenderness in his eyes that she flushed. That amused him. But not in a bad way.

She was so happy that her heart was overflowing, and she remembered something her mother was fond of saying: after the cut, the kiss. Her grandfather's death, her traumatic experience with Will, had been the cut. This, Cane paying attention to her, wanting to be with her, that was the kiss. It was mind-shattering.

When they got home, Cane stopped at the hardware store in Catelow to order supplies for the ranch. It was such a small community that most everybody knew everybody else, and their families had been acquainted for generations. The Kirks were relative newcomers to the community, but Bodie's people had been in it for over a hundred years.

"Jack's grandfather used to sell hardware supplies to my grandfather when he was first married," Bodie whispered to Cane, indicating the man behind the counter. "Gossip was that they got in a terrible fight over a woman and bruised each other up. Then they became best friends and ignored the woman." She laughed.

"Good thing for your grandmother," Cane teased.

She nodded. "A very good thing. She loved my grandfather dearly. She was one of the best cooks I ever knew. I'd love to be a good cook," she remarked with a sigh, "but I'm too busy trying to get an education to learn."

She hadn't thought about school until then. There had been so much going on in her life, so many upsets and a major tragedy. From the time her grandfather was diagnosed with heart failure until now, things had been unsettled and frightening. The episode with her stepfather and his friend had only made things worse.

"You're brooding again," Cane murmured. "You have to stop that. I know all too much about brooding and the results."

"In your case," she remarked with twinkling eyes, "brooding results in broken things."

He shrugged. "We all handle stress in our own individual ways." He leaned down. "At least usually it's just broken bottles and glasses instead of broken jaws."

"Usually." She laughed.

He grimaced. "Well, there are times..."

"Can I help you?" Jack asked, noticing the two people at his counter.

"Yes. I have a list," Cane said, handing it to the man. "It's a little larger than our usual order, but we're not in a hurry this time. Some of our men will be on vacation for a week, so we won't be doing as much."

"We've heard about the benefits at the Rancho Real." Jack chuckled. "Maybe I should learn to ride a horse and hit you up for a job. Be a cold day in a hot place when I get offered a week off with pay."

Cane smiled. "We work our employees hard. We feel they should derive some benefit from their sacrifices."

"Two weeks paid vacation a year, retirement, insurance...." Jack ticked them off on his fingers. "I know ranchers who pay half what you do and people who take Christmas day off get a day's cut in pay."

"We've been lucky," Cane commented diplomatically. "A lot of ranchers are hurting in this flat economy. They do what they have to do, to stay in business."

"That's true," Jack replied, nodding. "Nobody has job security. Not even us. We're just fortunate that no big-time franchise wants to set up business in such a small community, or all these little shops would go under. I've seen it happen elsewhere."

"So have I," Cane said. "It's a real shame."

"Well, we can have most of this by next week," Jack said, glancing at the list. "These tools are specialized and we'll have to get them from a supplier back East, so it will take maybe ten days. Unless you want it overnighted," he added.

"Not necessary. Just give us a call as it comes in, and we'll send somebody into town to pick it up."

"My pleasure," Jack said. "And thanks for the business."

"We always trade locally when it's possible," Cane told him. "We want to keep you open as much as you do."

Jack chuckled. "Yes. My wife and kids appreciate it, as well."

Cane just smiled.

ON THE WAY BACK TO THE ranch, he was thoughtful.

"You're very quiet," Bodie remarked.

"I was thinking."

"About what?"

"A family."

She blinked.

He glanced at her and laughed a little self-consciously. "I've never thought about settling down. A wife, kids, the responsibility for maintaining a family...it's pretty extreme."

Her heart sank, but she smiled, anyway. "I don't think it's a responsibility that people really choose. It sort of chooses you, in the right setting."

"In other words, some woman gets her hooks into you and holds out with promises of nightly delight until she gets a wedding ring on her finger."

He sounded so bitter that she knew it was a situation he'd dealt with in the past.

"Well, there are women with ideals," she began.

He glanced at her with a world-weary smile. "Ideals are dispensable in the right situation, Bodie. And you know it."

She went red. She averted her face and folded her arms over her chest defensively. She'd never forget what she'd been forced to do, trying to save her grandfather. Now she had to live not only with the decision, but the contempt of the one man in the world whose opinion really mattered.

"I did what I thought I had to do," she said tightly. "Will was threatening to throw us into the streets, and my grandfather's heart condition was so dangerous…"

"Oh, my God!"

He turned the truck onto the side of the road and cut the engine. "I didn't mean that," he bit off, his face taut with anguish. "Bodie, I didn't mean it like that!"

She swallowed. She couldn't look at him. "I did a horrible thing. I did tell them I'd only go so far. I let Larry kiss me…" She closed her eyes. "It was awful. I hated having him touch me, having Will film it…he promised me it was only for private use and nobody would ever know. He'd let us stay in the house if I did it just that one time, and he'd pay my grandfather's pharmacy bill. I still had the specialist to pay and no money left for anything…." She bit her lip. "I felt like a prostitute!"

He wanted to drag her into his arms and comfort her. But if he did, while she was dealing with that memory, one he'd helped her make with his bad attitude, it would tarnish what was building between them.

"Listen," he said heavily, "I know why you made the decision, and so do you. It was a sacrifice you made for love of your grandfather, not for the sake of money. And it was my fault. Do you think it's any easier for me to live with what you had to do? I lie awake nights thinking what a fool I was, thinking of the damage I did to you because I classed you with that woman who only wanted money from me. It's a mistake I keep making," he groaned.

She wiped her eyes. "You've had your own tragedies to work through," she conceded.

"Yes." He looked out the windshield, his eyes dark and sad. "I'm not dealing with any of it. Not with the accident, not with the loss of my arm, not with…anything." He leaned his head back against the seat. "I can't talk about it with anybody. I don't trust people. The therapists they send me to, they all want me to open up at once and start spilling out my private thoughts to them, like I'm on some social networking page." His face went taut again. "You can't imagine how repulsive it is to me, reading the most intimate things about other people on a page that the whole world has access to. What the hell is wrong with people? They can't tell such things to their families? They have to share sordid stories with the whole world to feel absolution?"

"Don't ask me. I don't do social networking. I have a private page, for friends only."

He raised an eyebrow. "And your friends don't share what you tell them with *their* friends?" he asked cynically.

She stared at him. She felt uneasy. "Well, I don't know…"

"And just how much private information do you share with them?"

She shifted on the seat. "Not much. I mean, I haven't really done much that anybody would find interesting. It's mostly stuff about school and news in anthropology, my thoughts on new finds, that sort of thing. Nothing you'd say was really personal or intimate."

"Kudos to you," he said. "I know a guy who posted a rant about his boss. The boss read it and fired him. He's still out of work."

"I see what you mean. About sharing too much information, I mean. I'll be more careful."

"See that you do. Once that information is out there, it's out there. You can wipe it out, but not without specialized computer services. Someone like our cattle foreman, Red Davis, could do that." He chuckled. "Even the CIA respects his abilities."

"How do you know that?" she asked curiously.

"Oh, they told us, the night they took him off in handcuffs for hacking their files on Al Qaeda." He laughed. "They still arrested him, though."

"What happened then?" she asked, fascinated.

"He managed to talk his way out of it, by sharing a little program he'd written. I have no idea what it did, but apparently it was adopted as a new tool of the intelligence gathering trade. They tried to hire him. He said he liked cattle better than offices, and he came home."

She laughed. "Good for you, that was." She sighed. "My friend Beth once posted a photograph of herself in her undies that only her fiancé was supposed to see," Bodie recalled suddenly. "And it turned up all over the internet. She had to write to about ten sites and beg them to take it down."

"Idiocy," he pronounced.

She nodded. "Beth's religious, but she's really not as staunchly so as I am. Her fiancé, Ted, is." She laughed. "He was horrified. He won't even sleep with her until they're married."

"I see."

She glowered at him. "Yes, he's holding out for a wedding ring. See? It's men, too, sometimes, not just women. People of faith have a different view of the world."

"Nothing wrong with a friendly night in some kind stranger's bed," he said, just to irritate her.

She glared at him with pure venom. "Sure. Go right ahead. Share an anonymous encounter, risk STDs and God knows what else then inflict them on some innocent woman who's never indulged at all. Do all that with a clear conscience and no remorse. And imagine having it show up on a social network one day, and having your family see it."

He studied her quietly. "You paint one sad picture."

"It is sad. People think free sex is a counterpoint to a life of chastity, devotion to one person, a life together that includes children and security and love."

"Some people don't think that magic formula exists."

"Well, it does," she retorted. "And you don't find it in bars with strange women."

His eyes narrowed coldly. "Point to you," he returned.

Her lips made a thin line. "You hit me first."

"I never raised a hand to you!"

"Yes, you did. You said ideals can be sold out for the right reason!"

He turned his eyes away and started the truck. His mouth was a thin line as he pulled back onto the highway. He didn't say another word all the way home.

Morie was on the porch when they drove up. She knew with a look that there had been one hot argument between the two taciturn people getting out of the truck.

"Something wrong?" she asked gently.

"I'm not getting married," Cane said harshly.

"Nobody asked you to get married!" Bodie shot back.

"Furthermore, I'll sleep around if I feel like it, and I won't have a guilty conscience or catch some social disease!"

"Fine! Do what you please and see if I care!"

He turned and stomped off toward the barn.

Morie started to speak to Bodie, but she thought better of it. The younger woman grimaced, gave her an apologetic look and went quickly up to her room.

It was grim at the dinner table. Bodie ate without tasting anything and wouldn't even look at Cane. He, in turn, pretended she wasn't in the house. It made things difficult for the rest of the family.

After dessert, they filed into the living room. But instead of turning on the television, Tank sat down at the piano.

"I think a little music might have soothing properties," he remarked, with a pointed glance from a silent Cane to a stiff and unapproachable Bodie. "Calming savage breasts and such."

"I thought it was savage beasts," Mallory murmured, tongue in cheek.

"Whatever." Tank began to play Rachmaninoff's "Rhapsody on a Theme of Paganini." As the powerful music filled the room, Bodie uncrossed her arms and sat, entranced, at the impromptu concert.

The beauty of the selection brought tears to her eyes. It did every single time she heard it.

By the time Tank finished playing, she was openly wiping her eyes. So was Morie.

"I swear, you get better by the day," Cane told his brother, and he even smiled. "It's a gift, to be able to play like that."

"Yes," Mallory said with pursed lips and twinkling dark eyes. "In fact, he's almost as good as I am. I've been practicing for months. He's slacked off." He chuckled.

"Challenge him," Morie prodded. "Go on. Do it."

Mallory made a grimace, but Tank stood up and gave a flourish with his hand, indicating the piano seat.

"Well, all right," Mallory said as he moved to sit at the piano. "But if he starts looking around for a sharp object to use on himself, somebody be prepared to stop him. Egos are serious things."

Everybody laughed.

Mallory drew his fingers over the keys, thought for a moment and then launched into the beautiful theme song of the movie *August Rush,* presenting Mark Mancina's haunting, exquisite combination of harmony and discord.

When he finished, he stood up and bowed.

Tank made a face. "Okay. I surrender. Anybody got a white handkerchief?"

Morie laughed. "I heard the organ theme played in a theater. It absolutely rocked the seats. It's one of the finest compositions I've ever heard."

"What's your favorite piece, Bodie?" Tank asked.

She shifted in her chair. "You'll laugh."

"We won't," Tank promised and smiled at her. "Come on. Give."

"'The Firebird' by Igor Stravinsky."

"I won't laugh," Cane remarked. "That's one of my favorites, too."

Mavie, bringing second cups of coffee in on a tray, smiled as she sat it down. "I'm for Harry-Gregson Williams. The music for the Narnia movies?"

"Oh, yes," Bodie enthused. "Beautiful!"

"Don't forget 'Basil Poledouris'—the theme from the original *Lonesome Dove* television mini-series, and movies like *Red October,*" Mavie remarked. "He was always one of my favorites."

"Jerry Goldsmith, the themes from *Patton* and *The Secret of NIMH* and various *Star Trek* movies," Tank added.

"Respighi, 'Pines of Rome: Pines Near a Catacomb,'" Bodie said with a grin. "I can hear the Roman legions marching when I hear it."

"I like Debussy," Morie added.

"Nothing wrong with Toby Keith," Mavie interjected as she started to leave. "Wish I was rich and famous, and I'd call up a boy I used to date and ask him 'How do you like me now?'" She laughed after alluding to one of Keith's more famous early songs.

"I like one of Brad Paisley's songs about being so much cooler online." Bodie chuckled. "Great video. There's another one, where he's trying to be a singing star on a TV talent show and William Shatner is the judge. It's hilarious!"

"Music moves the world," Mallory agreed. "I've always been fond of James Horner—who did the *Don Juan Demarco* theme, and Alan Silvestri's *Polar Express.*"

"Howard Shore—*The Lord of the Rings* trilogy," Cane inserted.

"David Arnold, *Last of the Dogmen,*" Tank countered. "And Trevor Rabin, who did *Race to Witch Mountain.* 'The Rock,' Dwayne Johnson, was in that one. My favorite actor—well, him and Vin Diesel."

They all laughed. Tank was a die-hard action film fan, and he watched professional wrestling weekly.

"Speaking of which," Mallory remarked, checking the television listing, "they're rerunning *Pitch Black,* that sci-fi movie Vin starred in."

"See if you can find *The Chronicles of Riddick* anywhere," Tank replied. "It's the sequel to *Pitch Black*—my favorite movie. It has some incredible special effects, too."

Mallory turned on the television and started searching through the paid movie on-demand listings.

"It's in there," Morie said. "I recorded it. Look in that section. It's one of my favorites, too," she told Tank.

Cane got up from his seat and stretched. "I think I'll go for a drive. I'm too wired to sit down and relax."

Bodie didn't look up. She half hoped he'd ask her to go along and maybe they could make up. But he didn't even look at her. He just walked out.

The men sat down in front of the television as the movie started. Morie motioned to Bodie and led her into the study and closed the door.

"Okay, what's going on with you and Cane?" she asked gently. "I know you've argued."

Bodie bit her lip. "It was a stupid thing. He got to talking about marriage and how he'd rather sleep around than settle down, and I shot back at him that some women did still have morals about such things. He threw up what I did to me," she said finally and with a long, wistful sigh. "I'm never going to live it down, I guess. I was only trying to save my grandfather. I didn't even accomplish that...."

"Oh, Bodie, nobody blames you for what happened," Morie said, hugging her tight. "Listen, no one is so perfect that we can afford to throw stones at anybody else. Life is about forgiveness. You know more than most people about anthropology. Hunter-gatherers lived in groups of less than fifty people, in close proximity. People did have conflicts."

"Yes, but they had to resolve them," Bodie agreed. "If one man killed another man, he brought offerings to the family of the dead man and tried to make amends. There were punishments, but people were rarely banished forever, even for terrible offenses." She smiled. "They were more tolerant, as well. There were men in the community who didn't want to hunt, who preferred the life the women lived. So they were permitted to do what they pleased without censure. People got along because they had to. Their survival depended on it."

"You're going to make a wonderful instructor one day," Morie told her. "If you need help with tuition, I'll take care of it," she added, "and don't fuss. You know I can afford it."

Bodie flushed. "It's very kind of you..."

"It isn't. My family funds scholarships at two colleges," she said. "We're very big on education. It would be my pleasure to help in any way I can. You're family," she said gently.

"That means so much to me right now," Bodie said, and from the heart. "I'm still used to getting along without my grandfather. It's hard."

"I loved my granddaddy, too," Morie told her. "He was such a funny man. He and my dad would have these ridiculous arguments. Mom told me that they were having dinner when she was dating my uncle Danny, long before she married Dad, and my father let out a cuss word. His dad pulled him up for it, and my grandmother piped in and said that he, my grandfather, cussed at the table, too. And Big Jim, my granddaddy, said, 'the hell I do!'" She laughed. "He was wonderful. He taught me to fish."

"They say your father was a holy terror when he was Cane's age," Bodie remarked.

"He was. He still has a terrible temper. He and Mallory hit head-on at the cattle sale," she recalled. "Mallory said that he wasn't marrying into any family that my father belonged to. Fortunately for me, he changed his mind." She laughed softly.

"Mallory is terrific. So is Tank," she replied. "He should marry some really nice girl and settle down."

"He's still dealing with his own tragedy," Morie told her quietly. "He isn't as obvious with his problems as Cane is, but if you stand near him when a car backfires…"

"He dives to the ground," Bodie replied. "I know."

Morie sighed. "I didn't. I laughed, and Darby told me what happened and why Tank reacted that way. I felt very small. It's rather odd, that Tank went through the war in the Middle East and came home unscathed, only to get shot to pieces by a Mexican drug cartel while he was a border agent."

"It's scary," Bodie said. "And a miracle that he lived."

"I expect he has injuries that aren't apparent," Morie said thoughtfully. "Maybe scars he's afraid to show to a woman he doesn't know." She gave Bodie a curious look. "He likes you."

"I like him, too," Bodie said, smiling. "He's like the big brother I never had."

"I see."

"Cane is like the big brother I'm glad I never had," Bodie added coldly.

"No, I don't think you consider him a brother," Morie mused aloud, and smiled at Bodie's scarlet blush. "I thought so."

"Well, if I don't, it's definitely going to be one-sided," Bodie said firmly. "I'm not getting serious about a man who sees women as party favors!"

"Some men take time to settle down."

"That one will never settle down," Bodie said curtly. "He thinks marriage is for idiots. He even said so."

"He might change his mind, with the right incentive," Morie coaxed. "Give it time, Bodie. He's dealing with his own issues right now."

"He won't talk to the mental health people," Bodie confided. "He said he can't open up to them instantly, like they want him to."

"Then, he might do better to talk to someone he trusts," Morie suggested.

"Like his brothers, you mean?"

"Like you, Bodie," Morie said.

The younger woman laughed hollowly. "He won't talk to me about anything personal unless he's been drinking," she said.

"Ever consider that maybe he gets drunk so that he can talk to you and tell you about things that are bothering him? Things he'd never have the inclination to speak of when he's cold sober?"

Bodie thought back to some of the more intense subjects Cane had spoken to her about when he was in his cups. She blushed when she recalled the more intimate ones.

"So he does, doesn't he?" Morie persisted.

"I don't know. Maybe he does. But I don't have the experience to deal with all that," she replied worriedly. "I don't know what to tell him, how to help him."

"What if I got you in touch with a psychologist I know? She might be able to give you some advice on how to deal with it."

"That might be helpful. But I don't want to make things worse for him by saying the wrong thing."

"I'm sure she won't advise you to psychoanalyze him." Morie laughed. "But she can tell you some things that might help."

Bodie nodded. "Okay, then. I think…"

Morie's phone went off, with the theme of a popular movie. She pulled it out of her jeans and opened it. "Morie," she said into the receiver.

"Mrs. Kirk, can you send somebody over here to get Cane?" the worried bartender of a nearby establishment asked plaintively. "He's wrecking the place!"

Bodie, overhearing the plea, grimaced.

"I'll send someone right over," Morie promised. "And we'll make it all right financially, okay?"

"Okay. But please hurry!"

"That's your cue," Morie told Bodie. She grimaced again. "Sorry. I'll get Darby to drive you."

"Get him to hide the tire tool," Bodie advised grimly. "The temptation just might be too much for me!"

CHAPTER NINE

IT STARTED TO SNOW AS Darby pulled up in front of the country bar and grill with Bodie.

"Now, don't hit him," Darby advised as he opened the door for her.

"Chance would be a fine thing," she muttered.

She strode into the bar. It was very late, and only a couple of men were still there. On the bar was a shattered display of glasses and bottles.

But Cane was nowhere in sight. She frowned and went to speak to the bartender. "Isn't Cane Kirk here?" she asked tentatively.

He glowered at her. "Come and gone," he said. He waved his hand around the room. "Hundreds of dollars worth of damage, again. Listen, Bodie, you tell his brothers if he does this one more time, I'm calling the law. Enough is enough. I sympathize with the man, I do, but we're going to lose customers if this doesn't stop. Besides that—" he sighed "—maybe a few days in jail will turn him around."

She grimaced. "I don't think so," she confessed. "He's totally out of control. Do you have any idea where he might have gone?" she added, worried now, because if Cane was that drunk and driving, he could kill himself or somebody else.

"No idea," the bartender replied. "Except that he started north, toward Jackson Hole."

"Thanks, Sid," she told him with a wan smile.

"Hey, no problem. I'm sorry about your grandfather," he said gently. "He was a good man."

"Yes. He was."

"That stepfather of yours," he muttered. "There's talk of an investigation. They say he's operating a porn site and using underage girls."

Her eyes widened. "Will?" she stammered, horrified. She'd known he filmed things for his own amusement, but she had no idea he was capable of something like that.

"He's denying it, of course, but one of the girls was forced to come forward by her mother. She was sixteen when she was posing for Will, although she said she never told him her real age. Not that he asked. Damned shame. Sweet, innocent girl, now her body's plastered all over the internet, thanks to Will, in some shameful ways. Or at least, that's the gossip," he elaborated. "I don't visit websites like that. But plenty do. Even around here."

"Can't they take the pictures of her down?"

Bodie asked. She was worried in case Will doctored the film he had of her and put it out in some obscene fashion on the web, to get even with her for involving the Kirk brothers.

"Not really," Sid replied. "They've spread around too far, or that's what the sheriff told me. He said he didn't know what she could do about it, except her parents could sue Will. But it's going to make things really hard on her around here. Her mother said she guessed she'd send her to college up in Oregon, where hopefully nobody will recognize her. She's changed her hair color and all." He shrugged. "Maybe it will help."

"Poor kid!"

He nodded. "Adult judgment requires age," he said quietly. "Will's friend Larry sweet-talked her, promised her a film career...said he had connections on the West Coast. She and her family are poor. She wanted more. So she did what they said. Now here she is, her reputation in tatters, her family disgraced." He wiped at a spot on the bar. "Thing is, what people do has effects on everyone around them. Like tossing a rock into a river. Ripples spread out far from the impact."

She smiled. "You're a philosopher, Sid."

"Learn a lot about human nature, working in a place like this."

"Have they arrested Will?"

He shook his head, and his face hardened. "Can't get enough evidence to indict just yet. But the girl's willing to testify, and her mother says they're getting an attorney. Even if Will doesn't get prosecuted for lack of evidence, they're going to sue him all the same." He laughed hollowly. "Can't see what good it will do, except to bring what he's doing out in the open. Can't get blood out of a turnip."

"So they say." She looked around again. "Mallory will take care of the bill," she promised.

"Somebody needs to take care of Cane," Sid said. "He needs help."

"Everybody knows that except him."

"I guess some folk are hardheaded."

"I guess they are. Thanks, Sid."

He nodded. "Hope you find him."

"If I do, he'll hope I didn't," she said with just a touch of belligerence.

Sid laughed. "Atta girl." He grinned. "Go get him!"

"I intend to." She went back out to the truck. Darby frowned as she climbed in beside him. "Where's Cane? You need help getting him in the truck?" he asked her.

"He's not there," she said. "Somebody saw him go north, toward Jackson Hole. We'd better drive along the highway and see if he stopped and passed out."

What she didn't say was that they might find him in some other condition. Darby knew it, too. He started the vehicle without a word and pulled out on the highway toward Jackson.

THEY WENT SLOWLY. It was very dark, no moon, and they had to look on both sides of the highway for Cane's truck. The road was deserted this time of night. It wasn't unusual to drive for many miles and never even see another vehicle. It was some of the most open country in the state, beautiful and wild. It had snowed, but even the faint glimmer of reflected light from the snow didn't help them spot Cane's truck.

"Maybe he went home," Darby speculated.

He stopped the truck and used his cell phone, which was connected to a communications system installed in the vehicle. It allowed everyone in the vehicle to hear both sides of the conversation and it was hands-free.

"Mal?" he asked when Mallory answered. "Any chance Cane came home?"

"No. Wasn't he at the bar?" Mallory queried.

"He was already gone when we got there. Somebody saw him start toward Jackson Hole, so that's the direction we're headed in."

Mallory was quiet. "He shouldn't be driving at all."

"I totally agree," Darby said. "But we have to convince him."

"Easier said than done," Mallory replied heavily. "I'll wake up some of the men and send them out to help you search. He could be on any of the side roads that lead north."

"Thanks, boss," Darby replied.

"He's my brother, warts and all," Mallory reminded him. "Can't turn my back on family, even if I'm tempted. But he's going to get a thumping, I promise you. This can't continue. We've already let it go on too long."

"Sid said he needed more than a night in jail to take a look at his life," Bodie joined in. "It's drastic, I know, but he's never going to change unless he has something to turn him around before it's too late."

"I agree," Darby said. "Instead of picking up the pieces and paying the bills, we should let the sheriff do his job."

There was a hesitation.

"You know I'm right, Mal," Darby said after a minute of silence. "We're doing him no favors, letting him get away with this behavior."

"I suppose you're right," Mallory said heavily.

"It might be better to get him into rehab," Bodie

countered. She couldn't bear the thought of Cane in jail, no matter what she'd said in anger.

"Yes," Mallory said. "It might, indeed. Okay, I'll send the boys out. Keep in touch."

"Will do," Darby replied and cut off the phone. He glanced at a silent Bodie. "Going to be a long night," he prophesized.

IT WAS. COWBOYS FROM Rancho Real joined the search party, each one taking a different road on the many branches that led from the Jackson highway. Bodie and Darby kept along the main road, their eyes peeled for any sign of a ranch truck off the road in a ditch or in the median.

After an hour of fruitless searching, Bodie was tired and sleepy and out of sorts.

"I really do want to thump him," she muttered.

"Mallory will do that, when we find him." He chuckled. He sobered. "It's worrying," he said. "Cane used to be the most levelheaded one of the Kirks. He was the marketing specialist, the go-to guy. Mallory had to take over after Cane was injured. Then, when Mallory got involved in the daily operations and Tank retired from the Border Patrol after his own trauma, Tank took over the marketing. Cane was left with showing cattle. It's rather demeaning, for a man with his brain. He graduated top of his class in anthropology," he added, surprising Bodie. "Brilliant man, with a great future. He was invited to a dig in Egypt, and it would have made him famous after the newer discoveries there. But he went to war instead, became a patriot. It was a huge sacrifice that he made of his life."

"I didn't know, about his grades. He was a summa?" she asked, referring to the highest honor graduates, *summa cum laude*.

"Yes."

"What a waste of a good life," she murmured. "All because he lost an arm. You know, a lot of people came home from the Middle East missing arms or legs. They learned to deal with it and get on with their lives. I don't understand why Cane can't."

"Pride." Darby sighed. "He's too proud to ask for help. We had to force him to take a man with him to help show the cattle. He tried it, but one of the bulls balked and knocked him down. He didn't have enough strength in his one good arm to stop it. Humiliated him, especially when a drunk buyer made a remark about the 'cripple.'"

"What a bozo," she muttered, angry.

"He did apologize, after Cane knocked out one of his front teeth," Darby mused.

"Good for Cane!"

He laughed. "But it didn't shield him from the

fact that he just wasn't physically able to deal with a huge bull in an arena."

"I guess not. It would have hurt him."

Darby nodded. "The way women treat him hurts more," he said bluntly. "He's had two bad experiences, over that lost arm. Now he's vindictive. He takes it out on you."

She swallowed. "Yeah. I noticed."

He glanced at her. "You've got guts, to stick around here. We like the company, but you shouldn't take any guff from Cane."

She managed a smile. "I don't, really." She sighed and looked out the window intently. "Isn't Christmas supposed to be a time for being kind to your fellow man?"

"Supposed to be," he replied. "Maybe we should stand Cane up in the living room next to the Christmas tree and decorate him with holly."

She laughed at the word picture. "Wouldn't that be a hoot? We could use rope and spurs for decorations."

"He'd be purty, all right," he drawled. "Not long until Christmas... Oh, dear God!"

He stopped the truck in midsentence. There, on the side of the road, was the ranch truck. It was upside down, steam rising from the engine in the cold.

Darby pulled onto the side of the highway, cut

the engine and followed Bodie, running, to the wreck.

"Don't look!" Darby told her firmly, trying to head her off. He had a horrible feeling that he was going to find Cane's mangled body inside. He wanted to spare her.

"In your dreams," she bit off frantically. She dived for the door, upside down with the glass broken out. "Help me!" she cried.

Darby helped her force open the door. Inside, Cane was still strapped into his seat, his head bleeding, his eyes closed, his powerful body slumped, hanging upside down.

Darby fumbled with the seat belt but couldn't budge the mechanism. He pulled out his pocket knife and cut it, easing Cane down and pulling him gently from the wreckage.

Bodie hovered, worried.

"I know, we're not supposed to move accident victims," Darby replied grimly, "but in that position he was in even more danger. Get my blanket out of the truck, we'll cover him up. I'll call for help." He pulled out his cell phone.

Bodie, frozen in place, looked at Cane's still form with horror.

"Hurry," Darby said gently.

She ran.

Darby checked the younger man's injuries as he dialed.

"Carson County 911," a voice came over the intercom. "What is your emergency?"

Darby explained the situation, and tried to pinpoint the location. "Just a sec," he said, putting the operator on hold while he used the GPS in his phone. He gave her the coordinates. It was such a big state that a rescue unit would have fits trying to find them by landmarks. It was a straight stretch of highway, with no significant landmarks anywhere in sight.

The operator was asking him questions. He pulled out Cane's wallet and gave her everything he could.

"We have a unit en route," the operator said a minute later. "Stay on the line."

"You bet," Darby replied.

Bodie had returned with the blanket while Darby was talking to 911. She pulled it gently over Cane, grimacing as she saw all the blood. It brought back horrible memories of the wreck in which her father had died. He'd been bleeding, too, just like this. Nobody had been able to save him. It was too much trauma for her, all this stuff that had happened in her life in the past two weeks. Her grandfather's death, the funeral, before that, the episode with Will. Now, here was Cane, possibly mortally hurt, and after they'd quarreled. His last memory of her would be one of disgust and anger. And she could never change it. If he died, the light would go out of the world. How would she go on?

Darby watched her with visible compassion. "Don't give up on him, girl," he told Bodie. "He's a Kirk. He's tough."

She bit her lip and nodded, but tears were rolling down her cheeks. "How long?" she asked plaintively.

"Our unit's about ten miles from you," the operator said gently, overhearing. "They're coming as fast as they can. Hold on."

Bodie's tears fell faster. "Thanks," she whispered, her voice choked.

"That's what we're here for," the operator replied.

"Look, Bodie," Darby said, indicating Cane.

The younger man groaned and he moved his head.

"Be still," Bodie said, smoothing back his bloodstained hair. "It's all right. It's all right, Cane."

He blinked. The alcohol fogged his mind and his reflexes. He tried to sit up, but Bodie pushed him gently back down.

"You have to be still," Bodie told him. "The EMTs are on their way."

Cane swallowed. He looked up at Bodie and frowned. "What are you doing here?" he asked curtly.

So much for hoping he'd forgotten their last argument. "Trying to save lives," she said pertly.

He made a rough sound in his throat and glanced at Darby. "How bad is it?"

"Truck seems to be totaled," Darby said philosophically. "And I'd say you're going to be in some trouble when the sheriff's deputy gets here."

Bodie paled. "Sheriff's deputy?" she asked huskily.

Darby nodded. "They always send a law enforcement unit with the EMTs, in case there's trouble."

"I'll show them trouble," Cane said, disoriented.

"You shut up," Bodie said curtly. "If they lock you up, I'll go see the judge and beg him to put you away for fifty years!"

"You coldhearted, acid-tongued little...!" Cane began.

"Ahhh-ahhh!" Darby intervened. "None of that," he said firmly.

Cane glared at them both, but he shut up. He frowned. There was a lot of pain. He moved and winced. "Damn," he whispered, his good hand going to his rib cage. "I think I've got a busted rib."

"Well, let's hope it's not the same one you got

when the bull kicked you six months ago," Darby replied.

Cane drew in laboring breaths and looked up at the night sky. "There's Orion," he remarked heavily. "It looks real bright, doesn't..." His eyes closed.

"Did he faint?" Bodie asked frantically. "How can he faint when he's lying down? Cane! Cane?"

"Concussion, most likely," Darby said, and now he was really worried.

"Turn his head," the operator advised quickly. "In case he throws up. You don't want him aspirating that into his lungs."

"Good idea." Darby reached down and gently turned Cane's head to the side.

It was just in time. The younger man suddenly lurched and heaved into the grass. When he finished, he collapsed back into the ground, unconscious.

"Oh, dear God," Bodie sobbed.

"Don't panic," Darby said gently. "Concussion can be treated." He was careful not to add that he'd seen men die of concussions less obvious than Cane's. Bodie was scared to death already. No need to add to her worry.

SCANT MINUTES LATER, flashing red-and-blue lights came into focus over a rise in the road. Darby stood up and flagged them down. They could see the wreck, but they couldn't see Cane, who was prone. The sheriff's deputy got out of his car as the EMTs jumped from their truck and ran to the patient.

Darby greeted the man and woman, uniformed, as they bent over Cane.

"He was conscious for a couple of minutes," Darby told them. "Then he lapsed into unconsciousness, threw up and went out again."

The EMTs went to work on him. One ran for a gurney and wheeled it over.

"You can hang up now," the 911 operator said kindly. "I hope everything works out okay."

"Thanks a million," Darby told her. "You guys are worth your weight in gold."

"Thank you," she replied with a chuckle. "I'll tell my supervisor you said so."

She hung up.

The EMTs got Cane into the truck and fed a needle into the artery at his elbow to start a drip. They were already in touch with a doctor in the emergency room, describing Cane's symptoms and getting orders.

"We'll follow you to the hospital," Darby said. "I'll phone his brothers to come and admit him."

"Thanks," the driver said. "Don't speed," he cautioned. "We don't need another wreck."

Darby nodded. "I won't," he promised.

Beside him, Bodie was going insane. She wanted to force her way into the ambulance, to sit with Cane, to take care of him. It drove off, and she stood watching it, too upset even for tears as she contemplated a future without that hard-headed, difficult man in the ambulance. It didn't bear thinking about.

The sheriff's deputy had been getting 28s and 29s on the wrecked truck—wants and warrants—checking the damage and calling for a tow truck to pick it up and bring it to impound.

"Going to be some charges, I'm afraid," the deputy told Darby. "I'm sorry, but DWI is no laughing matter. I've pulled too many victims out of wrecks like this, many of them involving innocent people. Even children. They're the worst."

"I imagine so," Darby said. "He's lucky to be alive."

"Very lucky, considering the damage. Drive carefully," he told Darby. "You family?"

"In a sense," Darby said. "I work for him."

Bodie didn't add anything. Let the officer think what he liked. She'd been raging that Cane needed to be locked up, but now that it was a possibility, she was sorry and depressed. She turned away toward the truck. "Can we go?" she asked Darby worriedly.

"Yes. Right now. See you," he called to the deputy.

The deputy nodded and went back to his patrol car.

Darby drove to the hospital, which was in Jackson Hole. Until then, Bodie hadn't realized how far they'd come.

"This is miles from home," she told Darby, surprised.

"Yes. I'm just glad he didn't kill himself or somebody else." He'd already dialed the Kirk ranch and was waiting for someone to answer.

"Mallory," came a voice over the line. "That you, Darby? Did you find him?"

"Yes. He was in a wreck. A bad one," Darby said gently.

"Is he alive?" Mallory shot back, horrified.

"Yes, but concussed and unconscious," Darby replied, his voice grim. "You'd better get Dalton and get up to the medical center in Jackson Hole as fast as you can." He didn't want to say that, to worry Bodie any more, but it was imperative that he make Mallory understand how bad things were. Mallory, too, had seen head injuries lead to death. The family might not have much time to see Cane, if that happened.

"We're already on the way," Mallory said. "I'll call you when we get to the hospital."

"Drive carefully," Darby said.

"How's Bodie?" Mallory inquired gently.

Darby glanced at her, sitting stiff and terrified beside him. "Holding up. But not well."

"We'll be there soon."

Mallory hung up.

"You have to have faith," Darby told his companion in a gentle tone. "Cane's tough. He really is. He'll beat this."

She swallowed. "I yelled at him."

"Hey. He yelled at you first," he returned. "Don't do that. Don't punish yourself."

She closed her eyes. "If he dies..."

"He isn't going to die," he said firmly. "Believe it."

She shifted in the seat. "I'll try."

"And fasten that seat belt," he added curtly.

"Oh." She put it on. "I didn't realize..."

"You're upset," he said softly. "Yes, I know that. Cane is one huge pain in the neck. But none of us want to lose him."

"Not even me," she agreed.

Especially you, by the look of it, Darby thought, but he didn't say it aloud. He'd never realized how much Cane meant to the quiet young woman beside him. That was a tragedy in the making. Cane was a rounder. He wasn't the sort of man to settle down and raise kids. He'd break Bodie's heart and leave her numb, given the chance. Darby hoped she already knew that, because he wasn't going to say it to her. He had a soft spot for Bodie, like all the Kirks. It was a pity that Cane was so hostile toward her. A real shame.

DARBY AND BODIE SAT in the emergency room waiting area. Well, Darby sat. Bodie paced, arms folded across her chest, her face drawn and white while they waited for the resident who was working on Cane to come out and tell them something.

"Why is it taking so long?" Bodie worried, casting glances at the door behind which the medical personnel were dealing with Cane.

"Tests, I imagine," Darby replied. "They'll have to find out the extent of the damage before they can treat it."

"Concussion," she murmured. "How do they treat a concussion?"

"Depends on how bad it is," he replied evasively.

"What if it's real bad?"

"ICU," he speculated. "Maybe for a couple of days, until he's stabilized."

"ICU," she murmured again. She glanced toward the treatment area again. "It's taking so long," she repeated dully.

The door opened and Mallory, Dalton and

Morie came through it, all wearing worried expressions.

Morie went at once to Bodie and hugged her close. "You poor thing," she whispered. "I'm so sorry you had to see it."

Bodie broke down. The sympathy was too much for her shattered reserve. "I yelled at him," she cried. "I said I hoped they locked him up…!"

"And what did he say to you before you said that to him?" Morie asked wisely.

Bodie pulled away and wiped at her eyes with a tissue from a box placed strategically in the waiting room. "He said a lot," she replied.

"I thought so." She turned to Darby, who was talking to the other men in a hushed tone. "How bad is it?" she asked them, keeping her arm around Bodie.

"The doctors haven't come out, but I believe he had a massive concussion," Darby said quietly. "It could go either way." He couldn't pull punches with the brothers, but he hated having Bodie know just how desperate Cane's situation really was.

"He could die?" Bodie asked, and her pale brown eyes were drenched in tears.

"There is that possibility," Mallory said grimly. "But let's try to think positively. He's got good medical care, and he was conscious when you first found him," he added, indicating that Darby had filled him in on the details earlier.

"He was very conscious," Bodie said. "Then he just went out like a light, threw up and went out again."

"Not a good sign," Tank murmured, shoving his hands into his jeans. His own face was as taut as Mallory's. He'd seen combat. He'd seen men die of head injuries. He knew the prognosis, or possible prognosis, better than anybody else in the room.

"They have excellent staff here," Mallory replied gently. He patted his brother on the shoulder. "He's a Kirk. He's come through worse than this."

"I know." Dalton stretched. "Well, it wouldn't hurt to say a prayer. They got a chapel here?"

"I'll ask someone," Morie said, and went looking for the chaplain service.

Bodie folded her arms across her chest. She was already praying. Hard.

THEY WENT TO THE CHAPEL and stayed there for several minutes, silent and worried sick, while one of the chaplains stood discreetly outside the room, waiting for them. When they came out, she escorted them back to the waiting room and stayed with them.

It was a kindness, but Mallory understood it better than anyone else. The chaplain had spoken with the doctor treating Cane. When she put away her phone, her face was grim before she forced a smile and said encouraging things.

But Mallory knew why she was hovering. They didn't expect Cane to live. The chaplain might be needed by the family, which was why she stayed with them. It was vaguely terrifying, despite the comfort of it.

Mallory didn't say what he was thinking. Bodie was already near collapse as minutes turned to hours, and still the doctor didn't come out to speak to them.

"Do you think you could call them again and see what's going on?" Mallory asked the chaplain.

"Certainly I can," she said softly. "Just a moment." She went to use a stationary telephone, instead of her cell phone. That worried Mallory. She obviously didn't want them to overhear what she was saying, or what she might be told.

Around them, people came and went, some with hopeful faces, some in tears. A family sitting nearby glanced at Bodie and the woman, an elderly lady, smiled softly. It was an unspoken comfort. People in desperate situations, afraid for loved ones, became family in a way that was inexplicable to those who hadn't experienced it. Bodie smiled back, trying to convey her own sympathy.

Inside, she was shaking. This was as bad as

losing her grandfather. His death had been quick, merciful in its way. But she remembered the doctor's office, the terror she'd felt. It was like this. Only this was worse. Waiting. The waiting was terrible. It was torment.

She glanced toward the chaplain, who had her back turned to the family. She was listening, nodding, nodding some more. Finally she hung up. Her expression was briefly worried and tense.

She turned and came back toward the Kirks. Bodie watched her walk with stark terror in her eyes. That look on the chaplain's drawn face—it meant Cane wasn't going to make it. It meant he was going to die…!

CHAPTER TEN

BODIE'S HEART BEAT IN concert with the chaplain's steps, harder and harder. Her eyes clouded. *Don't say it,* she wanted to say aloud. *Don't tell us. Just let us hope. Let us hope...!*

She ground her teeth together and stood rigidly along with the Kirks, who were also dreading her approach.

But the chaplain didn't stop at them. She only smiled and went past them, to the elderly woman who was waiting, nearby. She spoke gently. The woman burst into tears, and the chaplain hugged her, whispering words of comfort. Beside her, an elderly man was also crying. They spoke again to the chaplain, nodded and walked out of the room, slowly.

The chaplain came back to the Kirks. "I'm sorry. I was getting news about your brother when the physician told me they'd lost the woman's mother. She was very old, but that doesn't matter when you love someone."

"I'm so sorry," Bodie said, looking after the elderly couple as they left the room.

"So am I. Now. About your brother," the chaplain said, and she smiled, "he's conscious and yelling at the doctor. It is a concussion, but not fatal. They're moving him to ICU overnight, to be sure. It's just a precaution," she assured them. "I wouldn't lie to you if it was a dire situation."

"Thanks," Mallory said. Dalton nodded. Morie smiled.

Bodie let the tears roll down her cheeks unashamed. "Thanks!" she added.

The chaplain smiled again. "This is what we're here for, to make things a little easier for the family. I'm glad I had good news for you."

"So are we," Mallory said. "Although I'm sorry for the other people."

"We all are," Morie said.

"Death and life are opposite sides of the same coin," the chaplain replied. "We deal with both here. It's nice when I can give a happy report, instead of a sad one."

"Nice for us, certainly. When can we see him?" Mallory asked.

"I'll find out. They're moving him to ICU now. It will limit the number of people who can go in to two, I'm afraid," she added as she walked away.

"Tank and Bodie," Mallory and Morie said al-

most at the same time. They laughed at their co-
ordination.

"I'm...not family, though," Bodie stammered.

"Yes, you are," Morie said gently. "Cane may
be an idiot, but you have feelings for him. We all
know it, even if he doesn't. You go with Tank."

"Thanks," she said, her eyes lifting to Mallory
to include him.

"I'll see him later, with Morie," he said softly.
"Tell him that," he told Tank. "He's more fond of
you than the rest of us. It will do him good to see
you."

Tank smiled. "Okay."

Bodie wiped her eyes again and managed a
smile. Thank God. Cane would live, even if he
never wanted to get married or have a family, even
if he hated her. He would live. It was enough. For
now.

When they were finally allowed into the cubicle in ICU where Cane was lying on white sheets,
covered with a light blanket, Bodie had to grit her
teeth. Her mother had been in ICU just at the last,
connected by tubes and wires to all sorts of machinery that made regular beeping sounds. There
was an oxygen tube in Cane's nose, a drip IV in
his arm. He had cuts on his head and stitches just
below his hairline. He was white as a sheet and
his eyes were closed. Bodie looked at the thick,

black lashes, and wondered at the expression on his face. He was always so tense, so wired. He never seemed to relax and his face reflected that stress. But here, on the bed in the hospital, all the harsh lines were softened. He looked younger, handsomer. He looked almost fragile.

Until he opened his eyes and saw Bodie. "Why did they let her in here?" he asked with ice dripping from every husky syllable.

Bodie stood her ground. She didn't snap at him. She didn't say anything.

"She and Darby found you," Tank said. "Stop grumbling. They saved your life. If they hadn't found you, it would have been too late by morning."

Cane blinked and shifted on the bed, groaning. "I busted a rib they said."

"You busted three, I heard," Tank replied complacently. "Well, you fractured three. You'll be wearing a rib belt and doing very little until after the new year."

"I had a show next week in Denver," he muttered.

"Red Davis will show the bulls," Tank replied easily. "He's good at it."

"He'll hack into the FBI files at night and get arrested," Cane grumbled. "My bulls will be left in their stalls while we try to spring Davis and arrange transport home."

"We won't let him take his laptop along," Tank promised.

"The FBI, too? In addition to the CIA?" Bodie asked, fascinated, as she recalled what Darby had told her about the daring cattle foreman.

"He likes to walk in fire." Tank chuckled. "The FBI was last year. But he was taken off in handcuffs three months ago by the CIA for just hacking their main website. He talked his way out of that. But now he's trying to dig out classified information about a specific terrorism incident from the CIA." He shook his head. "I know one of their agents. Davis really, really, shouldn't mess with those guys."

"They should offer him a job in their cyber terrorism unit," Bodie remarked.

"They already did and he turned them down. Bite your tongue, girl," Cane murmured. "He's the best hand we've got, next to Darby."

He spoke to her without venom. At least he was going to be civil, she thought. "Sorry," she whispered, averting her eyes.

"When can you get me out of here?" Cane asked, nodding toward all the equipment. "I feel like a cyborg."

"They're keeping you in here overnight," Tank told him.

"Yeah. So they can save me if I start to slip away, right? I know all about concussions. One killed Jamie Franklin," he added.

"Jamie was old and he got kicked in the head by a bull and stomped, as well," Tank replied.

"That was back in Arizona," Cane recalled. "Years ago, when we were teenagers."

"Were you ever a teenager?" Bodie mused, studying him.

"I was even a kid, once," he returned.

She managed a smile. "Hard to imagine that."

Cane searched her taut face for a minute then turned his attention back to his brother. "I'm sleepy. Did they give me something?"

Tank nodded. "For pain. You're going to be all right. Honest."

Cane smiled wanly and closed his eyes. "Okay. If you say so." His voice slurred. After a minute, he drifted off.

Tank walked out. But Bodie didn't follow. She stood by the bed, staring at Cane, frowning and frightened.

She smoothed back Cane's thick black hair with a tender hand, biting her tongue. "I'm sorry," she whispered. "Sorry for it all."

He didn't stir. She bent and drew her lips so

gently over his forehead, careful to barely touch him. Tears stung her eyes. "You have to live," she whispered. "I can't live…if you don't. You know?"

She swallowed, hard, and forced herself to turn and leave the room. But she wouldn't leave the hospital. She sat in the waiting room while the others went for food. They finally forced her into the cafeteria to have a sandwich, but she went right back to the waiting room, even when they told her they had a motel room nearby for the night. She just smiled and settled into her chair even more firmly. They gave up eventually and left her.

IN THE WEE HOURS OF THE morning, a veteran nurse spotted her sitting there. Cane Kirk was at a critical stage. The nurse had seen many cases like his, concussions that went suddenly wrong, tragically wrong. Cane was slipping.

She approached Bodie and smiled. "How's it going?"

Bodie noted the floral pattern of the woman's shirt and the stethoscope she wore around her neck. A nurse, she decided. "Not so good," she replied and forced a smile. "I'm worried about my…friend, in ICU."

"Would you like to sit with him for a little while?" the nurse asked.

Bodie blinked. "I thought that wasn't allowed—

that we could only see him every few hours, and just briefly...?"

The nurse smiled. "We make exceptions sometimes. Come on. I'll clear it with my supervisor."

It took a lot of convincing, but the older woman knew, as her nurse did, that the patient wasn't responding the way she would have liked. She'd already phoned the attending physician and asked him to stop by the room when he was free. So she understood the urgency of the nurse's request, and the reason for it. The young woman was pale and drawn, obviously involved somehow with the patient lying so still in the cubicle. The woman thought they were allowing the visit for her sake, but they were really doing it for the patient, to give him every chance to pull through.

"All right," the supervisor said after a minute. "But you must be very quiet and not get in the way of my nurses. And only for a few minutes."

Bodie nodded. "I'll be like a mouse. Honest. Thanks," she stammered nervously.

The supervisor smiled. Had she ever been that young? "You're welcome."

The nurse, relieved, ushered Bodie into Cane's cubicle.

Bodie curled up in a chair beside the bed, in her blue jeans. She noted that Cane had lost color, and he looked really bad. The nurse did her observations, charted them and glanced at Bodie.

"There's always hope," she told the younger woman gently.

Bodie nodded again.

When she was alone with Cane, she moved the chair carefully closer to the bed and curled up in it again, looking small and very vulnerable to the nurse monitoring the cubicles at the central desk. She reached out and slid her fingers around Cane's big, warm hand, holding it tight. The IV needle and tube were taped to a board around the hand, to hold it steady so that he didn't upset the drip.

Her fingers moved gently over his. "So many arguments," she said softly. "You always win them, because I never know how to fight back. And I've wished terrible things on you. But I never meant them. I think you know. I think you always knew."

He didn't stir. She knew he couldn't hear her. He wasn't responding at all.

Her fingers curled tighter around his. "You have to fight, Cane," she whispered brokenly. "So a woman turned you down because you lost an arm. You were a hero. You sacrificed yourself to save your men. That should count for something! Even with a stupid woman who couldn't see past the prosthesis...."

She had to stop. She was choking on emotion.

She hated the thought of Cane with other women, she hated it! But he'd already made sure that she knew she had no place in his life or his future. She, with her tarnished ideals and stubborn illusions, was so different from him.

"You can meet nice women," she said, hurting as she said the words. "You just don't find them in bars, mostly. You could go to cattlemen's meetings. Lots of nice women there who love the land and animals, who could love you.... Of course, you don't want that, do you? You don't want to be loved. You just want...women from time to time."

She swallowed. She stared at his hand, lying so still with her small fingers curled around it. "It's your life. I had no right to say things, to judge you. If I'd been through what you have, maybe I'd be the same." She hesitated. "Well, no, I wouldn't. You think I'm old-fashioned and out of step with the world, and I guess I am. But some people have to be conventional, to keep society solvent, you know. It's order, faith, duty, that keep us from reverting to savagery."

She smiled. "I know, I'm being philosophical. Stupid. I'm just trying to explain how I feel. Not that it matters to you, I know. You think I'm an idiot."

She smoothed over his fingers. His hand was beautiful. Big and sculpted, with flat, immaculate, trimmed nails. Olive complexion. He was so handsome that he made her ache. When his body had been whole, people said, women followed him everywhere he went. He never had any trouble getting a date. That Cane wouldn't have looked twice at Bodie. But, in his present condition, with his ego bruised, perhaps he'd come on to her simply because he wanted reassurance that a woman, any woman, could still think of him as a man. He'd touched her, kissed her...said outrageous things to her. She'd responded to them because...

She swallowed, hard. Because she loved him. She felt the blood drain out of her face. It was hopeless. He was never going to be able to return those feelings. He didn't really want love, or marriage. Bodie would never be able to settle for a loose arrangement, even if he went crazy and offered her one.

"Aren't we a pair?" she asked him huskily. "You're the original Don Juan and I'm like someone raised in a convent."

He didn't stir. She bent her head to his hand and kissed the back of it, tenderly. "I just want you to live," she whispered. "Even if you spend the next twenty years racking up notches on your bedpost with every single woman you can find. It will be enough if you're alive and in the same world with me. Really, it will."

She lifted her head and looked at him. Odd, that he seemed less pale. She squeezed his hand as hard as she dared. "I've never… Well, I've never really done anything with men, except with you. Everything I know, you taught me." She looked down at his hand. "I know you don't like me. I get in your way, I'm rude, I'm volatile." She swallowed. "I'm not pretty, I don't have social skills, I'll never win prizes for being witty or brilliant. But I love you." She laughed, not looking at his face. "For all the good it does either of us. I can't ever tell you. It would make you double over laughing. Or maybe it would insult you. I don't know. It's my secret, anyway," she whispered brokenly. "My burden. Nobody will ever know except me. I'll pretend that it doesn't matter when you call me names and laugh at my morals and snap at me. But each time I'll die a little more inside…."

She sat back in the chair and took a deep breath. "You just have to live, that's all," she said firmly, fighting tears. "It was never about me or my feelings. You can't help how you are. Some men just like beautiful women, nothing wrong with that. Except that I'm not beautiful." She laughed hollowly. "I'm like a comfortable old shoe that you hide in the closet when people come by. I don't threaten you in any way. I'd never toss off insults at you because you're disabled or make you feel small. I'm just the girl next door who's always around when you need someone to talk to."

She smoothed over his big hand with the tips of her fingers. "You do talk to me, too, don't you? About the most embarrassing things, too," she said, smiling. "At first I didn't know what you were talking about until I looked it up online." She sighed. "Gosh, you were graphic. I guess it could count as sex education, what you told me." She blushed and stared at his immaculate fingernails, tracing them with her fingers. "It's about as close as I'll ever get to that sort of thing. I'm not a good-time girl. Not even for you. I'm old-fashioned and set in my ways. I'll never fit anywhere." She swallowed again. "So I'll be a famous anthropologist one day," she mused and laughed softly. "Maybe I'll get to teach students at some famous university or something. Or maybe I'll dig up the missing link or find something controversial." She looked up at his still face. "You're so beautiful, Cane," she whispered. "Just beautiful. I never get tired of looking at you."

He stirred, just barely, and his thick, dark eyebrows drew together.

She worried for a minute that he might actually be hearing her, but she knew he was asleep. His heartbeat sounded on the monitor, strong and steady. Well, maybe a little fast, but that was because of the head injury, she imagined, putting stress on all his systems.

There was a gentle tap on the door facing.

"Time to go, I'm afraid," the nurse said softly. "I'll give you another minute." She smiled and left.

"They're making me leave," Bodie told Cane. She grimaced. "I'd stay with you all night if they'd let me. I'd never leave you." Her voice broke. She stood up. "You have to fight, do you hear me?" she managed gruffly. "You have to! Don't you dare give up! If you do, I'll…I'll…" She swallowed her tears. "I don't know what I'll do," she whispered, fear making her voice shake. "I can't…live without you."

He stirred again. There was a soft explosion of breath from him, but he didn't open his eyes and she was certain that he didn't really hear her. She hoped not. She was suddenly embarrassed at what she was saying so openly.

"Well, I've got to go," she said in a whisper. "Tomorrow you'll be awake and yelling at people, just like old times. Yes. You'll be fine tomorrow. I know you will."

She bent over and pressed her lips to his forehead, beside the stitches. "Sleep and dream of all those beautiful women out there, just waiting for you to wake up and take them on dates. You'll find one someday that you can love, maybe. You'll be happy. That's all I want. I just want you to live and be happy. Whatever it takes." She stood up, her face drawn and pale.

Cane's face was different suddenly. It had more color. His breathing was stronger. His heartbeat was stronger. It was odd, when she'd come into the room at first he'd looked...pale and dangerously still.

"The others will be back to see you tomorrow," she said quietly. "I won't come back. You need to get well. I just...make you angry, upset you. That's the last thing you need. Sleep well. So long, Cane."

She turned and left, refusing to look back. She was sick at heart. Scared to death.

The nurse was waiting. She was smiling. "His vital signs are improving," she said softly. "They're getting stronger by the minute."

Bodie looked at her oddly. "I thought he looked a little better when I left."

"Head injuries are tricky," the nurse said as she walked Bodie out of the unit. "Sometimes it takes a little boost to bring patients through." She turned and looked at the younger woman. "It isn't scientific, but sometimes the human touch can make the difference."

"Will he live? Please say yes." Bodie choked.

The nurse smiled again. "None of us can be certain of anything in cases like this. But what do

I think? I think he'll pull through just fine. Now you go get some rest, okay?"

"Okay," Bodie said. And she smiled back.

But she didn't leave the hospital. She sat up in one of the most uncomfortable chairs she'd ever occupied and slept fitfully.

When Mallory and Tank and Morie came in, very early, she was still sitting there.

"Good Lord, why didn't you come back to the motel and sleep in a bed?" Tank exclaimed when they woke her.

"Too far away," she whispered, and managed a smile. "The nurses let me sit with him for a while last night."

"Did they," Mallory said, surprised.

She nodded. "Can we ask somebody how he is this morning?" she wondered aloud, still worried. "I'm not family so I didn't know who to ask."

"I'll find out," Mallory said, and went toward the desk.

"You look terrible," Morie told her, holding her hand. "It's been a long night for all of us."

"Very long." Bodie sighed.

Mallory was back in a minute, smiling. "He wants bacon and eggs," he said, and laughed out loud, prompting the others to laugh with him. "The doctor says he's almost out of danger. They'll be moving him out into a room later this morning."

"Oh, thank God," Bodie exclaimed, bursting into tears.

Morie hugged her. "Now, will you go back to the motel and get some proper sleep?" she asked.

"Of course," Bodie said, and stood up with a sigh.

"You can come back and see him later," Tank mused, smiling.

"No, that's not a good idea," Bodie said gently. "I just upset him. That's the last thing he needs, in his condition. He needs to get well." She forced a smile. "I thought I'd go back to the ranch, if nobody minds?"

"Nobody minds," Mallory said quietly. "If you're sure that's what you want?"

"It's what's best for Cane," she replied.

"I'll drive you," Morie said. She reached up and kissed Mallory. "I'll be back in an hour or two, okay?"

"Okay. Drive carefully."

"You know I will." A secret smile passed between them, missed by everybody, as if something was going on that the others weren't privy to.

"Anything you want us to tell Cane?" Tank asked.

"Just…that I'm glad he's better," Bodie said. "Just that."

"See you later, then," Tank said.

She nodded, following Morie out of the building.

Cane was subdued when his brothers went in to see him. He was quiet and thoughtful, and he didn't say much.

"You going to be okay?" Tank asked worriedly.

"I think so," Cane said. "Where's Bodie?" he asked, glancing past his brothers with an odd expression on his drawn face. "Wouldn't they let her come in with you?"

"Morie took her back to the ranch," Mallory replied quietly.

Cane's face grew hard. "Is she disappointed that I made it?"

"What a vile thing to say," Tank muttered.

"Especially considering that she spent the night in the lobby," Mallory added coolly.

Cane averted his eyes. "Guilty conscience, probably," he said irritably, "from starting a fight with me before the wreck."

"You snapped at her first, I'll remind you," Tank told him, with a bite in his voice. "She doesn't start trouble. You do."

Cane glared at him. "Shows what you know! She's always sniping at me, always on about marriage and kids and picket fences...!"

"I kind of like those things," Tank said solemnly. "And Bodie's a sweet kid. She's got a heart as big as Wyoming."

Cane's black eyes flashed. "She's too young for you."

Tank's eyebrows arched up. "I'm younger than you by two years." He pursed his lips. "Just right for her. Besides, she likes me."

Cane's face went hard as stone. "If you have anything to do with her, I'll never speak to you again!"

"What I do with her is my business," Tank shot back.

Mallory moved in between them. "This is a hospital and you're in no condition to start a fight," he told Cane firmly. "You're here to get better."

Cane made a sound deep in his throat. He glared at Tank, who glared right back.

"She's poor and you've got money," Cane told Tank after a minute, with unusual venom in his tone. "It's easy to love a rich man, isn't it?"

"You think money is my only attribute?" Tank growled.

"I know it's mine," Cane bit off. He lay back on the pillows and looked up at the ceiling. "It's the only thing about me that women like."

Mallory and Tank exchanged worried looks.

"I wish I had a drink," Cane grumbled.

"You're going into rehab when you get out of here," Mallory said shortly. "I've had enough. You need to stop wallowing in self-pity and get a life."

Cane gaped at him. So did Tank.

"I mean it," Mallory replied tersely. "You're my brother and I love you. I'm not going to stand by while you self-destruct. You need to come to grips with the fact that you're disabled and learn to cope. The world hasn't ended. You're still alive. You were spared for a reason. You need to find out what it was."

Cane was still gaping at him.

Mallory shifted uncomfortably. "Yes, I'm getting religious," he said self-consciously. "Stress does that to people. We've been out of our minds with worry. We were told that you might not make it. We didn't tell Bodie, but she refused to leave the hospital just the same." He jerked his head toward the door. "The doctor said that the ICU nurse was concerned enough to let Bodie sit in here with you for a few minutes. Whatever she said to you, it brought you back when you were drifting away. You can't find anything better to do than insult her, but she's very likely the reason you're well enough to grumble about her this morning."

Cane averted his eyes. He was hearing something in the back of his mind, a soft voice, laced with tears, whispering to him. He remembered with a jolt what he'd heard. Bodie had said that she...

He caught his breath. He couldn't even say the

words in the privacy of his own thoughts. It was
too overwhelming. What she'd said shamed and
embarrassed him. It tantalized him with possibilities. It made him feel…whole again. But she wasn't
here and he was being unreasonable because he
wanted Bodie and she'd deserted him.

The nurse came in, smiling. "We're moving you
to a room, Mr. Kirk. Sorry, but you'll have to leave
while we get everything ready. You can see him
again in a few minutes."

Mallory chuckled. "No need to apologize. We'll
see you later," he told Cane.

"I could use some coffee," Tank remarked.

"Me, too," Cane replied.

"No," the nurse said. "Not just yet. No caffeine."

Cane made a face at her.

She laughed. "If you're nice, you can have ice
cream for lunch."

Cane's eyebrows lifted. He grinned at her.
"Okay. I'll be good."

She smiled back, flushing a little, because he
was very handsome.

Cane saw her interest and his black eyes twinkled.

Mallory and Tank shook their heads. Cane was
already getting back to normal, flirting with the
nurse. It wasn't a good sign for poor Bodie.

LATER, SETTLED IN HIS ROOM, Cane was more animated, although his fractured ribs were giving him some problems.

"That sure hurts," he murmured, touching the rib belt.

"It will get easier," Tank said. "I had broken ribs, after the shoot-out," he said. It was the first time he'd spoken of it in a long time.

Cane frowned. "I'd forgotten. Sorry."

Tank shrugged. "It gets easier. Once you face it."

Cane grimaced. "I haven't done that. Not yet."

"Isn't it about time you did?" Tank asked gently. "Breaking up bars and wrecking cars isn't going to do it for you."

"Which reminds me, we had a call from the sheriff's deputy who worked the wreck last night," Mallory said solemnly. "You're being charged with driving under the influence."

Cane sighed, grimacing as it lifted his rib cage and provoked more pain. "Nothing less than I deserve," he confessed sheepishly. "Better call our attorneys. I'm going to need representation."

"Already did," Mallory replied. "He said it's possible we might plead it down if you'll promise to get help."

Cane looked irritated, but he didn't speak. He moved his head on the pillow. "I've tried to get help," he said after a minute. "They send me to people who hang out on social networks and expect me to talk to them like an old friend as soon as we're introduced."

"You need to talk to someone you trust."

"Ha!" Cane exclaimed. "Well, that will be a short list."

"How about us?" Tank asked. "We're your family. We won't judge."

Cane made a face. "Yes, we're family, and we're close. But there are things I...can't tell you."

"We can find a private psychologist."

Cane glared at Mallory when he suggested it. "Same problem I had with the military one. I can't open up to somebody I don't know. There are trust issues."

"There's one other possibility," Mallory said.

Tank glared at him. "Bad idea," he muttered.

Cane stared at his brothers. "What's a bad idea?"

"You're always talking to Bodie when you get drunk," Mallory said with a quiet smile. "Why can't you talk to her when you're sober?"

CHAPTER ELEVEN

"I DO NOT TALK TO BODIE!" Cane exploded. "Not even when I'm drunk."

"That's not what I hear," Mallory replied.

Cane averted his eyes, flushed with anger. "She's just a kid."

"Okay," Mallory said, placating him. "Bad idea. You were right," he said to Tank, who seemed to relax a little.

"Bodie's got her own problems," Tank said quietly. "She's still dealing with the loss of her grandfather. And if they do charge Will over his website, some of those pictures of Bodie may turn up somewhere. If they do, she'll never live it down. It will destroy her."

"Wait. What charges?" Cane asked, blinking.

"There's gossip that the sheriff's investigator found enough to indict Will Jones for trafficking in pornography involving underage women."

"Finally!" Cane said. "That's great news."

"Yes, except that it will put Bodie on the firing line," Tank returned curtly. "Will had a movie camera he was using to film her with his buddy. You knocked the computer off and probably broke the hard drive with the images, but he still has the camera and whatever's on it."

"If he puts any images of her on the internet, he'd better be wearing body armor," Cane said in such a cold tone that his brothers stared at him in surprise.

Neither of them said anything, but Tank looked irritated. Mallory knew that his youngest brother was nursing feelings for Bodie. But judging from the way Cane reacted, it was a growing possibility that he himself had feelings for her, as well. Feelings he wasn't admitting.

"Isn't it a good idea to head off trouble?" Cane asked, thinking aloud. "Find a computer expert who can search for any images of Bodie and wipe them?"

Mallory and Tank looked at each other. "Red Davis," they said in unison.

Cane nodded.

"I'll get him on it ASAP," Mallory replied. "Good idea."

"Except that it's a big internet and search strings aren't always reliable," Tank said worriedly. "I'd hate to have Bodie exposed like that for people to see."

"So would I," Mallory added.

"It's her own damned fault," Cane said angrily. "She should have told Will to take his computer fantasies and go to hell with them."

"She could have, if any of us had known how strapped for cash she and her grandfather were," Mallory said reasonably.

"And," Tank added with venom, "if you hadn't sent her running and made her feel cheap for asking you for help."

"I thought she was being frivolous," Cane bit off, "like every other damned woman who comes on to me and wanted money just because I have it!"

"Bodie's not like that, Cane," Tank told him flatly. "And if you can't see it, then that's your loss. She's one fine woman."

"She's a kid," Cane emphasized, and he wouldn't meet his brother's eyes.

"Some kid," Tank chuckled. "There's a community dance this Saturday. I'm going to ask her to go with me."

"Like hell you are!" Cane flashed furiously. "You're not dating her! Not while there's a breath in my body!"

"Well, she won't date you," Tank said smugly. "Not after how you've treated her."

Cane averted his eyes. "I have my doubts about that," he said quietly. He was remembering Bodie's soft voice, laced with tears, whispering to him in the silence of the hospital room. "I really do."

The brothers exchanged puzzled glances and then changed the subject.

BODIE WAS FEEDING THE chickens when the big car drove up, with Cane in the backseat nursing his ribs.

She carried the bucket with the chicken feed in it with her, standing quietly by the front steps as the men got out of the car. She was wearing jeans and a gray sweatshirt. She looked very small, and tired—and flushed with subdued excitement.

"How are you?" she asked Cane hesitantly.

He glared at her. "Better, no thanks to you!"

She flushed and turned on her heel to go back to the chickens, fighting tears.

"Bodie," Cane ground out. "Come back. I'm sorry."

She stopped, but she didn't go back. "It's okay," she said in a husky tone. "I've got...chores to do. Glad you're home." She kept walking.

"Damn!" Cane ground out. "Damn!"

"Keep it up," Tank mused, smiling. "Helps me out, a lot." He turned and started after Bodie.

"You ask her, and I'm moving out of the house!" Cane threatened.

"Your choice." Tank kept walking.

"Calm down," Mallory told his injured brother firmly. "You won't solve any problems by yelling at the top of your lungs. Come inside and let's get you settled. You don't need to start a fight the minute you set foot on the place."

Cane didn't reply. He was sick and sore and hurting, and he hated Tank. He really hated him. Tank was going to soothe Bodie's wounded feelings. She might turn to him, in her heartache. Cane was so unsettled by the thought that he tripped on the steps and had to have Mallory catch him.

"Okay, up to bed," Mallory said firmly. "You're in no shape to do anything yet."

"Maybe you're right." Cane let the older man help him up the staircase to his room. "Tank wants her," he muttered coldly.

"She's very pretty," Mallory said simply. "And Tank's been alone a long time. You don't want Bodie. You should be happy that your brother is finally getting involved with someone."

Cane turned and stared at his older brother. "She's mine," he bit off. "Mine!"

Mallory's eyebrows arched in surprise.

"And I'm not giving her up," Cane added. "Not until she tells me herself that I haven't got a chance with her. And that," he said curtly, "isn't even a possibility. She loves me."

"And you know that, how?" Mallory queried softly.

"Because she told me so, in the hospital, when she thought I was unconscious," Cane replied, his voice subdued and quiet. "I was slipping. I felt myself going. Then she held my hand and talked to me, told me to fight, told me I couldn't give up and die." He shifted down onto the bed with a heavy sigh. He looked up at Mallory with pure wonder in his tone. "She said that I was the handsomest man she'd ever known."

Mallory smiled. "You're not bad," he conceded. "Not a patch on me, of course."

Cane laughed, as he was meant to, because Mallory might be tough and capable, but he was the ugliest of the three brothers and everyone knew it.

"Nice of her to boost your spirits," Mallory said.

Cane flushed. "She wasn't saying it for that reason. She meant it," he replied.

"Then you don't have to worry about Tank cutting in on your territory, do you?" Mallory asked.

"I suppose not." He lay back on the bed after Mallory pulled off his street shoes for him. "Thanks," he said.

Mallory smiled. "You're welcome."

"I shouldn't have snapped at her like that," Cane said sadly. "I don't know why I go for her throat every chance I get. I mean, she's the only person outside my family who ever gave a damn about me. She's rescued me from bar brawls half a dozen times. She and Darby came looking for me after I left the bar, saved my life. First thing I say to her is an insult, after all that."

"Could be that you're conflicted," Mallory suggested. "You know how Bodie feels. But how do you feel?"

Cane lifted his eyes to the ceiling and frowned. "I don't want to get married."

"Well, Bodie's not the sort of girl you can have a loose relationship with," Mallory cautioned. "She doesn't just do lip service to her ideals. She really feels them."

"I know that. It complicates things." He sighed. "I want her," he confessed. "I have for a long time, ever since she was old enough for that sort of thing. I've kept it hidden, until recent days." He glanced at Mallory, who sat down on the bed beside him. "She doesn't care that I'm...disabled," he said after a minute. "I mean, she really doesn't mind it. Not like that woman in the bar who said she couldn't sleep with a one-armed man because the thought of it was repulsive to her." He clenched his teeth together. The memory still hurt.

"You never used to resort to trying to pick up women in bars," Mallory reminded him. His own face hardened. "And I'll remind you that that sort of woman isn't likely to use soft soap with any man—any more than a prostitute would. No woman who doesn't care for a man is going to be sympathetic."

"Unless the price is right," Cane said cynically. "Money talks."

"It shouts."

Mallory nodded. He cocked his head. "You know, as you get older, that playboy image is going to lose its sheen. You'll see kids playing in the yard here when mine come along, Tank's if he marries someone. You'll be left behind, living from bedroom to bedroom, with nobody to come home to who gives a damn if you live or die. It's a pretty dismal picture from my point of view."

"Marriage is a trap. Not for you," Cane added quickly. "You and Morie are like soul mates. I'm happy for you. But I can't give up my freedom for any woman."

"What is freedom?" Mallory asked philosophically.

"I can come and go as I please. Date anyone I please. Sleep with anyone I please." He laughed hollowly. "Except that I don't please anybody, like this." He indicated what was left of his arm. He bit his lip and drew in a deep breath. "Mal, I haven't… slept with a woman since this happened," he confessed heavily.

Mallory was shocked. "You've been very vocal about approaching women...."

"Approaching, yes. Trying to prove that I could still function as a man." Cane averted his eyes. "Nobody wants me like this."

"That's not true."

Cane sighed. "Bodie does, I know," he said. "But she comes with strings attached. A wedding ring. Marriage. A family." He looked at Mallory. "I'm not ready for that."

"You're thirty-four years old. You're ruining your life, Cane. Drinking isn't going to help. It's just going to land you in jail eventually. The wreck was a warning. You were tapped on the shoulder and reprimanded. Somewhere down the line, tragedy is waiting for you. And for us, because we're your family and we love you. This isn't an experience I ever want to repeat. You don't know what it took out of us, in the hospital waiting to see if you lived or died."

Cane frowned. He hadn't considered the feelings of the other people around him. He'd only been concerned with himself. He felt suddenly guilty as he recognized the unfamiliar strain on his brother's face, the new lines carved into it over the fraught few days.

"I think I'm beginning to," Cane said quietly.

"Your behavior doesn't just affect you," Mallory counseled. "It affects everyone who loves you."

"I've been pretty selfish."

"You've been troubled," Mallory replied gently. "I know what you've gone through because of the accident. Tank understands even better than I do, because he's been there himself. But Tank is coping and you're not. I don't want you to end up in jail."

Cane smiled wanly. "Thanks. I'm not keen on that idea myself."

"So you have to get help," Mallory finished. "God knows we can afford a private therapist, we've been very lucky in our diversified stocks and investments, not to mention the prices we command for our seed bulls."

"It's the same old problem," Cane replied. "I can't talk to strangers."

"Then we'll find someone you can talk to," Mallory promised. "Just work with me."

Cane hesitated. "Okay," he said finally. "On one condition."

Mallory raised his eyebrows inquisitively.

"Get out there and keep Tank away from my girl!" Cane said.

Mallory chuckled. He got to his feet. "I'll find something for him to do."

"Thanks. And…ask Bodie to come up here, will you?" Cane said, hesitation in his tone.

"I'll ask." He emphasized the last word.

"Tell her I'm sorry again. Then ask her."

Mallory chuckled again. "Okay. Anything for my brother."

"You guys really are the best. And I'm sorry I put you through this," Cane said quietly. "I'm going to try to get myself back on track."

"That's all I ask," Mallory replied. "I'll be back."

He walked out, leaving the door open.

Cane stared after him, quiet and reserved. He didn't know what he was going to say to Bodie, but he couldn't let Tank muscle in on his territory. Bodie was his. He was never going to let go of her. Somehow, he'd come to terms with the distance that separated them on moral issues. It wasn't as if he was overwhelmed with women who thought he was the handsomest man in the world. He smiled, remembering Bodie's soft voice in his ear. This, he thought as he noted the small Christmas tree lit on a table in his room, was going to be a Christmas to remember. One way or the other.

TANK WAS HELPING BODIE feed the chickens.

"At least I don't have to worry about putting my hand on a snake in here in winter." Bodie chuckled. "Of course, I don't have any eggs, either." She sighed. "I wish chickens laid year-round."

Tank looked around the henhouse thoughtfully. "We need to put a new roof on this thing. Can't have our girls getting wet," he added with a chuckle, indicating the mixed flock milling around the yard.

"I love chickens," Bodie remarked. "Granddaddy used to keep them, when Mama was still alive, before she married Will Jones. I miss having them. This sort of makes up for it. And these hens are friendly." She reached down and petted one. It made that odd sound that hens made when they were contented, almost like it was talking to her in a happy way.

"I like chickens, too," Tank remarked. "I miss the eggs. Store-bought ones just don't taste the same."

"I do agree."

Tank looked out over the huge yard. "I'm sorry Cane was so curt with you. I guess he doesn't realize you sat up with him all night in the hospital."

"Cane's always curt with me," she replied softly. "I guess I'm getting used to it. It's not his fault. He likes beautiful girls."

Tank turned to face her. "What's wrong with you?" he teased, smiling as he studied her elfin features, her pale brown eyes, her short, black hair. "I think you're dishy."

She flushed and averted her eyes. It was the first time Tank had ever said anything personal to her. It was flattering, but she only had brotherly feelings for him. She didn't know what to say.

"Easy, now," he said gently, sensing her discomfort. "I was only making a comment. Even a big brother can comment that his baby sister is pretty. Right?"

She looked up, relief in her features. She smiled shyly. "Right."

"Besides—" he sighed, shoving his hands into his jean pockets and looking wistful "—Cane's already threatened to pummel me if I flirt with you."

Her heart jumped into her throat. "What?"

"He said—"

"Bodie?" Mallory interrupted.

She turned, torn between wanting to know what Tank had been about to tell her and being rude to Mallory. "Yes?" she stammered.

"Cane wants to talk to you."

Bodie's eyes widened, but she didn't move. "What, he's thought up another insult and wants to share it?" she asked, trying to sound facetious.

"He said to apologize again for his bad manners," Mallory replied with a smile. "If he insults you, throw it right back at him. He's a man who walks all over people he can buffalo. Don't let him get away with anything."

She drew in a long breath. "I do try. He's very forceful."

"We all are." Tank chuckled. "But you can cope."

"You think so? I wonder." She handed Tank the container with the chicken feed. "Can you finish feeding the girls?" she asked. "And watch out for Charlie."

He blinked. "Charlie?"

She indicated a preening red rooster nearby. "I always carry a stick when I come out here. He's spurred me a couple of times. Lucky for me, jeans are thick." She indicated the stick, which was a small broken limb. "I use that for protection. Doesn't hurt him, but makes him back off," she said.

"I've had to use it a time or two, because Morie and Mavie have stopped coming out here at all," Mallory confessed. "Until you came along, I had to feed the girls. Nice to know Charlie's met his match."

"You should give him to somebody and get a nicer rooster," Tank commented.

"No such thing as a nice rooster," Mallory said dryly. "I've never seen one who wouldn't attack anything moving, especially around a flock of hens. They're very protective."

"Also very tasty," Tank said with pursed lips. "Remember when we were kids and that big white rooster attacked me and drew blood?"

Mallory laughed. "Dad went right out and wrung his neck. We had him for supper that night."

"He said 'wasn't any rooster hurting his baby,'" Tank reminisced. He sighed. "Best chicken dinner I ever had."

"Well, you can't eat Charlie," Bodie said firmly. "The hens would mourn."

"We can always get another rooster," Tank teased.

She made a face at him. "I'll go see what Cane wants." She sighed. She glanced at Mallory. "Should I take the stick with me?" she wondered aloud.

Both men laughed.

CANE WATCHED BODIE ENTER the room. She hesitated at the door, her brown eyes worried and uncertain.

"I won't bite," he said quietly. His black eyes scanned her face with an intensity she didn't remember from any past encounters. "Come on."

She moved into the room, to the foot of the bed and stayed there. "How are you?" she asked softly.

"Better. Ribs still hurt, head's still rocky, but I'm better."

She nodded. "I'm glad. Everybody was worried."

"You left me."

She flushed. The way he said it was like an accusation, as if it mattered that she hadn't gone back to see him in the hospital after the night she'd stayed by his bed. That was sheer fantasy. Cane didn't care about her. He never had.

"I was just upsetting you," she stammered. "You didn't need that."

His black eyes stabbed into hers. They narrowed with speculation. "You talked to me."

She went scarlet. She swallowed, visibly upset. "The nurses were worried, I think," she hedged. "I just told you to get better. That's all."

"Is it?"

She didn't like the look on his face. It was different. She felt suddenly vulnerable. How much did he remember? Had he heard her embarrassing speech?

He took pity on her. He didn't want to make her feel any worse than he already had. She thought her feelings were a well-kept secret. He decided it might be better to let her keep her illusions, especially since his own feelings were so conflicted. He didn't really know what to say to her. He just liked looking at her, for some odd reason. She gave him peace.

"I don't remember any of it," Cane lied with a straight face. "Mal told me you sat with me most of the night."

She looked relieved. "Just for a few minutes. The nurse let me in. I think they were concerned that you were slipping."

"I was," he confided. "I felt it. Then I heard your voice," he added in a deep, velvety tone, "telling me not to give up. I remember that, at least," he said to reassure her, because she was looking threatened again. "It brought me back."

She smiled. "I'm glad."

"You don't have any excitement in your life past dragging me out of bars, huh?" he teased, and laughed.

She shrugged. "It's a dirty job, but somebody has to do it."

Cane shifted on the bed. "Come around here, will you? I'm getting a crick in my neck trying to see you."

She wasn't keen on getting any closer. He made her nervous and he would be experienced enough to know the signs if he got a good look at them. She was more vulnerable than she'd ever been before. But she went because he wanted her to.

"Sit down, Bodie."

She started to drop into a nearby chair.

"No," he said, his voice lowering an octave. He patted the bed. "Here. Right next to me, so that I can see your eyes."

She was almost trembling with excitement. It was disturbing, that look on his face, that dark interest in his eyes. She sat down beside him. His arm went across her lap, his hand resting gently on her hip.

"What was Tank saying to you outside?" he asked pointedly.

"Oh. He was—he was just helping me feed the chickens," she stammered. His hand was smoothing over her rounded hip with some odd familiarity. She should probably protest. His thumb was moving against her belly where it joined her hip, and the sensations it caused were becoming visible.

"Was he now?" Cane asked. He smiled. He could see what his touch did to Bodie. She couldn't hide it. She wasn't pretending because he had money. She was really, violently, attracted to him. It didn't matter to her that he was missing an arm. She wanted him. His heart jumped as he realized just how deep her feelings went.

His thumb moved down in the furrow between her thigh and her hip, more intimate now. "What did he say to you?" he asked, his voice almost purring.

Bodie was slipping away into some sensual fantasy while he touched her in a way that she should protest. "He, uh, he said…"

"He said what?"

She shivered. She really should say something. This was getting…intimate!

She gasped. She grabbed his hand. "Cane," she whispered uneasily.

"Too far too soon? Okay." His hand slid up, but under the hem of her sweatshirt, around her rib cage. His fingers lingered there while his thumb eased under the band of her bra. "How about this, then?"

She was shaking. His touch reduced her to melted flesh. "How about…what?" she faltered, her mind centered on the sensations that thumb was arousing as it moved ever closer to a very hard nipple.

"Bodie?" he whispered.

"Wh-what?"

"Lean closer, baby."

She obeyed him mindlessly, one hand going to the pillow next to his black hair, to prop herself up so that she didn't fall.

As she moved, so did he. His hand pushed the

bra out of his way and cupped her full, firm breast hungrily.

She moaned so harshly that he felt his body go rigid with desire.

"Good…God," he whispered again reverently, shuddering. "Bodie!"

He pulled her down beside him, ignoring the sharp pain in his ribs as he rolled over and pushed up her sweatshirt and her bra so that he could see her soft, pink, perfect breasts. "Beautiful," he breathed roughly. "God, you're so beautiful, honey…."

He bent and smoothed his mouth over her breast, lingering where the hard tip thrust up into his open lips. He drew it inside, working it with his tongue, while Bodie stiffened and gasped and made noises that almost pushed him over the edge. He was so hungry that he forgot the door was standing wide-open.

Footsteps on the staircase went unnoticed by him, but Bodie, even in her dazed state, heard them.

"Somebody's…coming," she said, pushing at Cane's head.

"Somebody's about to, really," he whispered blatantly, and suckled her, hard.

She had to fight to draw away from him in time, and he protested, shuddering. She got to her feet and jerked the sweatshirt down just as Mavie came in the door with a tray, mercifully concentrating on not spilling the coffee so that she didn't pay attention to a flushed and very embarrassed Bodie.

Cane was quick. He groaned and held his rib cage. "God it hurts!" he moaned, diverting Mavie while Bodie got her bra fastened again and smoothed her ruffled hair.

"You poor thing," Mavie said worriedly. "Don't you have something for pain?"

"Yes, on the table here. Can you open the bottle for me?" he asked, and sounded so helpless that Bodie had to fight back a shocked laugh.

"Of course I can," Mavie cooed. Even she, at her age, wasn't immune to Cane's charm when he chose to exercise it. She smiled. "Here you go. I brought coffee and a slice of pound cake, too. Bodie, I didn't realize you were up here. Wouldn't you like coffee and cake, too?"

"Yes," Bodie said. "But I can get my own, no need to make you climb that staircase twice. I'll see you later, Cane," she added quickly, without looking at him.

"You bet you will," he replied, and his voice was like brushed velvet in her ears as she fled from the room.

SHE POURED COFFEE WITH a shaking hand and took it, and a slice of cake, to the dining room table.

She wasn't going back into Cane's room unless she took somebody with her for protection. Good heavens, the man was potent! He'd lured her close, touched her, kissed her, and all she'd done was help him get her clothes out of the way.

So much for trying to resist him. If he put on the pressure, she was going to go under like a sack of sand. She'd never be able to save herself.

That being the case, she was going to have to be inventive, and find ways to keep him at bay. It had been a near thing. If Mavie hadn't shown up when she did, things might have gotten completely out of hand.

She finished her cake and washed it down with black coffee, just as Mavie came back down the staircase, smiling.

"He is such a charmer!" The older woman laughed. And Mavie hardly ever laughed. Bodie had to fight down a twinge of jealousy, despite the fact that Mavie was old enough to be Cane's mother.

"Yes, he is," Bodie agreed. She forced a smile. "This is great cake, Mavie."

"Thanks. I'm glad you liked it. Cane wondered if you'd go back up and talk to him for a while."

Bodie swallowed, hard. "I'll go in a few minutes," she said, and smiled. "I really have to finish my chores outside."

"Oh, Mallory would do them for you, or even Tank. It's so nice of you to help out, child. You really pull your weight here."

"I try to. I like working around the animals," she said softly. "I'll just finish up and then I'll go see Cane."

"I'll tell him."

Bodie bolted for the back door. She would go back, but not until and unless she could persuade someone to go see Cane with her. No way was he luring her into a physical relationship. She wasn't going to join the notches on his bedpost, even if she was head over heels in love with him.

CHAPTER TWELVE

CHRISTMAS EVE WAS magical. The whole family gathered around the Christmas tree in the living room and turned on a holiday special on television. They were all singing along to the familiar carols, drinking hot chocolate and eating cake. Mavie and Darby Hanes joined them for the evening.

Cane sat on the sofa with Bodie beside him. Once in a while, his fingers tangled with hers, unseen by the rest of the family. His black eyes searched hers, looking for secrets, caressing, mysterious and thrilling.

Since their encounter in his bedroom, Bodie had carefully avoided being alone with him. He'd been irritated at first, but he seemed to be all right with her caution once he understood that it wasn't coyness. She wanted him. But she wasn't willing to compromise her principles by sleeping with him. He found himself oddly proud of her for that attitude, even as he was frustrated by it. His body was hungry for hers. It was all he thought about lately.

He became aroused if he got close to her, even when she met his eyes from across the room. It had never been like that before in his life. Women had aroused him from time to time when they came on to him. But Bodie could do it from a distance.

She noticed Cane's changing attitude. It thrilled her, even as it frightened her. Was he looking for new ways to complicate their relationship? Was he still focused on seduction, with no thought of a future between them? She didn't know. She was just living one day at a time now, watching him, wanting him, but hoping for a miracle that would make him love her. She could see that she was attractive to him. That was thrilling, flattering. But attraction didn't necessarily involve any finer, deeper feelings. A man could want a woman without loving her. Bodie was aware of that, and it made her more cautious. She didn't want to join the ranks of Cane's one-night stands.

Even so, the way he touched her, the way he looked at her, melted her.

Meanwhile, Tank, for reasons nobody understood, was keeping close to Bodie, as well, teasing her and flattering her at every opportunity. It irritated Cane and made him snap at his brother. Tank just grinned, as if Cane's frustration and jealousy amused him.

Cane's ribs were still giving him fits. He couldn't

do anything that he really wanted to, and that, un-
fortunately, included seducing Bodie. A man with
fractured ribs wasn't in any condition to become
a lover. That frustrated him, too. He wondered if
Bodie knew that he couldn't manage intimacy in
his condition. The way she kept people around indicated that she didn't. He was constantly amazed
at how naive she was for a woman her age.

He liked it, too.

When the others filed into the kitchen to bring
back more coffee, Bodie was left momentarily
alone with Cane.

"Never miss an opportunity is my motto," Cane
whispered, catching the back of Bodie's head with
a firm hand. "Come here."

He pulled her mouth under his and kissed her
with furious, instant passion, his mouth insistent
as it opened hers and his tongue shot inside with
slow, deep thrusts.

She moaned and pushed close to him. He
groaned and jerked away, lifting his mouth and
wincing.

"Oh, your poor ribs! I'm sorry," she said huskily.

He swallowed, his hand going to his rib cage.
"Not your fault. I started it." He looked into her
eyes hungrily. "You do realize that I can't have sex
until my ribs heal?"

She gaped at him, going scarlet.

He laughed. "Sorry. That's blunt. What I mean is, you don't have to have people to chaperone you. Not for a couple of weeks, at least. I can't do anything. Well," he purred, tugging her closer, but not completely against him, "I can do some things," he added, smoothing his hand blatantly over the thrust of her breast under her pretty red blouse. "This, for instance..."

She caught his hand as the sound of voices neared. "You can't..."

He bent and kissed her quickly, drawing away at the same time. "I want to," he whispered, and his black eyes looked straight into hers. "I'm going to, Bodie. That's fair warning."

"Please," she whispered, her eyes eloquent. "You know, you must know, that I can't resist you. Please don't take advantage of something I can't help. It's like eating and drinking to you, but I've never...I couldn't live with it," she faltered.

He touched her mouth with his fingertips. "I know that, sweetheart," he said softly. "I won't hurt you. Well, maybe a little. Just at first," he added, leaning toward her, lingering at her soft, full lips. "When I first go inside you..."

She made a hungry, helpless little sound at the graphic remark, and his lips closed on hers, tenderly, hungrily.

"Thinking about it makes me hard," he breathed into her mouth. "I want you, Bodie. I want you so damned much!"

She shivered as his hand came up to smooth around her breast. Even through the soft fabric, her body answered him, giving away secrets as the hard tip lifted to his fingertips.

"I'll bet you're swelling, too," he whispered as he kissed her. "In the same place I am..."

"Cane," she groaned.

"I haven't done it since I lost my arm," he confessed against her open lips. "I've been afraid to try, afraid of being ridiculed. I'd try, with you," he added in a soft groan. "I wouldn't be embarrassed if I fumbled."

She opened her eyes and looked into his, anguish visible in her face. "I...can't," she choked out. "I'm so sorry...!"

"You can." He drew back and lifted his hand to her face. He touched her swollen lips tenderly, just with his fingertips. "Bodie, I think you should marry me."

"Wh-what?"

Her lack of confidence made him even hungrier. Her helpless pleasure was visible in her bright, wide eyes. It made him feel more like a man than he'd felt since the loss of his arm. "Marry me," he repeated.

She almost said yes. She wanted to. But he wanted to prove he could still be a man, and she was attracted to him. It didn't mean he loved her.

"You don't...love me," she said bluntly.

He sighed. "I'm fond of you," he insisted.

She bit her lip. "It's not...enough."

"Yes, it is, you little liar," he murmured against her mouth. He hadn't liked the idea of proposing at all. But her resistance added spice to this. He wanted her. He wasn't likely to attract any other woman who wanted more than his wallet. Bodie wanted him. Wanted him badly. Loved him. If he didn't make a move, Tank would. Tank was already infatuated with her. He couldn't lose her to his brother. He couldn't lose her at all....

He crushed her mouth under his, forcing her head back against the sofa. "Marry me," he ground out. "Come on. Say yes. Say it. Say it!" He punctuated each demand with another hard kiss.

"All right," she exclaimed brokenly. "All right. Yes. Yes! I will!"

"No, you won't," Mallory said firmly as he walked into the room and glared at his brother. "Cane," he added warningly.

But Cane was grinning from ear to ear. "She wasn't saying yes to some illicit relationship," he informed his brother. He watched Tank as he walked into the room. "I asked her to marry me. She said yes."

Tank's face fell. Cane's eyes glittered with dark triumph. He didn't often win competitions with his brother, but he'd won this one, the important one.

"Well, congratulations," Mallory said, taken aback.

"Welcome to the family, baby sis," Tank added, and forced a smile.

"Thanks," Bodie said huskily. She laughed self-consciously and moved a little apart from Cane. Things had been heated. Now she was trying to calm down and look collected, when she was shattered by the unexpected proposal.

"Better take good care of her," Tank told his brother firmly. There was an unheard threat, as well—Tank would be waiting if Cane botched it. He wanted Bodie, too. Nobody else seemed to notice his disappointment, but Cane felt it. He also felt a little ashamed. He shouldn't feel a sense of victory at hurting his brother's chances with a woman. But Bodie was Cane's. There was no getting around that fact. It showed.

"When?" Mallory asked.

Cane blinked. "When what?"

"When are you getting married?"

Cane hesitated. He was feeling suddenly trapped by his own impulsive proposal. But he glanced at

Tank and saw cynicism there. Tank thought he'd put it off, postpone it. He was in for a shock.

"This week," Cane said abruptly. "As soon as we can get a license and a minister." He looked at Bodie. "We'll have a church wedding, even if it has to be rushed. We'll invite everyone. Well, almost everyone," he added coldly. "No former family members," he said, indicating her stepfather.

"So soon?" Bodie stammered. "But…but I have one more semester to go at college," she faltered.

Cane smiled. "And you'll go. I want you to finish. You can come home on weekends. We'll give you a car to drive back and forth. We can use your truck for scrap metal," he added maliciously. "I hate seeing you drive around in that aging tin can. It's dangerous."

She was going to defend her truck until he said that. She beamed. He cared about her that much, at least. He didn't want her hurt. It wasn't much. But it was a start.

"No honeymoon just yet, though," Cane said with a hard sigh. "I'm a walking basket case for the foreseeable future. You'll have to help me down the aisle," he told his brothers with a chuckle, "because I'm not going in a wheelchair."

"You know we will," Tank said, and the affection in his eyes made Cane feel less guilty.

Bodie was feeling less threatened. Cane couldn't

function just yet with his ribs and his leg in that condition and she felt safe, for a while. She'd cope with her hang-ups when she had to, but for the meantime, she and Cane could really get to know each other. They could talk without the intrusion of physical pleasure, just for a few weeks. It might help him to understand her, to care for her more, if he saw her as more than just a way to physical satisfaction.

Cane wasn't used to talking to women. She knew instinctively that he was more interested in bedroom antics than social chat. He probably hadn't ever really been in love. She knew he'd been briefly involved with some woman who'd chosen a law career over him and went away, but they'd never been engaged and it hadn't been really serious according to Tank.

She glanced at Tank with fleeting guilt. She hadn't realized until lately that he was really interested in her, and she was sorry about it. But she loved Cane. Nothing could stop that.

Tank knew. He smiled at her in a way that told her he wouldn't have hard feelings against her or his brother. She was now his little sister and he'd protect her and care for her, but not flirt with her. Never again.

She looked back at Cane, who was watching

her with a keen, unusual look. He smiled softly. "You're red as a beet, Bodie." He chuckled.

"I've never been proposed to before," she stammered.

"First time for everything."

"I guess so." She searched his black eyes. "Are you sure?"

He nodded. "I'm very sure." And suddenly, he was. Sure that it was the right thing to do, sure that he cared enough for her to really try to make the marriage work. And if it didn't work out, there was always divorce, he mused. Odd, how painful that thought was. He didn't love Bodie. He was very fond of her. Would it be enough? It would. He was certain it would. Almost certain, anyway.

THEY WERE MARRIED A week before New Year's at the local church where the Kirks attended services. The minister, a tall, silver-haired man with kind dark eyes, performed the ceremony while the Kirk brothers, Morie, all the ranch hands and more than a handful of local citizens sat in the pews.

Bodie wore a white wedding gown with simple lines and lace accents, and a fingertip veil covering her radiant face. She carried a bouquet of poinsettias, which accented the stark white of her gown in a very artistic way. Cane wore a dark suit with a white shirt and patterned tie. He also wore the prosthesis. He'd whispered to Bodie that they were having a professional photographer record the event and he wanted it to look like he had two arms even if he didn't. He smiled when he said it, though, for the first time talking about his disability without bitterness.

The photographer took his shots carefully and discreetly, without diverting attention from the couple at the altar.

After Cane slid a simple wide gold band on Bodie's finger, and she slid one on to his, the minister pronounced them man and wife. Cane lifted the veil back, and looked upon his bride for the first time as his wife.

He hadn't expected it to feel profound. But it did. He frowned at the sudden sense of possessiveness, protectiveness, that he felt with her all of a sudden.

She worried because he looked angry.

He bent and kissed her very tenderly. "Mrs. Kirk," he whispered against her lips.

She flushed and laughed nervously.

He grinned. Just that quickly, the tension was gone.

MAVIE HAD A CATERER come in to provide a feast for the guests in the large fellowship hall. Bodie stood next to Cane, all flustered and laughing, her face so radiant that she looked beautiful. Cane smiled at her. He still had reservations. He felt confined. It was a feeling he'd never experienced. He also felt possessive of his new wife, but he was confused and he couldn't quite sort out what he really felt.

Bodie slid her fingers around his a little nervously. She was unsure of him, and he looked odd, as if he wasn't happy about the decision he'd made to marry her.

"I won't be possessive," she said under her breath. "I won't hound you or…or demand things. I just wanted you to know how proud I am to be your wife."

His heart swelled. He looked down at her with quite black eyes. "I wasn't sure about this," he confessed, looking at their linked hands, at the wedding band on her finger. "Just…give me some time to adjust."

"You'll have lots of it when I go back to school, and get out of your hair," she teased lightly.

He scowled. "What about your master's work?"

She shrugged. "I can start that anytime. I just want to finish my undergraduate work and get my degree. There are all sorts of jobs I could do even with just a Bachelor of Science degree, you know."

"Jobs."

"I want to pull my weight around here," she said

firmly. "I'm not the sort to socialize. I don't really get along well with most people."

He laughed hollowly. "Me, neither," he said inelegantly.

"I noticed."

He pursed his lips.

"And I really would appreciate it if you could restrain yourself from attacking people in bars, just for the foreseeable future," she said demurely.

He sighed. "I guess I can try."

"I know I'm not old enough to understand a lot of things," she said, staring up at him. "But I can listen. I know you don't trust people you don't know. You can trust me. I'd never say a word about anything you tell me to another living soul. Not even your family."

He twirled her hand in his. "You're my family now, too."

Her heart lifted. "Yes. I guess I am." She smiled slowly.

He chuckled.

AFTER THE RECEPTION, Cane and Bodie changed clothes and the Kirk brothers loaded two suitcases into the hired limousine that was going to take them to Jackson Hole for a brief honeymoon in a luxurious hotel suite. Cane had wanted to take her somewhere exotic, but his injuries were still painful and they made it difficult for him to even move, much less get on a plane for an extended trip.

Bodie was very excited. She didn't care where they went. She only wanted to be alone with her new husband, even though she knew that Cane wasn't going to be able to do much as a lover. It didn't really matter. She was happier than she'd ever been in her life.

ALONE IN THE HOTEL ROOM, overlooking the sharp white crests of the Teton Mountains, Bodie put on a pretty red dress and waited for Cane to come back up from the little store in the lobby. She'd been looking at brochures and found a couple of places she wanted to go and see...if he felt up to it. It was almost lunchtime, so they could get something to eat along the way. The Kirks had paid the limousine driver's expenses to stay in the same hotel and be available to take them sightseeing. It would save Bodie the trouble of having to drive, since Cane wasn't able just yet.

Thirty minutes later, she wondered where he'd gone. She had a fear that the overwhelming newness of marriage might be wearing on him. She went downstairs, putting the room card key in her pocket and locking up behind her, to look for him.

He wasn't in the small souvenir shop. Worried,

she headed for the only other place he might be. The bar.

Sure enough, he was leaning against the bar, very relaxed, talking to an exceptionally pretty woman with long blond hair wearing a stark white wool dress that ended five inches above her knees. She had an exquisite figure and beautiful long legs.

Bodie felt dowdy in her inexpensive, off-the-rack red dress. She hesitated in the doorway, feeling betrayed. Just married, and her husband was in the bar marking time with another woman.

Even as she watched, Cane laughed and bent his head, and kissed the blonde woman.

Bodie felt sick. She turned and went back up to the hotel room. She should have waited for an explanation. She should have barged in and yelled at him. She should have done…something!

What she did was grab her suitcase, call the driver, and go home.

HER CELL PHONE RANG WHEN the limousine was halfway there. She looked at the number, recognized Cane's cell phone and turned the phone off.

The driver's phone rang. She could see him talking, see him looking in the rearview mirror and grimacing. He opened the electric window between them.

"Mrs. Kirk, your husband said would you please turn on your phone?"

"You tell my husband to go to hell with his new blonde friend!" she raged. "And close that window!"

The driver flushed. He powered the window up, grimaced again, spoke into the phone, grimaced once more, nodded and hung up. He drove somberly all the way back to the ranch and stopped at the front door.

Bodie was fighting tears. She'd never felt so humiliated in her whole life. It was worse because when she got out of the car both Kirk brothers and Morie were waiting for her.

"Cane's sorry," Morie said at once, coming forward with a worried expression. "Really sorry. He was talking to someone he knew from the cattlemen's association...."

"Yes, someone blonde and sexy and knockout gorgeous, in the bar," Bodie said through her teeth. "He kissed her...!"

She took off her wedding ring and put it in Morie's hand. "You wait right there," she told the driver, still fuming. "You're driving me to Billings right now."

"Bodie," Morie tried to reason with her.

"No," Bodie said icily. "I was a fool! I knew what he was and I fooled myself into thinking it doesn't matter. But it matters! I'm the only one who got married today. He just put on a wedding ring. He left me sitting in the room waiting for him while he was passing the time with another woman. How do you think I feel right now?"

Morie sighed. "Betrayed."

"Exactly. I'm going to stay with Beth until classes start next week. I'm sorry," she told the brothers. "I'm so sorry. I just can't deal with this. I made a mistake."

"It just needs time," Mallory said gently. "It's a big step for both of you."

"Especially for Cane," Tank tried to reason with her.

"Yes. One woman instead of several, I can see how big a step that was for him," she agreed. She bit her lip. Tears were threatening. "I can't stay here. I'm sorry to ruin the rest of the holidays for you."

Morie hugged her close. "I'm sorry it's ruined for you. Come on. I'll help you pack. We can Skype on New Year's Eve. Okay?"

Bodie choked back tears. "Okay."

"It will be all right," Morie promised. "You'll see."

CANE CAME HOME FUMING and cursing at the top of his lungs. "She walked out on me on our wedding day!" he raged when he was back in the house. He was furious that he'd had to wait all day while the limo driver took Bodie all the way to Billings and then came back to Jackson Hole for him. It was after midnight when he got to the ranch.

Morie darted upstairs to avoid the confrontation she knew was coming. She didn't need any more upsets in her fragile condition.

Mallory put his hands on his hips and glared at his brother. "And you did nothing at all to deserve it."

Cane frowned. "I went down to get a bottle of aspirin and when I got back to the room, she was gone. I tried to call her on my cell phone and she wouldn't even answer. I called the driver and he said she said she was leaving and she didn't want to talk to me." He threw up his hands. "I don't know what the hell happened!"

"She walked into the bar and saw you kissing a beautiful blonde woman," Tank said icily. "That's what happened."

Cane averted his face. He couldn't tell his brothers the truth. He'd been feeling trapped in the hotel and he'd wanted to escape. He'd used Laura to show Bodie that he wasn't about to be hog-tied by any woman, not even his wife. Now, his manufactured escape clause was hitting him right in the gut.

"Bodie went looking for you," Mallory agreed, "and she thought…well, you can imagine what she thought. You've never been a one-woman sort of man."

Cane was devastated at the way his muddled thinking had backfired. He'd seen Laura and they'd started talking…he'd met her at a cattle convention several years back and they were friendly. Just friendly. He'd seen Bodie coming out of the elevator. It had irritated him that she'd come looking for him, and, impulsively, he'd thought of a way to hit back. But now he felt guilty, and defensive.

"I was just talking to Laura," he said.

"And kissing her," Tank shot back. "Nice move, on your wedding day."

"Listen, pal," Cane returned, and moved closer belligerently.

"No, you listen," Mallory said icily, moving between them. "You blew it. Bodie's gone back to school and when she can afford it, she's seeing a divorce attorney. Don't worry," he added when Cane looked even more furious, "she isn't going to ask for anything except an annulment. She wanted you to understand that."

Cane felt even worse. He'd failed Bodie, in the worst way. Of course he'd felt trapped, as if he'd been dragged to the altar. But it had been his own idea, not Bodie's. Her only fault was to love him.

He turned away from his brothers, feeling sick. He should have realized she might come looking for him. Of course he should. He had. Then he'd deliberately let her find him in a compromising situation, so that she'd leave him. He'd set himself up for it, because he felt trapped. Bodie and her sterling ideals, Cane and his black-sheep morals. She'd deserved better.

He looked out the window at the threatening skies. "She won't even have a way to get to work," Cane said heavily. "Her truck, if you can call that piece of junk a truck, is still here."

"I had Darby and Fred run one of the ranch pickups to the apartment she shared with Beth."

The way he said it made Cane strangely uneasy. He turned and looked at his brother. "What do you mean, the one she shared, past tense?"

Mallory was somber. "There have been a few developments today."

"Developments?"

"Will Jones has been busy," Tank said in an icy tone.

Cane had a premonition. He didn't even want to voice it.

Mallory took a deep breath. "The sheriff arrested Will a few days ago for trafficking in pornography and using an underage model."

"That's good news. Isn't it?" Cane asked.

"It was, until we found out just how angry Will was about all his problems. I suppose he figured that Bodie was the most vulnerable, and he knew exactly how to make her pay for what happened to him. Apparently he did this some time ago, and we only just found out."

Cane swallowed, hard. "What did he do?"

"This."

Mallory turned his open laptop around. There, on the page, was a picture of a nude woman in a gross pose with a man, her face laughing as she looked into the camera. It was Bodie.

"She said she never posed in any such way for Will!" Cane exploded. "How could she do such a thing? Didn't she realize it would ruin her in this community?"

"Cane, that's not Bodie."

"The hell it's not!" Cane raged. "That's her face!"

"Yes, but it's not her body," Tank replied coolly. "It was changed with Photoshop."

"And how would you know that, unless you've seen her without her clothes?" Cane demanded, unreasonably jealous.

"Because I know a genius computer tech and I had him do the legwork to find out," Tank said.

"Red Davis," Mallory added. "We had him trace the photo. Will put an old picture of Bodie's face on this body. Davis even found the source of the picture. It was one her mother took on a digital camera and transferred to the computer before she died."

"I'll kill him," Cane said in a tone that sent chills up Mallory's spine.

"The law will take care of Will. I've got Davis working on the photograph. He had to provide a copy to law enforcement, because it's identity theft and that's another charge he'll face in court. But Davis is working the internet to find every trace of that photograph and erase it."

"Can he really do that?" Cane asked through his teeth.

"We hope so," Tank said. "Davis is really good and he has contacts in government agencies who deal with cyber terrorism. He's certain that he can get rid of the photograph."

"Does she know?" Cane asked, worried. "Does Bodie know?"

Mallory was grim. "She didn't until she walked up to her apartment and found all her things sitting on the doorstep. Beth didn't even speak to her. She left a note on the door saying she was sorry but Bodie couldn't live there anymore. She wasn't living with a roommate who was putting nude pictures of herself with strange men all over the internet. Bodie was shattered."

"Where is she now?" Cane asked, even more furious at her roommate.

"We set her up in a hotel near the campus. I'm afraid her classmates will have found that link, though," Mallory replied quietly.

"I'm sure her so-called friend Beth will make sure they do," Tank muttered. "Some friend! She could have at least given her the benefit of the doubt."

"Yes, like Bodie could have given me the benefit of the doubt," Cane replied somberly. "Talk about what goes around comes around," he added.

"Well, the damage is done," Tank said. "Now it's up to us to do what we can for Bodie."

"Isn't she coming back home?" Cane asked.

"You're kidding, right?" Tank replied and even smiled. "She told the driver she wasn't going to be driven away in shame for something she didn't do, and she was going right up to the campus to tell the whole world what her idiot stepfather did to her. In fact," he added, going to the computer and pulling up Bodie's Facebook page, "she's already done it."

He indicated the screen. Bodie had laid it all out, her stepfather's ultimatum, her grandfather's death, her shame at accepting his conditions but in a discreet way to pay the rent, right up to her discovery that Will had paid her back for his arrest with a bogus photo, which even her friend, she'd added acidly, believed without question.

"Wow." Cane chuckled. "That's one in the teeth for friend Beth."

"Well deserved," Mallory said.

Cane stared at the screen and felt a sense of loss. He was remembering the incident at the truck stop, the truckers leering at Bodie—they must have seen the photograph even that long ago. Poor kid...and she didn't even know. Bodie, with her sweet nature and innocence, pasted on computer screens all over the world in a lewd photo that she hadn't even posed for. He was ashamed of himself for what he'd thought when he first saw it. How in the world must she be feeling now?

He remembered how cruel he'd been to Bodie, to the wife he'd married reluctantly and betrayed on her wedding day. First that, then the internet fiasco. He was more ashamed of himself than he'd ever been in his life.

"Now the question is, what are you going to do?" Mallory asked Cane.

He drew in a long breath. "I don't know," he said. His voice had lost all its self-confidence. "I honestly don't know."

CHAPTER THIRTEEN

BODIE HAD BEEN DEVASTATED when she found her
clothes in cardboard boxes, along with her small
treasures, sitting on the porch of the apartment
she'd shared with Beth through almost four years
of college. The note had made her sick, because
she knew at once what Will had done. She recalled the two drivers at the truck stop leering at
her, and now she knew why. How long had that
disgusting photo been making the rounds of the
internet already? And, worse, how was she ever
going to stop it?

She told the driver what had happened. He
phoned Mallory, who spoke to Bodie gently and
then to the driver. She was taken to a nearby hotel
and installed there, and Darby left a truck outside
in the parking lot and gave her the keys. He also
handed her an envelope with cash and told her to
hush when she protested. She hugged him.

She went inside and opened her laptop and
pulled up the photograph. Then she went into the

bathroom and threw up. It had been the absolute worst day of her life next to losing her father, and, more recently, her mother and grandfather.

IN THE WEEK BEFORE classes began, she used her time to try to undo what Will had done to her reputation. Her little-used Facebook page became a public forum as she explained the motivation for the vicious internet attack by her stepfather. She ended a post by pointing out that it was never kind to push someone out of your life without hearing both sides of the story first.

Beth called her the night after the post was published.

"You're right," Beth said quietly. "I was unreasonable and I'm very ashamed. I sent Ted a photo of me in my underwear that went all over the internet before I got it stopped and you were supportive of me even though it was my fault. I judged you without asking you anything. I'm very sorry." She hesitated. "Will you come back and share the apartment?"

"No," Bodie replied. "Thank you for the offer, but I'm comfortable here."

"I'm really sorry, Bodie." The other woman sounded close to tears. "Especially when I know why you posed for your stepfather in the first place. I didn't know your grandfather had died…."

"I didn't pose for the photograph, Beth. My stepfather used Photoshop to change it. There's proof and he's being charged for doing it."

"Oh!" Beth really sounded shocked now. "Oh, my gosh...!"

"You believed what you saw, didn't you? I go to church, I don't even date. But you believed it, after living with me for almost four years." Bodie's voice was less accusative than sad.

"I'm so sorry," Beth said again.

"Thanks." Bodie hung up.

She and Beth had been friends, but never close ones. Still, it was hard to think that her roommate had believed such lies about her. She wondered how many of their classmates Beth had talked to. Well, people would read her posts and know the truth. Some might still believe what they'd seen, and Bodie might take some heat for it. But she was going to get her degree, one way or the other, despite the obstacles.

She thought about Cane with much more heartache. She'd seen him kissing another woman. She'd believed he was being unfaithful. Perhaps she, too, was judging on scant evidence. It was a sickening thought. She'd told Mallory to tell Cane she was divorcing him, but she didn't see an attorney. She could let Cane do that, when he pleased. She was going to put the past away and try to get on with her future. She'd never stop loving him, but trust was another matter. Even if he hadn't planned to cheat on her, the fact remained that he was flirting with another woman on his wedding day. She couldn't get past that, no matter how hard she tried.

BODIE USED SKYPE TO TALK to Morie on New Year's Eve. She was concerned about her sister-in-law. That concern made Bodie feel warm inside. After a minute, she asked the question she had to ask.

"How is he?" she asked the other woman, who was using the computer in her bedroom, not where Cane could eavesdrop.

"Somber," Morie replied quietly. "He goes through the motions, but he doesn't smile anymore. He has gone back into therapy, with a psychologist who's a combat vet. He says the guy is easy to talk to, and he's helping him. He hasn't had a drink since you went back to Montana."

"That's good news," Bodie said softly. "Has he…talked to a lawyer?"

"No. He said you could divorce him but he's not divorcing you. He thinks you might forgive him and come home one day."

Bodie's heart jumped. "He said that?"

"Well, not in those words," Morie admitted. "But he said he's not seeing a lawyer."

Bodie shrugged. "I see."

"Mal thinks Cane did it deliberately because he got cold feet about being married. He knew you'd go looking for him. He might have seen you coming down the elevator."

"You mean, he might have staged the whole thing?" Bodie asked hesitantly.

"It's possible, isn't it?" Morie said. "Cane wanted you, but he wasn't sure about getting married so soon. On the other hand, he knew Tank wanted you, too, and he was afraid not to do something. But then when the rings were in place, he felt trapped and started looking for exits. That's what Mal thinks, anyway."

"It's not so far-fetched," Bodie said. "So... there's still hope."

"There's always hope," Morie replied gently. "I had a rocky road to marriage myself. It takes time for people to learn to trust each other. Cane definitely has feelings for you. He just doesn't quite know how to deal with them. He's never been in love, to hear his brothers tell it."

"He just wants me," Bodie blurted out.

"For men, that's a start." Morie laughed. "Be patient. Just let life happen."

"Good advice." She sighed. "Well, happy New Year. I'm going to register at the end of the week and classes start after. Wish me luck."

"You don't need luck. You're smart. But I'll

wish you luck with your reluctant husband." She laughed again.

"That I'll need. Thank Mallory for the truck and the hotel room. I'll pay him back however long it takes, I swear I will!"

"You don't need to do that." She hesitated. "Did your friend see your Facebook page?"

"Yes. She called to apologize, but during the conversation she stumbled and admitted she thought it was me in that photograph and that I posed for it."

"Some friend."

"That's why I'm staying in the hotel. I dread classes. Some of my classmates may have seen the photographs and not seen my Facebook page."

"You'll deal with that," Morie said. "I have faith in you. Just hold your head high and ignore them."

"I'll try. You know, it's hard living in the world."

"Yes. But we cope."

Bodie smiled. "We cope. Thanks."

"You're welcome!"

THE FIRST DAY OF CLASSES, Bodie was withdrawn and nervous. But nobody said anything to her about the internet photos. She'd already gone to the dean and told him what happened, just in case there were any incidents. He only smiled and said his own daughter had been a victim of a similar incident, and the case was going to trial soon. He told her not to worry about it. She left his office in better spirits.

But things didn't go as well for Beth. Oddly she came in for censure when word got around campus about what she'd done to Bodie. In fact, Bodie was walking to her class when she overheard one comment in the hallway.

"Putting her things out in the rain, like she was some homeless person you took in," a woman who wasn't even a friend to Bodie snapped at Beth, who flushed. "And you call yourself a person of faith? What sort of faith is that?" She turned and walked off.

Beth looked at Bodie, flushed even more and almost ran the other way. Two days later, word was going around that Beth had left the campus and transferred to a college back East. Bodie felt sorry for her. She'd been angry that Beth believed Will's filthy propaganda, but she'd never have wished that on her. After all, Bodie had taken Cane's philandering for gospel without hearing his side of the story. It didn't put her in a better light.

A MONTH AFTER SHE STARTED classes, there had been no whispers, no gossip about her. Nobody had trolled her or made her feel uncomfortable. She'd looked for traces of those photographs on the internet and found absolutely nothing, not even a reference to them.

She contacted Morie late one night. While she waited for Skype to connect them, she rubbed her fingers over her lucky stone, liking its metallic feel. She really did have to have her friend in the geology department have a look at it. She thought, and not for the first time, what an unusually heavy rock it was.

"Hello," Morie said, smiling. "How's it going?"

"Much better," Bodie told her. "How are things there?"

"Cane's got a new prosthesis," Morie said with pursed lips and twinkling eyes. "It's a prototype. His psychologist has a friend in AI research. The prosthesis is being created to link to a person's brain so that it's controlled just like a real arm. Cane won't let them attach electrodes, but he's seen it done in the lab. It's very realistic."

"He's actually wearing it? Wow!" Bodie exclaimed.

"He's had a haircut. He shaves every day. He's boning up on anthropology, for some reason," she added with a chuckle. "And he has a photo of you in his room. Mavie saw it and told me."

Bodie flushed. "Well!"

"We're all coming up to see you graduate, you know."

Bodie made a face. "If I graduate." She swallowed. "How about Will and his friend Larry?"

"Both in jail," Morie said surprisingly. "They were arrested on new charges yesterday and bond hasn't been set. Red Davis got the evidence to convict him and turned it over to the sheriff personally. He's also erased every single trace of Will's notorious photo of you from the web."

"I love Red Davis."

"So do all of us. He really should be working for some government agency instead of being a ranch livestock foreman." Morie chuckled. "But he says he doesn't want to have to wear a suit and report to some guy in a tie."

"Can Will get out of jail do you think?" Bodie asked worriedly, because Will was vindictive. "Even if they put the bond high, he's always got the house and land to put up for it...."

"No, he doesn't," Morie said. "I was going to call you tonight, anyway, because this is the most exciting thing that's happened. When the sheriff's investigator tossed Will's house, he found a locked box and got a warrant to open it. Inside was your mother's real will, leaving the house and the land and everything else to you. It's in the hands of our lawyers and they're challenging the fake will that was filed after your mother's death. You'll be a woman of property."

Bodie sat down. "Gosh! How can I ever thank you? Ever?"

"You just graduate and come home, even if it's just for a few weeks," Morie said. She smiled secretly. "I've got some news, too."

"What is it?"

She laughed. "I'm pregnant."

"Morie! I'll be an aunt!" She hesitated. "Well, Cane will be an uncle."

"You'll be an aunt...you're still married to Cane. I'm so excited! The baby's due in August."

"I'm so, so happy for you."

"We're over the moon. They'll be able to tell the sex soon, but Mal and I agreed that we don't want to know. We want it to be a surprise."

"Now, that's restraint." Bodie laughed. "Congratulations. I'll bet your dad and mom are so excited they can't stand it."

"They are. Even Cort," Morie said, shaking her head. "My brother is full of surprises."

"How's he doing with Odalie Everett?" Bodie asked curiously.

She sighed. "Odalie has a real superiority complex. She doesn't want to go around with a man who, to use her words, smells like cow droppings."

"Good Lord! Her mother's not like that, is she?"

"No! Heather Everett is an angel. She could find one nice thing to say even about the devil himself. It's sort of tragic. Cort's mooning over Odalie, who's off to Italy soon to study with a famous voice trainer, and there's this sweet, cowgirlish sort of neighbor who'd die for him and he never sees her." She frowned. "Well, that's not quite true. He sees her every other day. He's usually cussing when he sees her...."

"Why?" Bodie asked, fascinated.

"She's got this pet rooster. Loves her. Hates men. Sort of like our big mean rooster out back, only worse. He goes over to my folks place where there are several hens but no rooster, to visit, you see. When he sees Cort in the yard, he goes at him, spurs and all. It's sort of funny," she said with a helpless laugh. "Cort can't catch the rooster. He's sort of a hit-and-run artist. So Cort's yelling his head off, running after this big red rooster, and the rooster's running around making that funny sound, like he's laughing."

Bodie burst out laughing. "Oh, my gosh!"

"It may end badly. Or in chicken soup. Or something. Anyway, you study hard and keep in touch. I'll keep you posted on things around here."

"Thanks, Morie. Congratulations again." She hesitated. "If Cane's sprucing himself up...is he seeing that girl in Jackson Hole, do you think?"

"He hasn't left the ranch since you did. No. He's

not seeing anyone. Want my opinion? He's waiting for his wife to come home." She smiled gently.

Bodie caught her breath. Her pale brown eyes
were sparkling. "Wow."

"Yes. Surprising, isn't it? Make us proud."

"I'll do my very best. I promise."

THE WEEKS WENT BY IN A rush. Bodie was so busy
studying that she lost track of time. She was determined to graduate. She had no social life, even
though classmates invited her to musical concerts
and special events around campus. She spent her
nights in her hotel room studying.

There had been a major development in her life,
though. She took her lucky rock to the geology
department and was astonished to discover that it
was part of a meteorite, and that it was worth almost a hundred thousand dollars.

"I know a collector who'd pay that or more,"
the geology professor, Dr. Gandres, told her. "It's
quite unusual, and very well preserved. Do you
want me to give you his number?"

She could only nod. She was almost in shock.

He smiled as he wrote it down.

"That's more than gold is worth," she stammered.

"Yes. Collectors will pay anything for a superior

specimen. Bodie, you really shouldn't be carrying it around in your pocket, though. It's too valuable."

She laughed hollowly. "Oh, yes, I do realize that now. Thank you!"

"My pleasure."

SHE WENT BACK TO HER hotel room in shock. That little rock would have spared her all the turmoil of the past weeks. It might have saved her grandfather's life. It would certainly have spared them so many upsets. But she hadn't realized it was valuable. She'd always carried it around, without knowing what sort of rock it really was. Now that she knew, she almost didn't want to part with it. But it would pay for college, a good vehicle of her own, graduate school—even, if necessary, a divorce. It would make her financially independent. So, yes, she had to sell it. She picked up the phone and called the collector.

A WEEK LATER SHE HAD A formidable check in her bank account. She paid her hotel bill and moved into a modest apartment near campus that was in a private home with an elderly couple. She had Darby come and get the ranch truck because she had a small, good used car of her own now.

"What's going on?" Morie asked that evening. Bodie laughed as she saw her friend's face on

Skype. "Remember my lucky rock, the one I always carried around in my pocket?"

"Yes. It was very unusual."

"It was part of a meteorite and I just sold it for a small fortune to a collector."

"Heavens! There's this show on TV about people who hunt those for a living."

"I don't watch TV—no time. I'll have to look that one up, though."

"You should. It's fascinating. These two guys go all over the world looking for fragments." She hesitated. "You still have your mother's property, you know, the deeds will be in your hands in a few weeks according to the attorneys."

"They were in touch with me," Bodie replied. "But I'm not selling the house and land, not for anything."

"I don't blame you. A home should stay in the family, if possible."

"So I'd still have been short of cash. I want to pay you all back for all you've done for me...."

"If you even try, there will be a big scene. I promise," Morie assured her.

She grimaced. "Well, thank you."

"You're welcome." She pursed her lips. "You're going to have company Friday night."

Bodie blinked. "What?"

"I heard from a reputable source that someone's

driving up to Billings Friday to pay you a visit. Someone tall, dark, handsome and determined."

"Cane?" Bodie gasped.

"I do believe that was his name...." Morie laughed.

Bodie almost dropped the cell phone in her excitement. "Friday? He's coming here?"

"Yes, he is."

"He didn't call me or anything," Bodie faltered.

Morie laughed again. "He thinks he's going to surprise you. So this call is a heads-up."

"Thanks a million, Morie. I'll put on my best dress...."

"No, no. You don't know he's coming. Or he'll know who told you."

"Wasn't thinking, sorry. Darn! What will I wear? What will I say? What will I do?"

"Calm down, take a deep breath and just let life happen."

Bodie took a deep breath. She didn't calm down. She was flushed and nervous and more excited than she'd been since Cane proposed. He was coming to see her. Wait...he'd said he didn't want a divorce. But what if he really did? What if he was coming to ask her for one, what if that beautiful blonde woman was back in his life...?

"Don't," Morie said after the long silence. "Stop tormenting yourself. You have to meet things head-on, sweetheart. Just wait until he gets there and talk to him."

"Sounds simple."

"It is simple."

Bodie took another deep breath. "Okay," she said finally. "I'll pretend I don't know a thing."

"Good girl. And good luck."

"You're the best friend I've ever had."

"Thanks. Same here. I'll talk to you soon, okay?"

"Okay."

Bodie hung up. She went to bed that night, but she didn't sleep until it was almost dawn. When the alarm clock woke her, she had circles under her eyes and she had to run to make it to her early class on time.

ALL WEEK SHE THOUGHT about what Cane would look like, what he'd say to her, what they'd do when he showed up at her apartment. She went through every single scenario she could imagine. And she could think up lots. But her supposing caused more worry than ever. She was convinced that he wanted to end their rocky relationship. He'd always said he didn't want any part of marriage, but Bodie had come up on his blind side. He'd married her to keep Tank from asking her. It had been a brotherly competition with Bodie as the prize in Cane's eyes. She was sure of it.

She wondered how his ribs were doing. It had been long enough that they should be completely healed by now. If she passed all her courses, she'd graduate in less than a month. That brought another worry. Where would she go when she got home? Then she remembered. She would have her house, the one she'd shared with Granddaddy, the one her mother had left her that Will had stolen.

Will was in jail with Larry. That meant a little less trouble for Bodie, a little less fear that she might run into her stepfather at a local store and have to deal with him. She still bristled at her own actions. Posing for a teasing photo. It was so out of character for her. But she'd done it to save her grandfather. It had been useless. She could have saved herself the anguish of the consequences. But she'd done what she thought she had to do, at the time. She'd have done anything for her grandfather, within limits. She still missed him, very much. She always would.

FRIDAY AFTERNOON, Bodie finished her last class and drove back to her apartment. She looked around for a car, or a ranch truck from Wyoming, but she didn't see a soul anywhere. She let out a sigh of relief. At least she had a little time to freshen up, tidy the apartment, maybe cook a few things to heat up later if Cane decided to stay for supper. Whatever he had to say, they could have a meal first.

She had it all planned out in her mind. She put her key in the lock and frowned when she found the door already unlocked. She must have forgotten to lock it when she went to her classes. Stupid mistake. Of course, the sweet elderly couple she lived with wouldn't have let anybody into her apartment. She knew that for a fact. They were very protective of her.

So she went into her apartment, hung up her sweater coat, humming a soundtrack from a new movie she liked, tossed her purse into a chair, went into her small kitchen unit—and came face-to-face with a man in jeans and a chambray shirt cooking steaks on her stove.

She caught her breath and almost passed out.

Cane turned his head and grinned at her. He was so handsome that he made her heart stop. It had been so long since those black eyes had twinkled at her, since he'd smiled at all. He smelled of spice and soap and his shirt was faultlessly pressed—Mavie's work, no doubt. He looked like every woman's dream of the perfect man. She couldn't stop staring. Her eyes were starved for him.

"I thought you might be hungry. Those late

classes are hard to get through. What was it, physical anthropology?"

She nodded. Words wouldn't form correctly in her mouth.

He turned the steaks one last time, cut off the stove and forked them onto a large platter. Nearby was a bowl full of hash brown potatoes that smelled lovely, and a bowl of Brussels sprouts. All of that together made up Bodie's favorite meal, and he knew it.

"Surprised to see me?" he murmured, coming closer.

She nodded again.

He cupped her face in his hands. One of them was a prosthesis so cleverly constructed that it actually felt real on her skin.

"It won't fool anyone up close," he whispered, looking at her mouth. "But it's not bad at a distance. It works like a real one. Lots of levers and pulleys and things…. Oh, God, I'll die if I can't kiss you!"

His mouth hit hers like a storm, furiously hungry, intense, his lips crushing hers apart as his arm swallowed her whole and riveted her to the length of his powerful body.

She whimpered at the anguish of passion he incited in her. She reached around him and pressed even closer, her lips opening to meet the feverish crush of his in the apartment where nothing felt real anymore except Cane in her arms.

He groaned. The robot arm held her while the other one found its way surely under her blouse and bra, and onto soft, firm flesh. He kissed her with pure intent, his lips teasing, provoking, while his fingers brushed lightly over a nub that grew hard and almost painful with the sweet torment. She lifted toward his hand, her eyes closed, her mouth clinging.

"Too many...clothes," he whispered roughly. "I'm starving to death!"

He tugged her into her bedroom, closed the door and piled down onto the unmade bed with her, struggling to get her shirt off. In the end, she helped him, stripping down to soft, flushed skin while he watched, his eyes intent, hungry.

She lay back on the pillow. He hung above her, looking at the soft pink beauty of her body.

"All of it," he said roughly.

She swallowed uneasily.

"All of yours," he said. "Then all of mine. You'll have to help me, Bodie," he said in a soft, tender tone. "I don't know if I can do this...."

"Of course you can do this," she whispered. His insecurity made her bold. Without thinking about her modesty, which tormented her, she stripped off her jeans and then went to undress him. It was exciting to take off his shirt, button by button, to see the thick hair that covered his chest, see the muscles rippling as she pulled it off his arms.

The prosthesis was held on with a harness. She learned to unfasten it, and noticed his hesitation.

"I'm not sure…" he began heavily.

"Men have lost limbs in wars since wars began," she said tenderly. "And women have coped. I'll cope. You wait and see. You can teach me."

"Teach you." He laughed huskily as her hands went to his belt. "Yes," he murmured, bending to her mouth. "I can do that."

It was difficult at first. She'd never even seen a man without his clothes, except in some furtively concealed magazines a girl had brought to high school once. She didn't watch foreign films or hang out on porn sites, so she was somewhat lacking in what seemed to be common knowledge for most modern women.

"You are a trip, honey," he mused as she fumbled off the last things that covered them both. "What an education this has been."

She swallowed and tried not to look at the obvious place. "Well, I'm repressed…"

"Not for long. I promise you." He eased her back on the sheets, one long leg sweeping between both of hers while he propped himself on what was left of his injured arm. He did it gracefully, without clumsiness, and his other hand went to a place that lifted her right off the bed with mingled embarrassment and pleasure.

"Don't panic," he whispered against her lips. "This is to get you ready for me. It's sweet and sexy and very exciting. Don't think. Just relax and let me touch you."

She hadn't planned to be so enthusiastic. It seemed to come naturally when he found a spot that made her mind explode with pleasure. She arched up to his hand, her eyes wide and shocked as she moved in ways she'd never dreamed she would. She wasn't thinking any longer. She was all sensation, bursting with pleasure, writhing on the clean sheets as he brought her to a sudden, shocking climax and looked into her eyes while it happened.

His face was flushed with pleasure. "You've never felt that," he said, surprised.

"No," she choked out.

"Then this," he murmured, easing down between her legs, "is really going to blow your mind. Move your legs around my hips. Let me show you how to love."

She followed his lead, her body protesting only a little as he began to penetrate it with slow, steady movements of his hips. All the time, he looked straight into her eyes. Once, embarrassed as the pleasure grew, she tried to close them.

"No," he whispered firmly. "Look at me. Let me watch."

"It's...so intimate..." she whispered brokenly.

"You're my wife," he whispered back, moving deeper inside her with every long, slow thrust. "You're everything. Share this with me. Share every second of it with me...!"

She choked back a scream. Suddenly it was urgent. So urgent. She gasped as her hips leaped up to meet the downward thrust of his, she felt him growing, swelling inside her. His teeth clenched as his hips ground down into hers.

"So...sweet," he bit off. "So sweet, Bodie, so sweet, so sweet... God!"

He shot down inside her like a gun going off, and she pushed up against him as hard, as fast, as she could, driving for the rhythm that would end the anguish of tension that was building, building, building...!

"Cane!" Her voice didn't even sound like her voice. It was so alien that she didn't recognize it.

"Look...at...me!" he managed to say in the last few seconds.

She saw his black eyes dilate even more as he began to convulse above her in rhythmic jerks that echoed the pistollike movement of his hips. When he climaxed, she felt him burst inside her, felt the heat of it, felt him become hers even as her own body fell and fell through endless layers of pleasure that almost sent her unconscious. Whatever her dreams of intimacy had been, the reality was so far beyond them that she couldn't believe the difference.

He collapsed on top of her, sweating, shivering, his mouth on her taut breasts. "Never in my life," he said. "Not like this."

She held him to her, swallowing hard. She looked past his black hair. The pleasure was still pulsing in her satisfied body, but as reality slowly asserted itself, she remembered.

"Not even with that long-legged blonde from Jackson Hole?" she managed to say at his ear.

He burst out laughing.

It was the last thing she expected.

He lifted his head and looked down at her. He was still inside her. He lifted just a little to let her see how completely they were still joined.

"I wouldn't know," he whispered. "Because I never had sex with her. She was just a friend's date at a cattle show I went to." He brushed his mouth over hers. "I saw you coming out of the elevator. I had cold feet and I felt trapped. So I did something incredibly stupid."

"Stupid." She was only repeating him, because

he was moving slowly and her body was catching fire.

"I pretended to be involved. I knew you'd run. I thought it was what I wanted. We'd get divorced and I'd be free. But I'm not free." He moved again, watching her gasp. "And neither are you. We belong to each other so completely that even when we're apart, we're still together. And, too," he said, "there's this…"

He moved insistently, so that she began to arch up to him convulsively, her teeth clenched as pleasure bit into her like a vise. She cried out.

"You made me a whole man," he breathed, kissing her. "And I made you a woman."

"I was already a woman, I think," she bit off, laughing through the pleasure.

"You were a virgin," he said into her mouth. "Sweet and chaste and shy. I loved it. I'll never forget how it felt, how you looked when you climaxed for the first time." He groaned as he moved closer. "I want to do it over and over and watch you every time, as long as I live. As long as you live." He pushed hard into her, his black eyes biting into her light brown ones. "I love you, Bodie. I love you!"

She tried to tell him, too, but the pleasure was so overwhelming that she could only cling to him and weep. It was the most exciting thing she'd ever done, and the sweetest. She went over a cliff and fell into the most explosive pleasure she'd experienced yet. Cane found his own fulfillment, but long after she'd had hers several times.

She wanted to talk to him, but all she could manage was an exhausted, "I love you so much."

He buried his face in her throat. "I love you, too, baby. I'll never stop."

They fell asleep in the dazed aftermath, with food still sitting on plates in the kitchen.

CHAPTER FOURTEEN

IT WAS AFTER MIDNIGHT when they woke up, showered and dragged into the kitchen to find food.

"However did you get in here?" Bodie asked, wearing his shirt while he wore his jeans and nothing else. He was so comfortable with her now that he didn't mind letting her see his injury. It was a testament to his feelings for her.

"I showed them this." He flashed his wedding band, and grinned. "I told them we'd had a fight but I wanted to make up. They just melted. Nice folks."

"Very nice," she agreed. She looked at him with wonder.

"I know," he murmured deeply, sliding an arm around her waist to draw her to him. "You're in awe of my bedroom skills." He bent and kissed her. "Just think, I'll even improve with practice."

"We should practice all the time," she whispered back, hugging him close.

"If we practice too much, the way we have tonight, we'll have a small companion very soon."

She blinked. "Companion?"

"What we're doing is how people make babies, Bodie," he teased.

She stared at him blankly. Then she remembered. She had no means of birth control and she was fairly certain that he hadn't used it, either.

"Will it matter?" he asked, and seemed concerned.

She pressed close, shivering at the thought of a baby. Cane's baby. "Oh, no," she said fervently. "It won't matter at all!"

He hugged her close. "A wife and a family. People who know me will faint at how easily I fit into that scenario."

"I almost did faint. Imagine, having to undress a man!"

He chuckled. "I thought you did very well for a woman embarrassed out of her mind. But it had to start somewhere."

"Yes."

He kissed her forehead. "I made you steak and potatoes and even Brussels sprouts." He looked over the top of her head and grimaced. "I expect it would kill us if we tried to eat it now."

She laughed. "How about bacon and eggs and biscuits instead?"

"Lovely."

She kissed him. "Coming right up."

THEY ATE AND THEN WENT back to bed, but they were too tired for any more experimentation. In the morning they dressed and drove home to Catelow.

Morie was on the porch waiting when they walked up the steps, holding hands.

"No need to ask how things went," she teased, grinning at them both.

They grinned back.

"No need at all," Cane agreed. "I seem to be happily married." He looked down at a radiant Bodie. "Imagine that."

"It's hard, but I'll give it my best shot," Morie said. "Come on in. Mavie's been cooking all morning. She has a surprise for you."

They walked into the kitchen and there, on the table, was a magnificent wedding cake, complete with a bride and groom on top.

"Mavie! It's beautiful!" Bodie exclaimed.

"I know you had one at the fellowship hall, but it wasn't the right kind," she said, brushing back her hair with a floury hand. "I wanted you to have a proper one, with three layers and a bride and groom on top—not a sheet cake from the bakery."

"We didn't plan on a sheet cake," Morie told them. "But everything went wrong."

"You can say that again," Cane replied heavily. "I helped mess it all up."

Bodie hugged him. "You made it up to me. Stop flogging yourself."

"I need ashes and sackcloth," Cane murmured.

"You need a shovel and a toothbrush," Bodie replied. "I've decided where I want to go on our honeymoon if I graduate."

"You'll graduate," Cane assured her.

She sighed. "I hope. Anyway, there's a special program in Colorado where you help established archaeologists in a dig."

"I haven't been on a dig in years," he said. He shifted restlessly. "I can't use a shovel anymore."

"You don't need to. You can use a trowel. And I happen to know that you've been doing some studying."

Cane laughed. "Brushing up on bones," he agreed.

"So you can help dig."

He sighed. "You're forcing me back into the world. I was doing a pretty good job of hiding from it."

"Not allowed," Bodie said, smiling up at him. "Not anymore."

He bent and kissed her. "Okay, boss."

She made a face at him.

Mavie picked up the cake and carried it into the

dining room. Cane took Bodie's hand in his and followed after her.

They took pictures with Morie's digital camera and then they sat down and proceeded to make inroads into the cake along with cups of French vanilla coffee.

"This is wonderful," Bodie exclaimed. "Absolutely delicious," she murmured as she put another bite of cake into her mouth.

"No, I'm delicious," Cane admonished with his fork. "The cake is good."

She laughed. So did the others.

Mallory and Tank came in a few minutes later, and noted the sudden intimacy of Cane and Bodie.

"Can we assume that you've made up?" Mallory asked with pursed lips.

"Yes, you can," Cane assured him. "We're going to graduate from college with honors and then we're having a honeymoon digging up old dead things in holes of dirt."

Bodie hit him. "We're going on a very dignified archaeological expedition," she corrected. She grinned. "Where we'll dig up old dead things in dirt holes."

They laughed. Cane hugged her close.

"Whatever you want, honey," he said, and

his eyes were possessive and dark with love and pride.

"You remember that," she told him, but she was grinning.

SHE DID GRADUATE, *magna cum laude,* and the whole family drove up to Billings for the graduation exercises. Afterward, with Bodie in her cap and gown, clutching her diploma, Cane strolled along with her to speak to her favorite professors and meet some of her classmates. At least one of the women gave him a speaking invitation, but he turned away without even looking at her again. He had eyes only for his wife, he told Bodie, and she was more certain of him now than she'd ever expected to be. He was a man in love.

They went to Colorado for two weeks, digging by day and loving by night. When they got back home, they were stiff and sore, but they told the family that it was the most fun they'd had together so far. Even if it was digging up bones in dirt holes.

WILL WAS CONVICTED OF identity theft and trafficking in pornography, including exploitation of a minor, along with his friend Larry. He was also indicted for theft by wrongful taking or disposition of property for hiding Bodie's mother's will. The two men were sentenced to several years in prison. Bodie had the deed to her family home and property, and she found a nice elderly couple who needed a place to live and let them stay rent-free.

Her mother's heirloom jewelry turned up on her dresser early one morning. She took it in to the breakfast table and showed it to Cane. "I pawned it," she stammered. "I meant to go and get it back…"

He pulled her close and kissed her. "One of the cowboys saw you pawn it. Even back then, I knew I couldn't let you turn loose of something so important. I bought it and swore the pawn shop owner to secrecy. I was waiting for the right time to give it to you. I think this is the right time."

He said it with a strange, wondrous look in his eyes. As he held hers, his hand went to her flat belly. "Isn't it time you told me, Bodie?" he said as he kissed her.

She gasped. "I only did the test this morning," she exclaimed, gaping up at him.

He smiled. "I saw the test in the trash can. I can read colors on a box, too, you know. Come on. Tell me."

She took a deep breath. Her face was radiant. "We made a baby," she whispered.

He drew her close, stared down into her wide eyes and bent and kissed her with breathless tenderness. "We made love." He touched her belly gently. "Real love."

She shivered and pressed close. "It's scary, to be so happy."

He kissed the top of her head. "Yes. But wonderful."

"Utterly wonderful." She laughed. "I have to go to the doctor, to make sure. But I just know."

"Me, too." He hugged her close. "I've been a lot of trouble," he said against her soft hair. "Was I worth it?"

"Worth every tear," she assured him. She looked up into his black eyes. "I'm so proud of you. Not one wrecked bar in months!"

He flushed a little. "Yes, well, I don't want to embarrass you."

She beamed. "Is that why?"

He shrugged. "That and the fact that I finally have a therapist I can relate to. I guess I'm learning to cope, after all."

"Coping beautifully," she whispered.

"Oh, so you like how I cope, do you?" he mused, his eyes twinkling as they met hers.

"You cope in so many...unusual ways," she said, clearing her throat and flushing a little.

He chuckled. "Blame my wicked youth."

She leaned into his arms and laid her cheek on

his chest. "I didn't think it would be like that. I mean, I didn't know it kept getting better."

"Better and better, every day." He sighed. His arm contracted. "You're the best thing that ever happened to me, sweetheart," he whispered. "And I love you madly."

"I love you madly."

He bent and kissed her with exquisite tenderness. "I think…"

"…that damned rooster is going to end up in a stewpot, and I'll put her in there with him!"

Cane and Bodie looked at each other with shock as a tall, dark man with wavy hair came storming into the house. He was wearing jeans and boots and a suit and a wildly expensive Stetson.

"Oh. Sorry." He stopped, looking self-conscious, and smiled. "I thought Mal said my sister was in here."

"She is," Morie said, coming out of the kitchen with a cup of coffee. "Cort! I didn't think you were coming until Thursday."

She hugged her brother.

"I wasn't, but the damned chicken spurred me and I left town so I wouldn't get arrested for assault."

"Oh, Cort." Morie laughed. "Is that rooster still after you?"

"You can laugh," he muttered. "The damned

thing chased me into my own damned house! On my property!"

"Can't you just catch it and eat it?" Cane chuckled.

"Chance would be a fine thing," Cort grumbled. "I had every ranch hand on the place chasing the stupid rooster. Jack fell into the water trough. Bill got kicked by a bull when he ran through the corral without looking. Andy got the worst of it. He jumped at the rooster and landed in a big pile of… well, it was bad."

Morie died laughing. "Poor Andy!"

"So I came up here early," Cort said, then grimaced. "I hope you don't mind if I stay for a while. I'm not going home until I get over it."

"Maybe a big chicken hawk will come by and save you," Bodie suggested.

"No such luck."

"Can't you just sue the owner?" Cane asked.

"The owner is a little cowgirl with only her great-aunt for company, on a miserable farm that's going bankrupt," Cort confessed. "You can't get blood out of a turnip." He sighed. "Even so, the neighborhood loves her. I'd never hear the end of it. Dad would lose business."

"Dad said you should just shoot the rooster," Morie reminded him.

"I tried!" Cort exclaimed. "I fired at point-blank

range five times and missed every damned time! When the pistol was empty, the damned rooster charged me. I swear to God he was laughing when I finally got into the house. I didn't even have a stick to fight him off with!"

Bodie and Cane burst out laughing.

"You'll be safe here," Morie assured him. "I only have hens. Well, I do have a rooster, but his wings are clipped and he's got no spurs since last week. Honest. All he can do is threaten you. Think of him as a toothless lion."

"Well, that's a relief. I may never leave," he added.

"You're welcome to stay," Morie replied. "How about some cake?"

"How about some coffee to go with it?" he pleaded. "I've had a long week."

"My pleasure!"

CANE AND BODIE SAT ON THE front porch in the swing later that evening, holding hands and watching the fireflies dart back and forth in the yard. All the flowers were blooming. The smell of them was subtle and sweet in the warm night air.

"Did you ever think you'd marry me, way back when we first met?" Bodie asked with a smile.

"Actually, I thought about it a lot," he confessed surprisingly. "But I wasn't coping with the war wound, or the drinking, and you were so young." He looked down at her. "I didn't realize at the time that you were an old soul in a young body." He bent and kissed her. "In hindsight, maybe I'm too young for you," he teased.

She kissed him back and sighed. "I never expected to be so happy."

"Honestly, honey, neither did I." He drew her close. "You and a baby to look forward to. And all the sweet times ahead."

She smiled and pressed close. "Yes. All the sweet times ahead."

In the distance, there was the sound of cars going along on the highway past the last fences. But all Bodie heard was the sound of Cane's heart, beating sure and strong at her ear. She closed her eyes and smiled, safe in the arms of her fierce Wyoming cowboy, tame at last.

* * * * *

If you love Diana Palmer,
don't miss MIDNIGHT RIDER,
a captivating historical romance
set in turn-of-the-century Texas.
Turn the page for a preview...

CHAPTER ONE

Southwestern Texas, 1900

IN ALL THE WORLD there was nothing Bernadette Barron loved more than her garden, despite the asthma that sometimes sent her running from it in the spring months. There were plenty of flowers in southwestern Texas, and many occasions to fill her father's elaborate Victorian home with them. Colston Barron owned at least half of Valladolid County, which was midway between the prosperous city of San Antonio and the smaller city of Del Rio on the Mexican border.

He had done extremely well for an Irish immigrant who got his start working on building the railroads. Now, thirty-three years after his arrival in the United States, he owned two. He had money to burn, but little family to spend it on.

Despite his wealth, there was one thing still lacking in his life—acceptance and respect from elite society. His rude Irish brogue and lack of conventional manners isolated him from the prominent families of the day, a situation he was determined to change. And Bernadette was going to be the means of it.

His beloved wife, Eloise, had died of an infection just after giving birth to Bernadette. His eldest daughter had died in childbirth. His only son, married with a small child, lived back East, worked as a fisherman and kept contact with his father to a minimum. Albert was in disgrace because he'd married for love, refusing the social match his father had planned for him. Only Bernadette was left at home now. Her brother could barely support his own small family, so running to him was not an option unless she was able to work, which was impossible because her health was too precarious to allow her to hold down a job, such as teaching. Meanwhile, she had to cope with her father's fanatical social aspirations.

It wasn't that Bernadette didn't want to marry, eventually. She had her own dreams of a home and family. But her father wanted to choose her husband—on the basis of his social prominence. Wealth alone would not do. Colston Barron was determined to marry off Bernadette to a man with a title or, if he were an American, to a man of immense social prestige. His first choice, a British duke, had been a total loss. The impoverished nobleman was willing enough. Then he was introduced to Bernadette, who had appeared at the first meeting, for reasons known only to herself and God, in her brother's tattered jeans, a dirty shirt, with two of her teeth blackened with wax and her long, beautiful, platinum hair smeared with what looked like axle grease. The duke had left immediately, excusing himself with the sudden news of an impending death in the family. Although how he could have known of it in this isolated region of southwest Texas...

All Colston's mad raving hadn't made Bernadette repent. She was not, she informed him saucily, marrying any man for a title. Her brother had left some of his old clothes at the ranch, and Bernadette wasn't a bit averse to dressing like a madwoman anytime her father brought a marriage prospect home. Today, though, she was off her guard. In a blue-checked dress with her platinum-blond hair in its familiar loose bun and her green eyes soft with affection for the roses she was tending, she didn't seem a virago at all. Not to the man watching her unseen from his elegant black stallion.

All at once she felt as if she were being watched...scrutinized...by a pair of fierce, dark eyes. His eyes, of course. Amazing, she thought, how she always seemed to sense him, no matter how quietly he came upon her.

She got to her feet and turned, her high cheek-
bones flushed, her pale green eyes glittering at the
elegant black-clad man in his working clothes—
jeans and boots and chaps, a chambray shirt under
a denim jacket, his straight black hair barely visible under a wide-brimmed hat that shadowed his
face from the hot sun.

"Shall I curtsy, your excellence?" she asked,
throwing down the gauntlet with a wicked smile.
There was always a slight antagonism between
them.

Eduardo Rodrigo Ramirez y Cortes gave her
a mocking nod of his head and a smile from his
thin, cruel-looking mouth. He was as handsome as
a dark angel, except for the slash down one cheek,
allegedly garnered in a knife fight in his youth. He
was thirty-six now, sharp-faced, olive-skinned,
black-eyed and dangerous.

His father, a titled Spanish nobleman, had been
dead for many years. His mother, a beautiful blond
San Antonio socialite, was in New York with her
second husband. Eduardo had no more inherited
his mother's looks than he had absorbed her behavior and temperament. He was in all ways Spanish. To the workers on his ranch he was El Jefe, the
patron or boss. In Spain, he was El Conde, a count
whose relatives could be found in all the royal
families across Europe. To Bernadette, he was the

enemy. Well, sometimes he was. She fought with him to make sure that he didn't realize what she really felt for him—emotions that had been harder these past two years to conceal than ever.

"If you're looking for my father, he's busy thinking of rich San Antonio families to invite to his ball a month from next Saturday evening," she informed him, silently seething. From the shadow his brim made on his lean face, the black glitter of his eyes was just visible. He looked her over insolently for such a gentleman, and then dismissively, as if he found nothing to interest him in her slender but rounded figure and small breasts. His late wife, she recalled, although a titled Spanish lady of high quality, had been nothing less than voluptuous. Bernadette had tried to gain weight so that she could appeal to him more, but her slender frame refused to add pounds despite her efforts.

"He has hopes of an alliance with a titled European family," Eduardo replied. "Have you?"

"I'd rather take poison," she said quietly. "I've already sent one potential suitor running for the border, but my father won't give up. He's planning a ball to celebrate his latest railroad acquisition—but more because he's found another two impoverished European noblemen to throw at my feet."

She took a deep breath and coughed helplessly until she was able to get her lungs under control.

The pollen sometimes affected her. She hated showing her weakness to Eduardo.

He crossed his forearms over the pommel of his saddle and leaned forward. "A garden is hardly a good place for an asthmatic," he pointed out.

"I like flowers." She took a frilled, embroidered handkerchief from her belt and held it to her mouth. Her eyes above it were green and hostile. "Why don't you go home and flog your serfs?" she retorted.

"I don't have serfs. Only loyal workers who tend my cattle and watch over my house." He ran a hand slowly over one powerful thigh while he studied her with unusual interest. "I thought your father had given up throwing you at every available titled man."

"He hasn't run out of candidates yet." She sighed and looked up at him with more of her concern showing than she realized. "Lucky you, not to be on the firing line."

"I beg your pardon?"

"Well, you're titled, aren't you?"

He laughed softly. "In a sense."

"You're a count—el conde," she persisted.

"I am. But your father knows that I have had no wish to marry since I lost my son. And my wife," he added bitterly.

"Well, it's reassuring that you don't want to get married again," she said.

She knew little of his tragedy except that for a space of days after it, the "ice man" had become a local legend for his rage, which was as majestic as his bloodlines. Grown men had hidden from him. On one occasion Bernadette had encountered him when he was dangerously intoxicated and wildly waving a revolver.... No one knew exactly what had happened, except that Eduardo had come home to find his infant son dead. His wife had died suddenly soon afterward of a gunshot wound to the head. No arrest had ever been made, no charges brought. Eduardo never spoke of what had happened, but inevitably there were whispers that he had blamed his wife for the child's death, and that he had killed her. Looking at him now she could almost believe him capable of murder. He was as hard a man as she'd ever known, and one she judged to be merciless when he had reason to become angry. He rarely lost his temper overtly, but his icy manner was somehow more threatening than yelling.

She herself had seen him shoot a man with cold nerve, a drunken cowboy in town who'd come at him with pistols blazing.

Eduardo hadn't even bothered to duck. He stood in a hail of bullets and calmly took aim and fired.

The man went down, wounded but not dead, and he was left at the doctor's office. Eduardo had been nicked in the arm and refused Bernadette's offer of first aid. Such a scratch, he'd said calmly, was hardly worth a fuss.

She had hoped against hope that her father might one day consider making a match for her with this man. Eduardo was the very reason her heart beat. Just the thought of those hard, cool hands on her bare skin made her tingle all over. But an alliance between the families had never been discussed. Her father had looked only to Europe for her prospective bridegrooms, not closer to home.

"You have no wish to marry?" he asked suddenly.

The question caught her unaware. "I have bad lungs," she said. "And I'm not even pretty. My father has money, which makes me very eligible, but only to fortune-seekers." She twisted a fold of her skirt unconsciously in her slender, pretty hands. "I want to be worth more than that."

"You want to be loved."

Shock brought her eyes up. How had he known that? He did know. It was in his face.

"Love is a rare and often dangerous thing," he continued carelessly. "One does well to avoid it."

"I've been avoiding it successfully all my life," she agreed with smothered humor.

His eyes narrowed. Still watching her, he pulled a thin black cigar from a gold-plated case in his jacket. He replaced the case deftly, struck a match to light the cigar and threw the spent match into the dust with careless grace. "All your life," he murmured. "Twenty years. You must have been ten when your family moved here," he added thoughtfully. "I remember your first ride on horse-back."

She did, too. The horse had pitched her over its head into a mud puddle. Eduardo had found her there, dazed. Ignoring the mud that covered her front liberally, he'd taken her up in the saddle before him and delivered her to her father.

She nodded uncomfortably. "You were forever finding me in embarrassing situations." She didn't even want to remember the last one....

"His name was Charles, wasn't it?" he asked, as if he'd read her mind, and he smiled mockingly.

She glared at him. "It could have happened to anyone! Buggy horses do run away, you know!"

"Yes. But that horse had the mark of a whip clearly on its flank. And the 'gentleman' in question had you flat on your back, struggling like a landed fish, and your dress—"

"Please!" She held a hand to her throat, horribly embarrassed.

His eyes went to her bodice with a smile that chilled her. He'd seen more than her corset. Charles had roughly exposed her small breasts from beneath her thin muslin chemise, and Eduardo had had a vivid glimpse of them before she struggled to get them covered again. Charles had barely had time to speak before el conde was on him.

In a very rare display of rage, the usually calm and collected Eduardo had knocked the younger man around with an utter disregard for his family's great wealth until the son of the shipping magnate was bleeding and begging on his knees for mercy. He'd headed for town, walking fast, and he hadn't been seen again. Naturally, Bernadette's father had been given a very smoothed-over explanation for Charles's absence and her own ruffled state. He'd accepted it, even if he hadn't believed it. But it hadn't stopped him from throwing titled men at her.

"Your father is obsessed," Eduardo murmured, taking a puff from the cigar and letting it out angrily. "He puts you at risk."

"If I'd had my pistol, Mr. Charles Ramsey would have been lying on the ground with a bullet in him!"

He only smiled. To his knowledge, Bernadette

couldn't even load a gun, much less shoot one. He smoked his cigar in silence as he studied her. "Did you ever hear from the unfortunate Charles again?" he asked abruptly.

"Not one word." She searched his hard, lean face and remembered graphically how it had looked when he hit Charles. "You were frightening."

"Surely not to you."

"You're so controlled most of the time," she said, underscoring the words *most of the time.*

Something moved in his face, something indefinable. "Any man is capable of strong passion. Even me."

The way he was looking at her made her heart skip. Unwelcome thoughts came into her mind, only to be banished immediately. They were too disturbing to entertain. She looked away and asked, "Are you coming to the ball?"

"If I'm invited," he said easily.

Her eyebrows arched. "Why wouldn't you be? You're one of the upper class that my father so envies."

His laughter was cold. "Me? I'm a half-breed, don't you remember?" He shifted in the saddle. "My grandmother can't make a match for me in Spain because my wife died under mysterious circumstances and I'm staring poverty in the face.

In my own way, I have as few opportunities for marriage as you do."

She hadn't thought of it that way. "You're titled."

"Of course," he conceded. "But only in Spain, and I have no plans to live there." He was looking at her, but now his mind was working on the problem of bankruptcy, which was staring him in the face. His late father had made a fortune, but his profligate mother had thrown it away. She had drained the financial resources of the ranch, and since he'd come of age Eduardo had been hardpressed to keep it solvent. Only his mother's marriage to some minor millionaire in New York had stopped her from bleeding the ranch dry. She had forfeited her inheritance the day she remarried, but the damage already had been done.

Eduardo stared down at Bernadette and wheels turned in his mind. Her father was rich. He wanted a titled son-in-law. Eduardo was upper-class, despite his mixed ancestry. Perhaps... Bernadette sighed heavily, smothering another cough. "At least you'll never have to worry about being married for your father's money."

"And this idea of marrying a title and a respected name has no appeal at all for you?" he asked slowly.

"None," she said honestly. She grimaced. "I'm so tired of being on display, like a bargain that my father's offering for sale," she said, drawing in a long, labored breath. She coughed suddenly, aware of a renewed tightness in her chest. She hadn't realized how long she'd been among her flowers, with their potent quantities of pollen. "I have to go in," she said as the cough came again. "The flowers smell wonderful, but they bother my lungs when I spend too much time with them."

He scowled. "Then why are you out here?"

She coughed once again. "The house... My father has men repainting the ballroom. The paint bothers me."

"Then going inside the front of the house is hardly a solution, is it?"

She tried to clear her throat enough to answer him, but thick mucus was all but choking her.

Eduardo threw his cigar down and swung gracefully out of the saddle. Seconds later, he lifted her into his arms.

"Eduardo!" she cried, shocked at the unaccustomed familiarity, the strength and hard warmth of those arms around her. She could see his eyes far too closely, feel his warm breath at her temple, touch, if she wished, the hard, cruel curve of his beautiful mouth....

"Calmarte," he murmured softly, searching her taut face. "I mean only to take you in through the kitchen to the conservatory. There are no blooming plants there to cause you discomfort." He shook her gently. "Put your arms around my neck, Bernadette. Don't lie like a log against me."

She shivered and obeyed him, secretly all but swooning at the pure joy of being so close to him. He smelled of leather and exotic cologne, a secret, intimate smell that wasn't noticeable at a distance. Oddly, it didn't disturb her lungs as some scents did.

She laid her cheek gingerly against his shoulder and closed her eyes with a tiny sigh that she hoped he wouldn't hear. It was all of heaven to be carried by him. She hadn't dreamed of such an unexpected pleasure coming to her out of the blue.

His strong, hard arms seemed to contract for an instant. Then, all too soon, they reached the kitchen. He put her down, opened the door and coaxed her through it. Maria was in the kitchen making a chicken dish for the midday meal. She glanced up, flustered to see their landed neighbor inside her own kitchen with his hat respectfully in his hand.

"Señor Conde! What an honor!" Maria gasped.

"I am only Mr. Ramirez, Maria," he said with an affectionate smile.

She made a gesture. "You are el conde to me. My son continues to please you with his work, I hope?"

"Your son is a master with unbroken horses," he said in rare praise. "I am fortunate to have him at the ranch."

"He is equally fortunate to serve you, Señor Conde."

Obviously, Eduardo thought, he wasn't destined to have much luck in persuading Maria to stop using his title.

Bernadette tried to smile, but the cough came back, worse than ever.

"Ay, ay, ay," Maria said, shaking her head. "Again, it is the flowers, and I fuss and fuss but you will not listen!"

"Strong coffee, Maria, black and strong," Eduardo instructed. "You will bring it to the conservatory, yes? And then inform Señor Barron that I am here?"

"But of course! He is in the barn with a new foal, but he will return shortly."

"Then I will find him myself, once I have made Bernadette comfortable. I am pressed for time." He took Bernadette's arm and propelled her down the long, tiled hall to a sunny room where green plants, but no flowering ones, grew in profusion and a water garden flourished in its glassed-in confines.

She sat down with her face in her hands, struggling to breathe.

He muttered something and knelt before her,

his hands capturing hers. "Breathe slowly, Bernadette. Slowly." His hands pressed hers firmly. "Try not to panic. It will pass, as it always does."

She tried, but it was an effort. Her tired eyes met his and she was surprised again at the concern there. How very odd that her enemy seemed at times like her best friend. And how much more odd that he seemed to know exactly what to do for her asthma. She said it aloud without thinking.

"Yes, we do fight sometimes, don't we?" he murmured, searching her face. "But the wounds always heal."

"Not all of them."

His eyebrows lifted.

"You say harsh things when you're angry," she reminded him, averting her eyes.

"And what have I said, most recently, that piques you?"

She shifted restlessly, unwilling to recall the blistering lecture she'd received from him after her unfortunate ride with Charles.

He tilted her face back to his. "Tell me."

"You can't remember?" she asked mutinously.

"I said that you had no judgment about men," he recalled. "And that it was just as well that…" His mouth closed abruptly.

"I see that you do remember," she muttered irritably, avoiding his dark, unblinking gaze.

"Bernadette," he began softly, pressing her hands more gently, and choosing his words very carefully, calculatingly, "didn't you realize that the words were more frustration than accusation? I barely arrived in time to save you from that lout, and I was upset."

"It was cruel."

"And untrue," he added. "Come on, look at me."

She did, still recalcitrant and resentful.

He leaned forward, his breath warm on her lips as he spoke. "I said it was just as well that you had money as you had so few attributes physically with which to tempt a man."

She started to speak, but his gloved finger pressed hard against her lips and stilled them. "The sight of you like that, so disheveled, stirred me," he said very quietly. "It isn't a thing that a gentleman should admit, and I was taking pains to conceal what I felt. I spoke in frustration. I didn't mean to hurt you."

She was horribly embarrassed now. "As if your opinion of my...of my body matters to me!"

"You have little enough self-esteem," he continued, as if she hadn't spoken at all. "It was unkind of me to do further damage to it." He brought her hand to his mouth and kissed it tenderly. "Forgive me."

She tried to pull her hand away. "Please...don't do that," she said breathlessly.

He looked into her eyes and held them with a suddenly glittery, piercing stare.

"Does it disturb you to feel my mouth on your skin, Bernadette?" he chided very softly.

She was terribly uncomfortable and it was showing. The breathlessness now was as much excitement as asthma, and his expression told her that he knew it.

His thumb smoothed over the back of her hand in a slow, sensuous tracing that made the breathlessness worse. "You're far too innocent," he said huskily. "Like a Spanish maiden cloistered with her duenna. You understand your own feelings even less than you understand mine."

"I don't understand anything," she choked out.

"I realize that." His fingers moved to her mouth and slowly, gently, traced its soft outline in a silence that throbbed with excitement and dark promise.

It was the first intimate contact she'd ever had with a man and it unnerved her. "Eduardo," she whispered uncertainly.

His thumb pressed hard against her lips, parting them. Something flashed in his eyes as he felt her mouth tremble under the sudden rough caress of his thumb bruising the inside of her lips back against her teeth.

She gasped, and he made a sound deep in his throat, somewhere between a groan and a growl.

The lace at her throat was shaking wildly. She saw his eyes go there and then, inexplicably, to her bodice. His breath drew in sharply. She looked down, curious even through her excitement, to see what had brought that sound from his lips.

She saw nothing except the sharp points of her nipples against the fabric, but why should that disturb him?

His eyes moved back up to hers. His fingers traced her chin and lifted it. His eyes fell to her soft mouth. He moved, just enough to bring him so close that she could taste the coffee scent and cigar smoke on his mouth as it hovered near hers.

She had a hold on his dark jacket. She didn't realize how tight a hold it was until she became aware of the cool cloth in her fingers.

"Bernadette," he whispered in a tone she'd never heard him use before. She was frozen in time, in space. She wanted his mouth to come down and cover hers. She wanted to taste it, as she'd wanted to so often in the past two years, even as she feared the change that it would bring to their turbulent relationship. But at the moment, the blood was surging through her veins and she was hungry for something she'd never known. The lack of restraint made her reckless.

Involuntarily, she leaned closer to him, her lips approaching his as she forgot all her upbringing in the heat of sudden desire.

He was tempted as he hadn't been in many years. He was painfully tempted.

Suddenly, he murmured something violent in Spanish, something she was certain he'd never have given voice to if he'd suspected how fluent she was in Spanish. She'd never told him that she had learned his language, for fear of him knowing the reason—that she wanted to speak it because it was his native tongue.

He drew back, his expression curiously taut and odd. He stared at her with narrowed eyes and she flushed at her own forward, outrageous behavior and dropped her gaze to his jacket in a flurry of embarrassment.

Tension flowed between them as the sudden sound of hard shoes on tile broke the pregnant silence like pistol shots. Eduardo moved away from her to the window and grasped the thick curtain in his lean hand as Maria came through the open doorway carrying a silver tray.

SHE WAS LOOKING AT IT, not at the occupants of the room, so Bernadette had a few precious seconds to compose herself. Her hands still shook badly, but she managed to clasp them in her lap while Maria put the cups and saucers along with a pitcher of cream and a sugar dish on the table against the wall. She poured thick coffee into the cups and then laid napkins and spoons beside them. By the time she brought the coffee to Bernadette, the younger woman was pale but smiling. "Thank you, Maria," she said hoarsely, and tried to sip the hot coffee, almost burning her mouth in the process.

"This disease of the lungs is something you must be careful about, *niña,*" Maria said firmly. "You must take better care of yourself. Is this not so, Señor Conde?"

He turned from the window and faced them with his usual composure. "Yes, it is," he agreed, although his voice sounded huskier than usual. "Will you stay with her, Maria?" he added curtly. "I'll go find her father myself. There's something I need to discuss with him."

"Do you not want your coffee?" she asked, surprised.

"Not at the moment, *graçias.*" He barely glanced at Bernadette. With a courteous nod, he left the room.

"What odd behavior," Maria murmured.

Bernadette didn't say a word. She'd shamed herself so badly that she wondered if she'd ever be able to look Eduardo in the eye again. Why couldn't she have controlled her wild heartbeat, her scant but rapid breathing, when he was so close? How could she have leaned so close to him, as if she were begging him to kiss her?

She groaned aloud, and Maria hovered worriedly. "I'm all right," she assured the servant. "It's just that…that the coffee is hot," she said finally.

"This is so, but it will help your lungs," Maria coaxed with a smile.

Yes, it would help the lungs. Strong black coffee often stopped an attack of asthma stone-cold.

But it wasn't going to do much for the renegade heart that was beating like a drum in her chest or the shame she'd brought on herself in a moment of ungoverned passion.

Amazing that she could feel such emotions with Eduardo. He didn't even want her. But if he didn't, then why had he come so close, spoken so seductively? It was the first time since she'd known him that he'd ever behaved in that way with her. They fought constantly. But there were times when he had been tender with her, concerned for her, as even her own father wasn't. But this, today, was different. He'd treated her for the first time as a woman he desired. It gave her an extraordinary feeling of power, of maturity.

She let herself dream, for a space of seconds, that he felt the same helpless attraction for her that she felt for him. Only a dream, but so sweet!